"WELCOME, CAPTAIN KIRK!"

The voice had the same commanding tone Kirk knew so well from his earlier encounter with the madman. "And Commander Spock, and of course the good Dr. McCoy! How good it is to see you again!" Garth bowed gracefully in the direction of Yeoman Wodehouse. "And I see that you've brought along your beautiful aide as well."

Kirk glanced at the other figure of Garth sitting by the fire, and saw him dissolve into the form of a fair-haired and muscular young male. The young Antosian looked up at Kirk with fear in his eyes, and Kirk understood why this Captain Garth had seemed so listless, so lacking in energy and charisma.

Kirk turned back to the remaining Garth and knew then that he was not speaking to his hero, to the rational captain who had traveled with him to this planet, but to the insane Lord Garth who had somehow reasserted himself in Garth's body.

STAR TREK®

GARTH of IZAR

Pamela Sargent
and
George Zebrowski

Based upon STAR TREK
created by Gene Roddenberry

POCKET BOOKS
New York London Toronto Sydney Singapore

An *Original* Publication of POCKET BOOKS

POCKET BOOKS, a division of Simon & Schuster, Inc.
1230 Avenue of the Americas, New York, NY 10020

ISBN: 0-7434-0641-9

First Pocket Books printing March 2003

10 9 8 7 6 5 4 3 2 1

Printed in the U.S.A.

To the memory of Steve Ihnat
(1934–1972),
who made Garth live

"A total of fifteen incurably insane out of billions is not what I would call an excessive figure."

—Mr. Spock, commenting on the Elba II asylum, "Whom Gods Destroy"

Chapter One

AS CAPTAIN GARTH brought the *U.S.S. Heisenberg* out of warp and prepared to enter standard orbit around Axanar, the ship's helmsman shouted, "There's a Romulan vessel in orbit around the planet!"

On the bridge viewscreen, the winged shape of a Romulan vessel, a raptor hovering over its prey, was now clearly visible against the pale blue orb of Axanar.

Garth stood up from his command chair and said calmly, "Prepare to retreat. Go to maximum warp."

"Retreat?" his first officer asked, watching Garth with a look of apprehension in his dark, almond-shaped eyes.

"Yes, retreat. At once!" There was no doubt in Garth's voice.

The *Heisenberg* accelerated beyond the orbital velocity toward which it had been slowing, outpaced the pull of the planet's gravitational well in a wide curve, and shot into warp.

"The Romulan is chasing us," the helmsman said softly, "and we can't outrun it."

Garth glanced back at his communications officer, a green-skinned but nonetheless beautiful woman with a cap of short dark hair. "Lieutenant," Garth said, "send a subspace message to Starbase at Tau Ceti, informing them of the Romulan presence."

"Yes, sir," the young woman replied.

As the *Heisenberg* went to maximum warp, the Romulan vessel kept pace. Ten hours passed while Garth sat at his station, silent and unmoving, an enigma to his officers and crew, all of whom knew that the Romulan battle cruiser could not only pace their ship but also match its firepower.

Was their captain simply trying to avoid a battle? From his navigator's station, James Kirk turned in his seat and looked aft at Garth, but could read nothing in his commanding officer's cold blue eyes and impassive face.

In the tenth hour, the Klingon vessel, straining at the limits of its warp drive, began to overtake the *Heisenberg*.

"Captain Garth," a voice called out. Kirk raised his eyes to the viewscreen as the face of a Romulan captain appeared, looking very much like Mr. Spock. *"I know that you are receiving my message. Drop out*

of warp and surrender, or we will destroy your ship."

"I hear you," Garth replied. Kirk turned toward the command station for a moment and saw that Captain Garth was smiling.

"Drop out of warp and surrender," the Romulan captain repeated, and then the image on the screen faded out.

"Bridge to engineering," Garth said. "I am ordering a complete and immediate warp shutdown."

"We canna do that, Captain," one of the officers in engineering called out over the intercom. *"The engines canna take it. We'll be at their mercy if we—"*

"Those are my orders," Garth said. "Shut it down now."

"Captain—"

"Now!"

The *Heisenberg* dropped out of warp, and Kirk realized that they were suddenly behind the Romulan vessel, which had come out of warp well ahead of Garth's ship. The Romulans would be confused now, seeing the Federation starship disappear without any of the usual deceleration signatures on their scan. But very soon the enemy would confirm that the *Heisenberg* was behind them, and the Romulan commander would open fire.

Garth would not fire upon the Romulans first; Kirk was sure of that. He would honor the book and wait until he was sure that his vessel was about to be attacked.

On the bridge viewscreen, the Romulan starship appeared.

Kirk noted the readings on his console. "Captain," he said, "enemy screen is down."

"Fire!" Garth shouted, knowing that the Romulan commander was about to do the same.

Kirk and the helmsman opened fire.

The Klingon cruiser blossomed into flame—

—and Kirk awoke from his dream, with the fireball still in his brain . . .

He lay on his bed in the captain's quarters of the *Enterprise,* reflecting on the exactitude of his recurring dream and the meaning of past events.

Some years earlier, Captain Garth, the legendary Starfleet officer, had taken his starship to Axanar to stop an extremely bloody civil war between the two colonial settlements on that planet. At the heart of the conflict, Garth had discovered the presence of a Romulan mission. The Romulans had seen an opportunity to seize control of this star system near Tau Ceti, and thereby to encroach upon Federation space; the arrival of their battle cruiser had promised victory to one side, which could then hope to rule Axanar under Romulan patronage.

But inexplicably, Garth had ordered his starship to flee, and the Romulan vessel had given chase, its commander clearly fearful that the Federation vessel would alert Starfleet. The Romulans could not have understood or guessed at what Garth was up to, but could only hope to catch and destroy his vessel before it could send off a subspace alarm to the nearest starbase.

Kirk had studied the entire incident at Starfleet Academy. Garth of Izar had been the kind of officer destined to become a famed and admired figure, one whose military exploits were required reading and whose writings were part of the Academy's curriculum. After a ten-hour pursuit at top warp speed, with the Klingon cruiser gaining on the Federation vessel, Garth had executed what later became famous as the Cochrane deceleration maneuver. Under certain circumstances, although with a risk of some damage to the engines, warp drive could be suddenly shut down. A starship being chased by an enemy vessel would drop back and then abruptly appear behind her pursuers, prepared to fire upon an enemy baffled by the sudden disappearance of its prey. That was another tricky part of this maneuver, firing before the enemy ship could put up its shields. The decisive tactical advantage of reappearing without warning behind the enemy was worth the risk of damage from the sudden shutdown of the drive.

That was all there had ever been to the so-called Battle of Axanar, Kirk thought as he came fully awake. He often dreamed of Captain Garth's maneuver, and his dream was usually as accurate as the account that he had studied at the Academy, except in a few particulars. The Klingon captain of the battle cruiser could not have been Koloth, since he was not yet a captain at the time, and would live to challenge

Kirk on the *Enterprise* on more than one occasion, most notably on Deep Space Station K-7. The first officer on the *Heisenberg*'s bridge would also not have been the stocky, dark-haired man Kirk saw in his dream: Dr. Donald Cory, the governor of the asylum and penal colony on Elba II. And the communications officer with Garth at Axanar, according to records, had not been a green-skinned Orion, as was the woman in Kirk's dream; the officer he had dreamed of looked exactly like the ill-fated Marta, one of the inmates Kirk had encountered during his mission to Elba II a couple of years ago.

He thought of that unfortunate woman for a moment; the serum he had brought to Elba II, that had promised a cure for the few criminally insane inmates of the asylum, might have helped poor Marta control and conquer her murderous impulses and heal her tormented mind.

He pushed his memories of Elba II aside.

Garth's deceleration maneuver, Kirk mused, had possessed great tactical beauty, concealing a completely unexpected action. What a pity that, in all likelihood, it could only be done once. Now no one in command of a starship-class vessel would be taken in by such a ruse, which amounted to nothing more than being fooled into outpacing one's prey.

As he lay in bed, with some minutes left before he had to rise and prepare for return to duty, Kirk wondered again whether there might be some situation in which Garth's inspired move might be made to work again, if only one more time, before that particular circumstance also became so well known that it could never be repeated. It was a game that he played with himself, trying to summon a set of conditions in which the Cochrane Deceleration Maneuver might still succeed. He had once dreamed that he had found the answer, but could not remember what had seemed so clear in his dream.

As a consequence of Captain Garth's action, the warring colonies on Axanar had finally made peace; without the Klingon presence to tip the balance of power in favor of one side, the two antagonists had put aside their differences and signed perpetual accords. Kirk, although still a cadet, had shown enough promise to be chosen as a member of the Federation's peacemaking delegation to the planet, for which he had been honored with the Palm Leaf of the Axanar Peace Mission.

Kirk's time on Axanar had marked the beginning of his career as a Starfleet officer. It had also been the last great accomplishment on record of the supremely gifted Garth. Whom the gods would destroy, they first make mad; that was part of Garth's story, too.

As he got up and began to dress, Kirk thought of the legends that had later grown up around the Axanar crisis. Garth's maneuver had been of short duration, but many tales stretched the pursuit of his starship across the whole quadrant, while the resolution of Axanar's civil war was often described as a major Federation victory, with Garth leading the victorious Starfleet forces.

Had Garth known that his destruction of the Klingon vessel would also defuse the civil war on Axanar? Historians liked to debate that one, but the man who might have answered the question directly was beyond questioning—at least he had been up to now. Kirk suspected that Captain Garth, had he been able, might have answered modestly by saying that he had not planned for any such result, had perhaps only guessed at how the struggle on Axanar might end, and had simply hoped for the best. Things might have turned out differently, with the two factions continuing their struggle even without a Klingon presence.

Kirk let out his breath as he straightened the sleeves of his uniform. He might soon be able to ask any questions he liked of the man he had so admired during his Academy days and had then come to fear during their violent encounter in the asylum on Elba II.

Garth, according to a recent message from Admiral José Mendez, was now in full recovery after his nearly two-year course of treatment. Dr. Cory had released him from the asylum at Elba II; indeed, with the success of the new serum and other innovative therapies, Cory was certain that the few remaining inmates of Elba II would soon be capable of leading normal and constructive lives. The governor would see the time when his asylum for criminally insane humanoids would at last be closed for good. Mendez was certain that Kirk would welcome the news.

Kirk was grateful for the message, but another question had immediately come to him: What kind of life could there now be for Garth of Izar, who had already lived one life as one of Starfleet's most brilliant officers and another as a murderous madman? Had his therapy healed him, or only made him into a man for whom there was no place, who would have to live on the margins of a society that might forever distrust him?

The new yeoman, Lesley Wodehouse, was waiting for Kirk when he came to the bridge of the *Enterprise.* The young woman had been on duty for only fourteen days, but Kirk had already come to appreciate her efficiency. Before he could ask for one, she had handed him a cup of coffee; by the time he was seated at his station, she had asked Lieutenant Uhura to call up a subspace message from Admiral Mendez, which had come in only a few moments ago.

"Admiral José Mendez to Captain James T. Kirk," the voice said over the comm. *"Just a message to let you know that I'm forwarding a petition we received from Captain Garth of Izar to you."* Kirk leaned forward, struck by the coincidence of hearing about the man who had so recently been on his mind. *"He's fully recovered now, and has been meeting with me and with other officers at Starfleet headquarters. As soon as you've looked over Captain Garth's petition, get back to me—I want to discuss it with you in more detail. Mendez out."*

Garth's petition was marked confidential and attached to the message in text form. Kirk was about to open the file when Yeoman Wodehouse murmured, "Garth of Izar—I remember reading about his exploits. There doesn't seem to be much on the record about his later life, only the fact that he was relieved from his command after a mission to Antos IV and sent to a medical facility for treatment."

"That is so," Commander Spock said from his computer station. "In fact, the captain and I had an encounter with Captain Garth nearly two years ago, on Elba II."

"Elba II?" The redhaired yeoman frowned. "But isn't that—"

"—the asylum for the criminally insane," Kirk finished. "Garth of Izar was an inmate there at the time I was ordered to Elba II with a new drug that promised a complete cure, when used with other treatments."

"Obviously the treatment was successful," Ensign Pavel Chekov said from his navigator's station, "since he has been released."

"So that was where he was sent after being relieved from command?" Yeoman Wodehouse asked.

"I'd better start at the beginning," Kirk said. "A few years ago, Captain Garth and his starship crew were sent on a mission to Antos IV. When he got there and beamed down to the surface, he was horribly injured in an accident caused by a transporter malfunction. The Antosians were able to heal Garth, but along with the cure, they taught him the techniques of cellular metamorphosis. Garth left the surface of Antos IV able to take on any shape he wished. He then ordered his crew to destroy the Antosians and their world."

"But why?" the yeoman asked. "We've always assumed that the Antosians are one of the most peaceful races in the galaxy."

"We do not know why Garth acted as he did," Spock replied, "but his officers refused to obey the order. By the time they were able to gain control of their ship, Captain Garth had killed his first and second officers. He called their actions mutiny, but given that his medical officer later claimed that Garth was mentally ill and had to be removed from command, his officers were considered justified in their actions, and the charge of mutiny was posthumously erased from their records."

"He was sent to Elba II," Kirk continued, "and it was expected that he would be confined there for the rest of his life. Fortunately, a new serum was developed that promised to cure even the most seriously ill and dangerous inmates. I was sent on a mission to deliver that drug to the medical staff. What I didn't realize until Spock and I had beamed down to the asylum was that Garth had assumed the appearance of Dr. Cory, the governor, and taken over the place. His objective was to force Spock and me to help him gain command of the *Enterprise.*"

"We were unarmed," Spock said, "and it was not possible for Lieutenant Commander Scott, who was left in command of our ship, to beam us up, since he could not penetrate the force field surrounding the asylum without risking the lives of everyone inside the facility. Captain Garth attempted to bend us to his will through threats, torture, and deception, and even tried to deceive me at one point by taking on the shape of Captain Kirk. His impersonation was most convincing."

"But fortunately not convincing enough," Kirk cut in. "We were able to subdue Garth and restore control of the asylum to Dr. Cory, and when we left, Garth was already beginning to recover thanks to the serum we brought. He had no memory afterward of anything he'd done to us, and perhaps that was a mercy."

There was no need, Kirk thought, to go into all the details of the encounter, the unsuccessful attempts of the beautiful Orion inmate Marta to seduce him into giving her the password that would enable Garth to board the *Enterprise,* the tortures Garth had inflicted on his captives. Garth, perhaps enraged by Marta's failure to get the information he wanted from Kirk, had finally had the poor woman dragged outside the asylum's dome and left there, gasping for breath in the poisonous atmosphere, before killing her with a powerful explosive he had managed to develop during his imprisonment. That the cruel Marta was herself a serial murderer with several victims to her credit did not excuse Garth's actions; she had been as insane and irrational as he.

"A madman and shape-changer in control of a starship," Yeoman Wodehouse murmured. "It's a good thing you and Mr. Spock were able to prevent that."

Kirk thought of the mystery of what had happened to Garth on Antos IV. Maybe Garth would finally be able to answer questions about Antos IV and explain why he had tried to destroy the people there who had saved his life.

Was it something about the techniques of cellular metamorphosis taught to him by the Antosians, so necessary to mend Garth's broken body, that had driven him insane? What had been the nature of his original mission to Antos IV? Coincidentally, the transporter accident had left him terribly broken but at the same time in the hands of the race most able to help him. Why then, upon his return to his ship, had Garth ordered the destruction of his benefactors' planet?

Donald Cory believed that the morphing abilities taught to Garth in order to save his life had unbalanced his mind in subtle ways. Others thought that Garth might have become extremely suspicious of the Antosians after he saw that they possessed the skill of cellular metamorphosis, because he viewed that talent as too great a temptation to the pursuit of power. Garth's own behavior certainly demonstrated the power of that temptation; fortunately, his officers and crew had refused to obey him. As he descended into mental illness, his original fear of the Antosians went with him, blossoming into a lust for power and glory divorced from all sanity.

Kirk had imagined it often, that scene on the

bridge of Garth's starship. Garth would have drawn his phaser and dissolved his second-in-command, and then the second officer. The horror of the scene so impressed Kirk that he regarded it almost as a personal memory. He saw himself in the place of one of the officers on the bridge, watching a respected and legendary officer transformed into a madman and a murderer, and knew how much courage it must have taken for them to stand against their commander.

"Lord Garth," the man had called himself while tormenting Kirk in the asylum, insisting on the title, his mood fluctuating wildly between serenity, even gentleness, and violent mania. There had been little chance of the insane "Lord Garth" escaping from his prison, but he and Spock might well have died preventing it. The hero of Kirk's cadet days might have killed him on Elba II, but he would not have escaped to command the *Enterprise;* there had been too many safeguards in place to defeat Garth's mad ingenuity and genius, even if stopping him had cost more lives.

Still, the nightmarish possibility, however slight, had existed—that of a starship taken over by a crew of criminally insane people and commanded by a rogue capable of taking the shape of anyone sent against him, of disguising himself as anyone who might further his dream of conquest. As was the case with his Cochrane deceleration maneuver, this might have been a ruse Garth could have used only once; like the invisible man of H. G. Wells's classic tale, his power would have become useless once others found out about it. But many might have died in the meantime.

Kirk knew that he might have died at his hero's hands, and yet his original admiration for Captain Garth had survived the troubling events on Elba II, and had only grown stronger with the possibility that the great commander might recover. Garth had been insane, unable to control himself, not responsible for his actions; Kirk had always tried to keep that in mind.

He recalled those last moments on Elba II, when Garth, after his first session of therapy with the new serum and free of the memory of his violent aberrations, had looked at Kirk and asked, "Should I know you, sir?" How Kirk had wanted to say "yes" to the hero of his youth, and he had almost said so, for no reason other than that he had admired Garth, once hoping to emulate him, and might be able to help him. And earlier in their encounter, when a raging Garth had heard that his works were still studied at Starfleet Academy and had said, "As well they should be!" Kirk had heard in the man's proud voice something of the heroic, logical mind whose spirit had been as strong as a sun.

By now, the Garth who had killed his officers, who had threatened a world with destruction, who had tortured him and Spock and Cory and had killed the madwoman Marta, was no more. He had died somewhere in the labyrinthine complexities of a powerful, maddened personality.

Chapter Two

"Captain Garth's petition," Kirk said, "seems straightforward enough to me." He leaned forward and rested his arms on the desk. "He is requesting to be assigned to active starship command." Kirk paused. "Is there a problem?"

Admiral Mendez's face on the small screen in Kirk's quarters showed an instant of surprise, and Kirk knew what it meant. The admiral had not expected that response from him. He glanced across the desk at Dr. Leonard McCoy; the chief medical officer lifted a brow, then looked back down at the screen.

José Mendez would have expected to have the physician be part of this discussion, and had quickly assented to McCoy's presence, but Kirk wanted McCoy in the conference room with him for his own reasons. McCoy had met Garth of Izar only after he was again under treatment and had been given his first dose of serum, just before Kirk and his officers had left Elba II. The doctor would be able to view Garth objectively, as a patient fully recovered from a serious illness; he had not known the madman.

"Captain Garth has followed all Starfleet regulations on rehab certification," Mendez said, *"and there is no reason, other than discretion, to deny him a command."*

"Discretion?" Kirk asked. "You mean . . ."

"You know exactly what I mean—endless bureaucratic delay, so that he would never see such a command. We could find plenty of reasons, all of them by the book. There are some in Starfleet Command who have floated the idea of dragging out the process of approval in the hope that Garth might give up after a while and decide to retire. I'm being frank with you, Jim."

"But he is qualified," Kirk said.

"In every outward sense. Exceptionally so."

"I've read all the medical and psychiatric reports you sent us, Admiral," McCoy said, "and Captain Garth gives every sign of being both physically and mentally sound. I've also looked at all of the studies about the effects of that new serum on the patients in the Elba II asylum, and they're even more remarkable than I expected. An Andorian and a Tellarite, both of whom were considered incurable for years, have been leading stable and normal lives on their homeworlds ever since their release, and another former patient is now a professor of mathematics at one of Earth's finest universities."

"That isn't the same as being a starship captain," Mendez said. *"Look, we do have human suspicions and instincts to deal with, even in Starfleet. A starship command is a lot to risk . . ."*

"On yesterday's madman?" Kirk asked, almost as if he were speaking with Garth's own voice.

"We can't see into his mind, Jim. There are those who will never trust him with so much power, despite the success of the new treatments and the low incidence of mental illness throughout the Federation. There are people who would remain suspicious even if he compels us, by the rules, to give him an assignment. Plus, there will always be personnel who won't be eager to follow him for fear of what happened at Antos happening a second time."

"The man has a clean bill of health," McCoy said, "and his Starfleet record, apart from the period of his mental illness, puts him right up there with the greatest commanders. If he pushes for an assignment, you'd have to give him one eventually, by your own rules and regulations."

"I know, Doctor," Mendez said. *"All our expert legal advisers say that we would have to violate our charter to deny him a return to active duty, and would then be ordered to assign him to a post."*

"There's always a desk assignment," Kirk said, even though he could not imagine Garth contentedly sitting in an obscure Starfleet office laboring at tedious administrative tasks. That, he thought, would also be an utter waste of the captain's abilities.

Admiral Mendez shook his head. *"I don't think so. You know how brilliant Garth is. He'd find some way to fight and win this battle just as he always has before, and I'd be on his side. Personally, I hope that he can return to us as one of our most valuable leaders, not as a desk jockey."*

Kirk nodded; they were in agreement on that. Captain Garth, he was sure, could find a way to hold Starfleet and the Federation to their own regulations on standards of health and fitness, and the right to serve despite ancient superstitions about mental health.

"And I also don't want a prolonged series of hearings," Mendez went on, *"with Garth pleading his case and other officers looking for even more excuses to deny him a post. Whether he wins out in the end, or just gives up and settles for an honorable discharge, there'd be so much bad feeling afterwards that Starfleet morale would be seriously damaged."*

"True," Kirk said. "The only way he can prove himself without a doubt is to return to service."

"And the sooner, the better," McCoy added. "Knowing that people are willing to give him a chance will be especially important to his mental health now."

"We agree, then." Mendez was silent for a bit. *"Good, because I'll need you for this. Garth has a particular project in mind."*

"Oh?" Kirk sat back. "So it's not a simple return to service on a starship."

"No," Mendez said. *"Garth is facing us with important unfinished business, with a proposal we can't ignore. It's important by any measure one cares to bring to it—and he's the best man for the job."* The admiral smiled. *"He's like you, Jim, most insistent when he's most right."*

Kirk folded his arms. "And exactly what do you want of me?"

Mendez hunched forward in his chair. *"This is going to sound devious, and I'll deny it officially if you ever bring it up, but what I want you to do is keep an eye on him and step in at the slightest sign of a problem."*

"I thought he'd made a full recovery," McCoy said.

"By every measure we've applied, he has," Mendez said, *"but occasionally even a seemingly well-balanced officer can have a lapse in judgment."*

Remembering his encounter with Captain Ronald Tracey and the *Exeter* on Omega IV—which began with Kirk finding the entire crew of the *Exeter* dead and ended with a crazed Tracey's arrest—Kirk was forced to silently agree.

Mendez continued, *"We're going to grant his request for a return to active duty and also approve his proposed mission. I'm convinced that he's fit, and nothing will go wrong, but if he runs into trouble, I have to be able to say that I had it covered. I'll need you to back me up, and you and Commander Spock are the logical choice to be Garth's watchdogs. After all, you were able to handle him on Elba II."*

Kirk was silent for a few moments. "Sir, what do you really think?" he asked at last.

"Exactly what I said. But we have to consider the possibility that Garth might appear to be unwell, or unbalanced and irrational, when in fact he's perfectly sane. If his mission doesn't go well, or fails completely, his actions could be misinterpreted, and the state of his mental health may have nothing to do with it. If enough officers on the general staff disagree with his judgment, a case could probably be made that Garth suffered a relapse."

"And that," McCoy said, "could open the door to removing him from duty permanently and forcing him to resign. Maybe there are even enough medieval minds at headquarters to force him back to Elba II for another stretch, just to be on the safe side."

"Are there that many doubts about Captain Garth?" Kirk asked.

"In certain circles, yes," Mendez replied. *"With so little mental illness during the last century, and so much success in treating it, we've grown too used to its absence. To have even the few cases we've had is like the return of an ancient infectious disease. Instability of the kind we saw in Garth—insanity on that scale—has shaken a lot of people in authority."*

Kirk recalled a line from *Hamlet,* "Madness in great ones should not unwatched go," and wondered how much invisible distress there might be in ordinary people who never sought help, and therefore were counted as being well. Again, his thoughts returned to Tracey and the crazed look in his eyes when Kirk had confronted him on Omega IV.

"Well, what is Garth's proposed mission?" Kirk asked. "Why exactly is he the most suitable person to carry it out?"

Mendez said, *"I'm sure you already suspect what this mission involves."*

Antos IV, Kirk thought, that had to be it. There had been almost no contact between the Antosians and the Federation since Garth's sojourn on their world; that much he knew. In spite of the reputation of the Antosians for being benevolent and peaceful, prudence had dictated avoiding Antos IV until more was known about what its inhabitants might have done to inadvertently—or deliberately—provoke Garth's instability.

"I'll be sending you the full description of Garth's proposed mission after we've discussed it," Mendez continued, *"along with transcripts of his debriefings after his discharge from Elba II. After that, I know you'll want to consult with Commander Spock."*

"Of course. So what is Garth's proposed mission?"

"His mission, which even those who worry about his reliability think is essential now, is to learn whether or not the people of Antos IV might have any dangerous ambitions, given their shape-changing powers, and whether they are ever likely to have ambitions beyond their own world that might threaten us."

Kirk had already guessed that this might have become a serious concern. If he had considered the possibility in the past, as he occasionally had, then so had other Starfleet officers and Federation officials. However peaceful the Antosians seemed, their encounters with other Federation races had been too few to give a complete picture.

"We have no evidence that the Antosians harbor such ambitions," he said, "at least not yet. Whether that will always be so is another matter."

Mendez nodded. *"They claim to have always been a peaceful race, but at one of our meetings, Garth asked me whether we could afford not to keep a close watch on the Antosians for any signs of aggression or instability."* He grimaced. *"I was about to say that we have the same problem with him, but he beat me to it."*

Kirk chuckled. "That must have been a moment."

"Yes, and Garth savored it. I assured him that he could tell me anything he liked in complete confidence, but he didn't seem all that upset. He just laughed and said that if I had all those doubts about him, then so would others, and he was prepared to face them. He emphasized that for others to trust him completely and without question, given his recent history, would be completely irrational."

"Sounds like a sane man to me," McCoy muttered.

"In any case, he has us pinned by our own regulations and ideals, and also by our concern for the Federation's welfare and security. So, in short, here's what we want you to do. You will deliver Garth to

Antos IV, on a diplomatic mission, and stand by to bring him home. He'll have the official status of a diplomat and representative of the Federation, but that won't fool him, since he already expects some supervision."

Kirk was puzzled. "But then you're not giving him an actual command after all."

"We are, after a fashion." Mendez looked distinctly uneasy. *"He will be in full command of this mission. You will remain in charge of the day-to-day operations of the* Enterprise, *but for anything mission-specific, his is the final word. I hope you understand—given his seniority, his experience as a fleet captain, and his longer record of service, he does outrank you."*

Kirk said nothing.

"It's only a technicality," Mendez went on. *"Naturally, if he shows signs of instability or of misusing his authority, you will step in."*

"If that's what the admiral orders," Kirk said, trying to keep the unease out of his voice.

"It is, I'm afraid. Look, Jim, I know you don't like giving up even a piece of your command, but it's necessary. To give him no more than the status of a diplomat wouldn't be convincing enough for the Antosians, especially if his fears about them prove to be true."

"So you do have reason to be suspicious of the Antosians?"

"I don't know. Garth and the Antosians know one another, and that should be very helpful to such a mission. It makes him the perfect intermediary, and

I've spent enough time with him to feel that he has no hidden agenda in mind. But a number of officers in Starfleet Command suspect that the Antosians may deeply regret ever having given their powers to Garth."

The proposed mission was definitely necessary, Kirk thought, and he did not doubt the ability of his crew and himself to control Garth should he prove troublesome—although if an officer of José Mendez's experience was this certain of Garth, then Garth's stability could be trusted. Kirk would be able to serve with an officer he had revered in his youth, and if Garth succeeded, his honor would be restored.

But he did not care for the idea of having the man in command of the *Enterprise,* even if only in part. He thought of his recurring dream about the captain and wondered if that was the Garth he was soon to meet, or if he would instead glimpse the madman behind the rational mask.

Kirk felt shame at the thought.

"He's aware of what he did when he was afflicted," Mendez said, *"including what happened on Elba II, since he's seen the records, but he apparently has no personal memory of those actions, only of his earlier deeds and his time among the Antosians. The man you see will be the Garth you read about at the Academy."*

"I have just one question left," Kirk said. "Does he still have the power to change his shape?"

"He hasn't used it," Mendez replied. *"Maintain-*

ing another shape requires a fair amount of energy, Garth claims, even for Antosians—a different shape can't be held indefinitely. You saw Cory's report—he hasn't seen Garth in any shape but his own since his successful course of treatment began, and he was under constant observation at the asylum until his release. Since arriving at Starfleet headquarters, he's rarely been alone, and he's always been himself. It's possible that his cure has suppressed his morphing ability."

"Or that he simply doesn't choose to use it," McCoy said, "in order to show that you can trust him."

"And maybe he's just waiting for the opportunity to change shape later on, for his own purposes." Kirk made the statement reluctantly, but it needed to be said. "The fact is that you don't know for sure."

"No," Admiral Mendez admitted, *"we don't."*

Alone with Spock in the briefing room, Kirk concluded his account of the meeting with José Mendez. "You've read all the reports now," he finished. "What do you think, Spock? Was Garth insane?"

Spock sat back and raised an eyebrow. "He was so diagnosed. We witnessed his behavior on Elba II. But perhaps you are asking a different question, namely whether or not his actions and state of mind were somehow misinterpreted by observers."

"What I'm asking is if he still might be insane."

"I am always surprised by human suspicion," Spock said after a moment. "It is so transcendent of the facts, so unconcerned with being wrong at the moment."

"So what do you think?"

"In another age," Spock said, "the fate of Captain Garth might have been deemed a tragedy, with so much intelligence, nobility, and grace brought so low."

"But today," Kirk said with a small smile, "the tragedy can have a happy ending, peace be to Shakespeare. The tragedians of past centuries might have been disturbed by our progress in these matters. It would certainly have deprived them of dramatic possibilities."

Spock nodded. "Indeed, they would have found our cure for Captain Garth's illness implausible, even though I would still say to them that the human beings of our time carry around enough remaining flaws for tragedies to be possible."

"But only rarely the tragedy of mental illness," Kirk said.

"There are still tragic circumstances, Captain, created by errors in judgment, where the flaw of character is not delusional in nature, but is lived as if it were a virtue."

"In which the villain of the piece is convinced that he is the hero," Kirk added, "and is not deluded or mentally ill, but is certain that he's right."

"And might have been right, or at least successful in his aims, right or wrong." Spock steepled his fingers. "It is possible to argue that Captain Garth was never insane, that he truly believed in his ambitions."

"Even that he believed that he was on a mission for the Antosians during his incarceration on Elba II," Kirk said.

"The problem of sanity," Spock continued, "as I have described it on occasion, divides into separate questions. A conqueror or political figure may perhaps not be deemed insane, aside from the empirically verifiable question of whether or not he has a physiological disorder that can cause insanity, if his ambitions are possible and can be achieved—in other words, if what is in his mind adheres to external reality. This is aside from the morality of his ambitions, since possible achievements may be moral, immoral, or amoral, desirable or undesirable, apart from the sanity of one who sees them as possible. Delusion, then, is always a lack of sanity in some sense, as distinct from ignorance, but even an apparent megalomania may not be insanity if served by an intellect capable of making its dreams a reality."

"And the case of Garth?" Kirk asked.

"Captain Garth was demonstrably insane before he received his treatments. He may be rational now, if not necessarily ethical. What does he propose to do on Antos IV to allay the Federation's suspicions of that people?"

"From what he proposes, he plans to talk to them and bring back assurances of their peaceful intentions, as well as assuring them that the Federation has no designs on their world. After that, presumably there would be a treaty and some sort of arrangement for diplomatic representatives. And if the treaty were violated—"

"There is not a shred of evidence," Spock said, "that the Antosians have ever had any ambitions beyond their own planet, or ever will. There has never been any such evidence. It is that mismatch between our experience with the Antosians and Garth's previous attempt at aggression against them that supported the diagnosis of insanity, a diagnosis confirmed by the evidence of structural and organic changes in his brain."

Kirk leaned back in his chair. Garth's medical records showed no sign of such changes now, no sign of any of the neurological alterations that had accompanied his insanity and contributed to it. That could have been an indication that he no longer possessed his shape-changing talents, but it was impossible to be sure.

"It is possible," Spock went on, "that Garth's instability was caused by his acquisition of the power of cellular metamorphosis that saved his life after his accident."

His first officer, Kirk thought as he listened, was apparently thinking along lines similar to his own.

"It is also possible," Spock continued, "that something of this instability lingers, and may express itself in certain resentments against the Antosians—suitably rationalized, of course. He may be projecting his own doubts about himself onto the Antosians, building them up into a menace, plausibly a minor threat now but growing larger later on. And by calling attention to that danger now, Garth's most secret self may imagine that he could become the savior of the Federation. The argument from pure possibility has no end, Captain. It may be both true and false, as revealed by time, even if the argument is given by a madman. One is reminded of your ancient Rome, which concluded that it could not tolerate two Romes on the shores of the Mediterranean basin, and so destroyed its rival, Carthage. But it took three wars for the Romans to do it."

"But was Garth insane when we first encountered him?" Kirk asked.

"If we mark insanity by the unrealistic dreams of conquest that he held at the asylum, then yes, he was insane. Garth might have acquired one starship to achieve his aims, though even that was unlikely, but he had no fleet, and no followers other than a few deranged fellow inmates. We might have concluded that he was merely mistaken in his aims, dangerous but not insane, had it not been for the detectable malfunctions in his physiology."

Kirk frowned. "But you were saying that his mad ambitions might have been completely sane."

"In other circumstances, yes."

"But what is he now, Spock? What is he now?"

"That is what we must learn," Spock said. "I see that you share some of the fears of Garth expressed by others."

"I have to go by the evidence," Kirk said, "and everything we have indicates that Garth is well and able to return to duty. Admiral Mendez has enough faith in that evidence to send Garth on an important mission, and that's reassuring. But I can't forget that he killed two of his own officers and caused the death of a woman as mad as himself. He might have killed us, too."

"That was when he was insane," Spock said, "when his affliction was forcing him to behave reprehensibly as surely as if his mind were being controlled by some powerful outside force. It would not be logical to assign blame to him for those deeds." He paused. "It troubles me now that so many in Starfleet Command and the Federation's diplomatic corps seem to share Garth's worries about the Antosians."

Kirk sighed. "I must share them, mustn't I? We can't risk doing nothing."

"That is the practical conclusion, Captain, but it may be wrong."

"And consider this," Kirk said. "Perhaps Garth knows that nothing will come of this mission, that no real danger exists, and he is merely undertaking a politically harmless mission in order to restore and build our trust in him."

"To what end?" Spock asked. "Other than of course to regain the trust of Starfleet."

"Perhaps against the day when he is in command of a starship again, perhaps a fleet."

"But will he not be in command of the *Enterprise?*"

"He'll be in charge of the mission. Strictly speaking, I'll be reporting to him, but only as it relates to the mission objectives."

"I see." Spock looked thoughtful for a moment. "But if we reason thus, then is it not possible that Captain Garth is playing a game of deep cover, and that somehow he will be in command despite all our safeguards—that he is, in fact, already in command?"

Kirk shook his head. "We're being a bit paranoid ourselves. Pretty soon I'll start wondering if McCoy and I were actually talking to Admiral Mendez. I'll start thinking that the admiral wasn't really there, that his image was an illusion. After all, we've had that experience with José Mendez before, when the Talosians were able to make us believe he was aboard my ship when he wasn't."

"That particular stratagem," Spock said, "is beyond Garth's abilities. I had the help of the Talosians then, who created that illusion, while Captain Garth has no such resource. It would not have been possible for him to take on the admiral's form and confer with you and Dr. McCoy without detection by Starfleet Command, and his call clearly came from Starfleet headquarters."

Kirk smiled. "You're right. The reports are thoroughly convincing, and I saw how Garth was beginning to recover even before we left the asylum." He had not seen the mad Lord Garth then, only a man grasping at sanity and apparently free of his demons. "There's no reason to think Captain Garth has anything in mind except for his stated purpose." Kirk sighed. "I guess this mission will just have to run its course."

"It would seem so, Captain."

Chapter Three

Captain Fatima Baksh, commanding officer of the *U.S.S. Gell-Mann,* was a dark-eyed woman with a direct, piercing gaze that was evident even on the viewscreen on the desk of Kirk's quarters. "*Captain Garth is prepared for his departure,*" she said, "*and we will be aboard the* Enterprise *in two hours. I will be piloting the shuttlecraft myself.*"

"I look forward to meeting you both," Kirk said to the image on the small screen above his desk. He had gone to his quarters to put on his formal uniform; he wanted Garth to have a proper reception, but had decided to keep the protocol to a minimum. How Garth responded to that might indicate whether he was dealing with a man who simply wanted to proceed with his mission or who still retained a little of the irrational pride of "Lord Garth."

"I will not be staying," Captain Baksh said, *"since the* Gell-mann *is due at Starbase 9 tomorrow."*

Kirk studied the woman. She had not betrayed any emotion during their brief discussion of the arrangements for Garth's arrival, but he had glanced at her record earlier. As a lieutenant, she had been one of the officers serving with Garth during his mission to Antos IV, and one of those on the bridge who had disabled Garth and then seized control of his ship. That she had been assigned to ferry Garth to the *Enterprise* was probably not a coincidence; Mendez would be testing them both, to see how they reacted.

"How is Captain Garth getting along?" Kirk asked, trying to keep his tone casual.

Captain Baksh narrowed her eyes. *"He appears to be doing well. I have not seen that much of him—I have my duties, and he has been absorbed in reading a great many volumes on history and diplomacy. We've played a few games of chess. He always checkmates me."* She let out her breath. *"I know what you are asking, Captain Kirk. You want to know if I have glimpsed any signs of the madman I saw on the bridge of the* Heisenberg."

"I didn't want to put it quite that bluntly." Kirk was, however, grateful that she had done so.

"I haven't seen that man," Baksh said, *"only the Captain Garth he was before his accident, the officer I admired and hoped to emulate. By all outward signs, he is completely recovered."*

"That's good to hear," Kirk said.

"Yet I keep having the feeling that he is hiding something, holding something back. It is perhaps a measure of my own weakness and intolerance that I cannot quite trust him, that I am glad he will not be in command of my starship, that I still cannot banish the memory of the man who shot two of my fellow officers and would have killed the rest of us if we hadn't stopped him."

"I understand," Kirk said, feeling the same.

"But he was very ill then, and not responsible for that. He was a man possessed. I was standing near him when he gave his order to destroy Antos IV, and he was terrified—I saw the fear in his eyes. I have no doubt that he truly believed that we were in great danger, and have often thought since then that we might have found some way to disarm him that would not have cost the lives of two of our officers. When he fired at them, I am sure that he thought he was acting in self-defense. Still . . ." Baksh paused. *"I have my sense of duty, and Starfleet has pronounced him fit for service. Every crew member aboard the* Gell-Mann *has been under strict orders to treat Garth with respect and honor."* Her mouth twisted. *"I wish you both a most successful mission, Captain."*

"Curious," Spock said, "that Captain Garth should still so fear transporters."

The shuttlecraft from the *Gell-Mann* had just arrived. Kirk stood with Spock and Yeoman Wodehouse in the shuttlebay, waiting to greet Garth and Baksh.

"I don't find it curious at all," Kirk said. "In fact, I sympathize with the man. Just think of what he went through physically. And if you consider what mastering cellular metamorphosis in order to save his life cost him in mental health, you can imagine the depth of his fear. No chance, however small, would seem worth risking such a catastrophe again."

"True, but the odds of another such accident are extremely remote."

Kirk glanced at his first officer. "Spock, no risk, however remote, may be worth it to him, given what he might lose again. A one in a trillion chance might seem too much to risk."

"The odds are much greater than that now, Captain."

"Please don't tell me the exact number."

"Several trillions to one," Spock said.

Kirk smiled at his friend's uncharacteristic imprecision, then turned his attention to the shuttlecraft, more apprehensive about this meeting than he had expected to be.

Captain Baksh left the craft and descended the ramp, followed by Captain Garth. Both captains wore their formal uniforms, and Garth his decorations: three Medals of Honor, several starbursts, the Palm Leaf and the Oak Leaf, the ribbons denoting several of his successful campaigns. Kirk felt a bit reassured by the sight of the decorations, and by knowing that Starfleet was allowing Garth to wear the medals his valor had earned him. He was an impressive figure; his tall form towered over the slight figure of Captain Baksh. His graying hair was slightly shorter than it had been during his time on Elba II. Kirk noticed then that Garth was smiling slightly, as the mad Lord Garth sometimes had just before launching into one of his rants, but there was no madness in this man's blue eyes, only a calm curiosity.

The three in the shuttlebay stood at attention. Yeoman Wodehouse lifted a whistle to her lips and sounded a brief ceremonial note to mark the arrival of the two captains, and then Kirk stepped forward. "Welcome aboard the *Enterprise,* Captain Baksh," he said. "Allow me to introduce my first officer, Mr. Spock, and my aide, Yeoman Lesley Wodehouse."

Captain Baksh said, "Captain Kirk, please allow me to present Captain Garth of Izar, returning to duty as a representative of the Federation to Antos IV."

Garth bowed his head slightly. If he was surprised by the small size of the *Enterprise*'s welcoming party, he gave no sign of it. "Ah, yes," Garth said in a low, even voice, "Captain Kirk and Mr. Spock. I am told that we have met before, when I was ill, but my memory is understandably vague on that point."

"Of course," Kirk said. "I'm pleased to see that you've recovered."

"Greetings, Captain Garth," Spock said. "I look forward to serving with you."

"We're holding a reception in your honor," Kirk

added, "in our recreation room. Our officers and crew are looking forward to meeting you, sir."

"I am so sorry that I cannot join you," Captain Baksh murmured, "but our mission to Starbase 9 cannot wait." She glanced at Garth. "Farewell, Captain, and may your mission succeed."

Garth bowed. "I shall miss our chess games, Fatima. You were a most worthy opponent."

"As shall I." Captain Baksh smiled, but Kirk had the feeling that she was relieved to be on her way.

Garth stood next to Kirk in silence until Baksh had disappeared into her shuttlecraft, then said, "Thank you for the welcome, Captain. Please lead the way."

The captain would, of course, be well aware of Starfleet's reservations about returning him to active duty; he would have picked up on the doubts about him either directly or indirectly. The man was no fool; everything that others might have thought must have long since played through his mind. Kirk's own conversation with Admiral Mendez had probably been only the tip of the iceberg; what had gone on below the surface had to have been much more contentious, and Kirk could easily imagine Garth confronting the doubts of others and then deflecting them in his own theatrical way. The Shakespearean cast of mind that Garth had shown as the mad Lord Garth, belonging as it did to a man who had grown to have confidence in his undeniable abilities and accomplishments, meant that he would not lose his sense of the dramatic, whether he was sane or insane.

That dramatic sense was part of what had made Garth a great leader in the first place.

Garth had made the rounds at the reception, greeting each officer and crew member in turn and presenting the same amiable and composed demeanor to each person. Kirk had been watching him while trying not to be obvious about it, but Garth, in the middle of a conversation with Lieutenant Uhura and Nurse Christine Chapel, had glanced briefly at Kirk with the amused look of an actor taking pride in a successful performance. Now he stood with Lieutenant Commander Montgomery Scott and Lieutenant Kyle as the three men sampled drams of Scotch.

Leonard McCoy came up to Kirk and handed him a glass of wine. "Garth seems to be charming almost everyone in sight," the physician said in a low voice.

"Yes, he is," Kirk replied. "Almost makes me think we should have laid on a full banquet for him after the reception." In spite of his words, he was content with keeping Garth's welcome on a smaller scale. He and Garth, along with Spock, had scheduled a meeting after the reception to discuss their mission in more detail, and there was always the chance that Garth, given the ambiguity of his position, might have found a more elaborate reception unsuitable, even subtly insulting.

A group of engineers were leaving the reception; others, including Spock, had already left. Garth drained his small glass of Scotch, nodded at Scott and Kyle, then made his way toward Kirk and McCoy.

"Thank you for your hospitality, Captain. I've enjoyed meeting your people, and much as I would like to prolong this occasion, I know we have a meeting ahead of us still."

Garth, Kirk thought, already seemed to be taking command. "Mr. Spock is probably already waiting for us in the conference room."

"And I have to get back to sickbay," McCoy murmured. "Good seeing you again, Captain Garth."

As McCoy left, Garth said, "I suppose that the good doctor feels that I am, in some small way, his handiwork."

"So you do remember him," Kirk said.

"I know that Dr. McCoy met me on Elba II at the onset of my successful therapy, and that he synthesized more of the serum you brought there for me and my fellow patients. But my memory of my first meeting with him is as vague as that of my earlier encounter with you and Mr. Spock. Perhaps that is just as well." For an instant, Kirk glimpsed grief in Garth's eyes, as if an unhappy memory had suddenly come to him, and then his unruffled expression returned. "Lead the way, Captain Kirk. Even though Vulcans are not capable of becoming impatient, perhaps it is time that we joined Commander Spock."

"Well, gentlemen," Garth said as he looked around the briefing room, "are we the only ones coming?"

Kirk nodded, then sat down at Spock's left. "No one else, Captain Garth."

"I would have no objection to the presence of others," Garth replied as he seated himself at the table across from them. "My mission is of great concern to the Federation and to Starfleet." Kirk noted that Garth seemed to be drawing a sharp distinction between Starfleet and the Federation.

"Captain Garth," Spock began, "please tell us exactly what you hope to accomplish on Antos IV."

Garth smiled. "Right to the point, eh, Mr. Spock?"

"Anything else would be pointless."

Garth seemed about to laugh, then folded his arms. "Quite right, Commander. I am already well acquainted with all the objections to my mission as voiced by Starfleet and the Federation's diplomatic corps, as well as all of the discreetly expressed doubts about me, and I am in complete sympathy with those doubts."

"Indeed?" Spock said, raising an eyebrow.

"I was a madman." A pensive, almost regretful look crossed Garth's face. "I may not be able to recall what happened to me when I was insane, but I have looked at all of the records of my deeds. I am well aware of what I did in that mad state, how much harm I caused, and how much more harm I might have brought about. That I retain no personal memory of those actions and am not held responsible for them is small consolation."

"And how will you address the doubts held about you?" Spock asked.

Garth shrugged. "How can I battle vague presuppositions, even outright fear of what I might do? I can only disprove the doubts of others through my actions, and even then there will still be those who will remain suspicious of me. And when I am gone, will others then claim, 'Garth was true after all, and all of our suspicions were wrong'? Or will they say instead that I simply ran out of time to carry out my schemes?"

"It is impossible to prove a negative," Spock replied. "An infinite amount of time would be required." Spock, Kirk knew, had his own way to probe and possibly reveal Garth's true state of mind.

Garth gazed at Spock for a few moments, then turned toward Kirk. "Perhaps I should ease your minds about questioning me this way. Be as harsh as you wish. It's necessary, and I'll do all that I can to answer you."

"Very well," Spock said. "Please tell us exactly how you propose to learn of any dangerous intentions on the part of the Antosians."

Garth smiled. "I see that Admiral Mendez left it to me to fill you in on many of the details."

"Go on," Kirk said.

"I know the Antosians better than anyone else who is not one of them," Garth said. "After my discharge from Elba II, on my way back to Earth and my meetings with Starfleet Command, I was able to stop at Antos IV for a time and visit those who had helped me there. I wanted to demonstrate to Starfleet that I could return to the place that had provoked my . . . illness without any deleterious effects, and was granted permission to do so, but my main reason for wanting to return was to apologize. I didn't know what to expect, but I felt that I had to atone for my threats somehow. To their everlasting credit, the Antosians greeted me warmly and made me feel most welcome. I was very sorry to leave again." He paused, then continued, "I intend to meet with the Antosian leaders and question them, and then I think I will perceive the truth."

"Indeed," Spock said.

"I will be standing before either a wall or a window," Garth said.

"That's it?" Kirk asked, unable to restrain himself.

Spock almost looked puzzled as he studied Garth. "But surely," Spock said, "you see how problematic your proposal seems to be, since we will have only your opinion by which to judge a people who have never threatened anyone, who are reputed to be most peaceful, and who show no interest in extending their influence beyond their own world."

"I wasn't trying to be vague," Garth murmured, "or cryptic. You have to know more in order to judge the complexity of what we will be attempting." He leaned forward and rested his arms on the table. "Captain Kirk, I must tell you and Commander Spock what Admiral Mendez did not."

Kirk took a deep breath. "Well, you certainly know how to pique my curiosity."

"That wasn't my intention," Garth said. "This entire mission is of such vital importance that it must proceed by stages, including a careful control of how much anyone involved with it can be told at any given stage. Right now, both of you need more information from me, but there is a point, as you'll see, beyond which no one, including myself, knows anything of what might happen with the Antosians and how the Federation might have to respond."

"Captain Garth," Spock said, "I find myself confused."

That, Kirk thought, was putting it mildly. Suspicion was taking hold of him again; what was Garth actually trying to do? Given his abilities, he might be attempting something far removed from what anyone assumed, even if his plan was a constructive one. Leaders often acted for the good of others even if their worthy goals were at first concealed, or had to be concealed, from those who would benefit most. There were factions at work at Starfleet Command and the Federation Council and in other halls of decision, and the same might be true of the Antosians. If so, Garth might be able to exploit such divisions on Antos IV; there was endless opportunity for a creative mind like Garth's to work toward purely private goals. Why had Garth been permitted to visit Antos IV? Who had decided that?

"I must tell you the whole story," Garth said, "and you'll be hearing it from one who is convinced that he understands it better than anyone else can, because he is the only living direct witness, apart from the Antosians."

"Go ahead, Captain." Fascinated as he was by the idea of hearing this tale from the man who had once been his hero, Kirk cautioned himself that Garth might be an unreliable narrator in spite of his closeness to the events. Garth might not be in command of all the facts, he might be misinterpreting what he had experienced, or he might be deliberately trying to mislead them.

"As you well know," Garth began, "a transporter accident can wreak havoc on a human being's structure—on any being's structure, for that matter. Organs can be displaced, limbs broken—any number of horrific things can happen. In a way, I was fortunate—I didn't die instantly, and I didn't suffer the most grotesque possible effects of such an accident, but I was damaged and deformed, and had to struggle even to breathe."

The man seemed to be looking through Kirk as he spoke, almost as though he was in a mild trance; perhaps Garth was remembering his ordeal.

"I had come to Antos IV," Garth continued, "because the Federation wished to establish relations with the people of that planet. All we knew about their culture was that they were humanoids like us, and that their few contacts with other races showed only peaceful aims. There had been few offworld visitors to Antos IV, but what they had seen there indicated that the Antosians were a most cooperative and pacifistic race. There was no sign of any advanced weaponry, and no indication that the Antosians were at all interested in violent pursuits."

Garth paused for a moment, and Kirk saw a

mournful look cross his face, as though he were sorrowing for something he had lost.

"I find myself wondering," Spock said in the silence, "why it is that you, a man known for your military exploits as a fleet commander, were sent there rather than a seasoned diplomat."

"Both Starfleet and the Federation Council wanted to demonstrate both our peaceful intentions toward Antos IV and our ability and willingness to protect the Antosians from any outside aggression." Garth opened his hands, palms up. "They thought that a Starfleet captain, one who had fought his battles only in the interests of restoring or furthering peace, would be the perfect representative. And I will confess that my superiors knew by then that I was already looking forward to another kind of life."

Spock arched his right eyebrow.

"I had won my victories," Garth said in answer to Spock's silent query. "I had been in Starfleet for my entire adult life. A man comes to a time when he must leave the battlefield to others and look for other challenges. I didn't know yet what might lie ahead, but I did not want to become an old warrior, living in the past, losing myself in thoughts of victories I might have had in past times."

Garth was being extremely honest, Kirk thought. He was in effect admitting that an aspect of the mad would-be conqueror Lord Garth had always lived inside him.

"In any case," Garth went on, "I made contact with

the Antosians and was asked to beam down alone—I believe only because the Antosians assumed that since I was the Federation's designated representative, anyone else accompanying me would be unnecessary or redundant. As it turned out, that was fortunate—it meant that only I was disabled and damaged in that freak transporter accident."

"A freak occurrence indeed," Spock said, "since the odds of it happening under normal circumstances—"

"—are several trillions to one at least," Garth finished. "Yes, I am well aware of being an extremely rare exception." He looked away for a moment. "I was dying. I couldn't breathe, and I imagined that I could feel the deformities in my body produced by the malfunctioning transporter. I don't quite know how to describe what happened next. The Antosians, in order to help me in my distress and begin my healing, sent me into myself. I believe they began this process by using a technique similar to your Vulcan mind-meld, Commander Spock, but I was in too much agony to sense exactly how they managed it. I was sent into, in effect, the mirror-memory of my own structure. They taught me, through cellular metamorphosis, to reverse the changes that had damaged me."

Kirk kept his eyes on Garth, wondering exactly how much of that knowledge the other captain still retained, and whether he still had the power to transform himself.

"I learned that I had to be extremely watchful of

my cellular structures," Garth said. "The Antosians could not tell me how long it would be before the original memory of my bodily integrity would again take hold and prevail against the disarray."

Garth bowed his head and was silent for a while. When he looked up once more, the mournful look had returned to his eyes. "With what I was taught, I healed myself, more quickly than I could have imagined possible. I remained among the Antosians for a short time, and by the time Liang Jin—he was my first officer—contacted me to see what orders I had for him, I assumed myself ready to return to my ship, and I gave him the order to beam me back aboard. I was physically whole, physically myself, but my brain was disordered, my nerves . . ." He passed a hand over his face, then rested his arms on the tabletop again, looking defeated. "But you know what happened after that."

Kirk again imagined the scene on the bridge of the *Heisenberg:* the raging Garth returning, screaming that the Antosians had to die, disintegrating Liang Jin and his second officer with his phaser. Something in him recoiled as he thought of the monstrosity that had possessed the man who sat before him, and yet he still felt the pull of loyalty that Garth had been able to exert on those under his command. It was the heritage of a psychological plumage, a personal style that could stand outside the morality of a particular context. It was good that Garth had not lived in past times; he might have been the kind of dedicated conqueror that the mad Lord Garth of Elba II had been too irrational and ill to become.

"Do you remember why you gave the order to destroy the Antosians and their world?" Kirk asked.

Garth shook his head. "Not exactly. All I can remember about my return to my ship is my absolute fear of them and my utter conviction that they were a danger to every inhabited planet in the galaxy. And of course that wasn't the case."

Spock said, "Captain Garth, either the Antosians are as peaceful as we have believed them to be—and all evidence points to this as a permanent condition—or there is evidence for something else. If they are a pacifistic race, then sending someone else to complete your original mission of establishing contact would have been quite enough. Therefore, I cannot believe that the Federation would be sending us on this particular mission without some evidence, or at least suspicion, of an upcoming problem. While such heights of paranoia are not unknown in human history, I am baffled by its presence in this case, with such an apparently benevolent race as the Antosians."

"Quite right, Commander," Garth said. "Now we come to the reason for my mission. The Antosians, thanks to me, are no slouches at paranoia themselves. They learned a lot about human beings in restoring me to myself. They also heard me raving about how, with their shape-changing abilities, they could rule the universe—how, with their power, we could not chance their very existence, that we had to destroy them to save ourselves, because even if it took ages, they might one day, sooner or later, begin to use their power against other cultures."

Garth leaned forward. "You see, gentlemen, it was my very presence among the Antosians that has changed matters. My last visit to their world has confirmed it. These peaceful people thought only of saving my life, and in return for that, they were treated to my ranting about their great power and how they might conquer the universe. They witnessed my fear of what they might do and heard my threats against them. And now—" He sighed. "A faction of Antosians has grown to believe that they should destroy us before we destroy them. They do not think that they can risk our ever having a change of heart about them. This was what I discovered when, after my discharge from Elba II, I visited those Antosians who had helped me, in order to express my gratitude properly. I found out that I have infected their people with my fear and paranoia, with my former madness. That is my greatest burden. That may be the worst of all my deeds."

Kirk noticed that Spock remained silent. It was his way of showing surprise. The captain broke the silence himself. "So now the Antosians are like us, holding many opinions, perhaps from one extreme to the other."

Garth nodded. "It was my own deranged presence that injected the virus of doubt into a vulnerable group of Antosian minds. And it is now up to me, with your help, to undo what has been done."

"And you are certain of this," Kirk said.

"A very small group of Federation and Starfleet officials are aware of what has happened. Admiral Mendez has also, with my help, exchanged messages with the leaders of the peaceful Antosian majority. They need us now as much as we will need them." Garth sat back in his chair. "At this point, Captain Kirk, you will undoubtedly wish to consult with the admiral. He asked me to recommend that you contact him, so that he can confirm what I've said."

Kirk tensed. "I'll do so at once. This is terrible news."

"Yes, it is." A look of sadness passed over Garth's face. "I am very unhappy at being the cause of these developments, however unwittingly. But the problem now before us only illustrates how the violent shadows of the evolutionary past of intelligent species wait to spill into their futures. I'm grateful that we've had the chance to glimpse what may be coming and to try to prevent it."

Kirk stood up. "Mr. Spock," he said, "I suggest that you show Captain Garth to his quarters while I contact the admiral."

Garth rose and left the room with Spock. As the door slid shut behind them, Kirk wondered if somehow he had been drawn into a subtle delusion of Garth's. Could he be misinterpreting the Antosians again? Was it even possible that Garth had somehow deceived a small group of Starfleet officers and Federation officials?

It was highly unlikely, but either way, the situation was a dangerous one.

"What Garth told you is true," Admiral Mendez said, *"and the mission he wishes to undertake is necessary. Garth has argued that, through his actions, he violated the Prime Directive by interfering with and altering the culture of Antos IV, and that the only way he can redeem himself is to repair the damage. But this mission isn't just a matter of Garth's personal redemption. Imagine the use the Klingons or the Romulans might make of any shape-changing Antosian allies who dream of conquest."*

Kirk glared at the image of Mendez on the three-screen viewer in the center of the briefing-room table. "Admiral, I would've appreciated being briefed on the *entire* mission before taking the captain on board."

"I'm sorry for leaving you partly in the dark, Jim, but I wanted you to hear about the Antosians straight from Garth without any presuppositions coloring your feelings on the matter. And I wanted your impressions of Garth's telling of the story."

"Fair enough," Kirk said, though he remained unhappy about the admiral's deception. "I hope we can trust Garth."

"What he's told us has checked out, and the peaceful Antosian majority would much rather deal with him than with anyone else. I suppose that's even more evidence of their peacefulness, that they're willing to forgive and welcome a man who tried to give an order

to destroy them. Garth's presence is also needed to convince the fearful Antosians that we mean them no harm. And I can't think of anyone better qualified to oversee his mission than you, Jim, and not just because you were able to deal with him on Elba II. You've bent the rules when you thought it was necessary, and you've turned out to be right. Starfleet has too often benefited by your willingness to flout orders when you believed we were wrong. You have a creative bent that sometimes, but only sometimes, exceeds Commander Spock's analytic abilities."

"You're saying that there's a bit of Garth in me."

Mendez smiled. *"I suppose I am. Keep a watchful eye on him, and don't hesitate to take over the mission if you find he can't handle it properly. With any luck, Garth will find a way to resolve the problem by himself, but as I told you before—"*

"—you want to be covered," Kirk finished. "Sad that our contact with the Antosians has planted the rotten fruit that now exists there."

"It was waiting to happen," Mendez said. *"If Garth hadn't contacted this civilization, others would have done so, and perhaps created a similar paranoia among groups of Antosians. And keep in mind that this particular violent group is still a very small minority."*

"Any more advice?" Kirk asked.

"Let Garth take the lead, but watch him carefully. Good luck, Jim." Mendez's smile seemed uncertain just before his image went dark.

Kirk stood up, wondering whether anyone really knew as much as he needed to know about what the mission to Antos IV might reveal. Garth, who had initiated this mission, probably had the best view of the matter, but his was a very personal view, linked as it was to his own recovery. Yet Garth was in command of this mission; he would either prove himself, or Kirk would have to do his best to prevent the situation from becoming even more threatening than it already was.

Chapter Four

ANTOS IV CIRCLED a G2 yellow-white star at a distance of nearly one hundred and fifty million kilometers. As the *Enterprise* entered standard orbit around the Class-M planet, Spock looked up at the bridge viewscreen and thought about how it was with intelligent beings when they began to look beyond their own worlds. Beings that looked beyond their own skies, and who happened to be in sectors of the galaxy that already had worlds with interstellar capacity, faced an immediate problem: how to get along with their neighbors.

This was not a problem with worlds in distant parts of the galaxy, where civilizations might be sparse, and a culture might emerge to find no one nearby—at least not in their immediate future. Nor was getting along with others a problem for the inhabitants of

Talos IV, whose mental powers and virtual reality choices were so advanced that they could conjure up whatever experiences they wished without ever posing a problem to their neighbors. In fact, had that planet not been placed off-limits by the Federation, other civilizations might have posed a problem to Talos IV. The prospect of a world where one could have whatever one wished was so seductive and potentially addictive that landing on Talos IV was punishable by the death penalty; it was the only offense within the Federation for which capital punishment was meted out. But Spock sometimes wondered how long such a ban could be enforced.

Had Garth of Izar suffered his transporter accident while beaming down to Talos IV, the Talosians would not have been able to heal his body, but they could have given him the mental illusion of health and strength, as they had with the human woman Vina. He might have lived out his life unaware of any deformities, as Spock's former commanding officer, Captain Christopher Pike, the only man allowed to violate the order forbidding contact with the Talosians, was now doing on Talos IV. Instead, Garth had acquired the physical ability to heal and transform his own body but had paid the price with temporary derangement.

"Standard orbit achieved," Lieutenant Hikaru Sulu said from his helmsman's station.

The planet below, except for six uninhabited and volcanically active islands known as the Tiresians, had only one land mass, a continent even larger than

Eurasia of Earth. The vast continent, according to records, was called Anatossia, with roughly half its land above the equator of Antos IV and half below. Anatossia's eastern coastline was dominated by high, sheer cliffs; in the west, the Illesa Mountains, a range of Himalayan height, ran from north to south, dividing the continent in two and indicating that Anatossia had been formed from two smaller continents that had drifted together. The regions closest to the equator were tropical, and there was an expanse of desert in northeastern Anatossia, but a moderate climate prevailed elsewhere, which made Spock wonder why, with so much habitable terrain available, all of the Antosians chose to live in or near one large inland city in the northeast, Pynesses, and its suburbs. Captain Garth had not been able to answer that question, not having spent enough time among the Antosians to find out.

Spock's opinion of the matter at hand was that shape-shifting, as demonstrated by Garth on Elba II, would require free circulation of Antosians throughout the Federation before the skill became a danger on either the criminal or the military scale. The best use of cellular metamorphosis might be as a secret weapon on the political level, wherein influential and powerful Federation functionaries and Starfleet officers might be covertly replaced. Still, once it was known that such a weapon existed, wielding it would become much more difficult.

The greatest danger, it seemed to Spock, lay in

close and continuous contact by others with the Antosian culture. The comings and goings of Federation citizens might in fact help to further the very kind of infection that Garth's presence and emotive threats had helped to create in the rebel Antosian faction. If so, Antos IV might join Talos IV as a planet under quarantine.

Spock did not care for such a solution. He did not care for anything that impeded the free flow of ideas among intelligent beings unless there was no alternative. Fortunately, the Antosian majority and its ruling body were apparently sane and also skeptical of military ambitions.

Captain Kirk, Spock noted, was being unusually silent. Captain Garth stood at his left, wearing the standard uniform of a starship captain on active duty.

"Captain Garth, Captain Kirk," Uhura said from her station, "we are being hailed from the city of Pynesses."

Garth nodded. "That will be the representatives we wish to contact—the First Minister and his Chief Adviser. Open a channel, Lieutenant Uhura."

The forward viewscreen flashed on. The two figures on the screen were humanoid adults of an age difficult for Spock to estimate, unfamiliar as he was with this culture and its biology, but they seemed almost assuredly to be male. Had they been Vulcans, he would have placed the pair in their middle years. Of course, he reminded himself, it was possible for shape-changers to present themselves in the appearance of any stage of life.

"We greet you, Captain Garth," the taller of the two Antosians said in a deep baritone with extremely precise pronunciation. The shorter humanoid only nodded. *"And welcome also to you, Captain James Tiberius Kirk."*

Kirk got to his feet. Garth made a motion with one hand that looked to Spock like a signal; the two Antosians made similar gestures.

"One club," Garth said.

"One heart," the tall Antosian responded.

"Two no trump," the shorter humanoid said in a tenor voice. Spock assumed that the subtle hand movements were signals, and that the contract bridge bids were passwords.

Garth smiled. "Time to play out our hands." He took a step forward. "How glad I am to see you, Empynes." He nodded in the direction of the taller dark-haired humanoid. "And also you, Gyneeses."

"Garth," Empynes said, *"we are prepared to welcome you back. There is much to tell you, so I hope you can get here as soon as possible."*

"I shall beam down right away," Garth said, obviously surprising Kirk. "It's time that I set that particular fear aside, and what better place to start? Ferrying me back and forth by shuttlecraft would be too cumbersome, and overcoming this last phobia of mine will be therapeutic."

"You will come alone, of course." Empynes looked

down for a moment. *"Forgive me, Captain Kirk, but we would rather explain how matters now stand to Captain Garth before you and any others of your crew beam down. He is, after all, the originator of this mission and your Federation's representative."*

Kirk nodded. "I understand."

"It's also a precaution," Garth said. "Empynes and Gyneeses will give me their report, and then I'll see a little more of their city. I want to make certain that being on Antos IV doesn't adversely affect my mental balance before you and your landing party join me."

Such a plan seemed reasonable to Spock, yet it would have been equally reasonable for all of the landing party to beam down together, in case Garth quickly began to show signs of instability and needed to be restrained. But the Antosians wanted this arrangement, and presumably they would be capable of keeping Garth under control should that prove necessary.

"We look forward to seeing you again," Empynes said, *"and to greeting you, Captain Kirk, and your party later on."*

Captain Kirk nodded. "We are at your disposal."

Gyneeses seemed to tense at those words, but Spock had no way to know what this might mean.

"I'll prepare to beam down," Garth said, "and be with you within the hour."

Empynes bowed his head slightly. *"And when we have concluded our discussion, I will ask your fellow captain to join us."*

"Farewell, Empynes and Gyneeses."

The screen went dark.

"Captain Garth," Kirk asked in what sounded like a hesitant voice, "how can we be sure that those two Antosians haven't already been replaced by rebel shape-shifters?"

Garth turned toward the captain. "But you saw our hand signals, and heard our passwords—they were all previously arranged. You can be sure that Gyneeses and Empynes are indeed themselves."

"I see," Kirk said. "And these signals and passwords could not have been obtained from them by their enemies?"

Garth smiled. "I admire your caution, Captain Kirk, but I think it's misplaced. You're granting the leaders of the dissident faction much too much credit."

"Perhaps."

"In any case, I know those two leaders fairly well by now, so my confidence in them isn't based solely on our prearranged signals. And my beaming down ahead of you is an extra measure of security."

As he listened to this exchange, Spock concluded that it proved nothing one way or the other. Only a person with an unreasoned suspicion, with no basis in fact, would refuse to accept Garth's statements.

Captain Kirk sat down at his station and thumbed the intercom. "Mr. Kyle, Captain Garth is on his way to the transporter room. Issue him a tricorder and communicator and beam him down to Antos IV." Kirk looked up at the other captain. "I don't think we should meet the Antosians with phasers, even hand phasers, given that we're here to further the cause of peace."

"I was just about to make the same suggestion," Garth replied quickly. "The Antosians do not need to be exposed to such advanced weapons, especially now, and you shouldn't need them for self-defense on a world that lacks such devices." He turned and strode aft toward the lift.

It was five days later that McCoy stood in the sickbay and announced, "I've been ordered to beam down with the landing party."

Nurse Christine Chapel and Dr. Ilsa Soong both nodded their heads in acknowledgment. McCoy glanced around the sickbay; except for two crew members recovering from minor but unpleasant viral infections, the medical facility was free of patients. "I'm actually looking forward to spending some time on Antos IV. Just think of what Antosian shape-changing techniques might mean for medicine."

"What they did for Captain Garth was little short of a miracle," Christine Chapel said.

McCoy smiled. "Repairing diseased organs and cells through cellular metamorphosis, reconstructing damaged limbs, ridding ourselves of deformities—it could be the end of another dark age of medicine."

"Maybe after Captain Garth completes his mission," Soong said, "Christine and I can beam down and see what we might learn about Antosian medical techniques. If Garth was able to master cellular metamorphosis, that may indicate that such an ability is latent in other human beings, even in all humanoids."

"I've been thinking the same thing," McCoy said, "but don't forget that Garth paid a heavy price for his cure with mental illness. The physical changes that shape-changing produces may lead to such derangement in other humanoids. Remember, Garth hasn't tried to change his shape since he was cured. The two might be linked. In any case, there's probably a lot we could learn from the Antosians."

"Good luck, Doctor," Christine said.

McCoy adjusted the strap of the tricorder hanging from his shoulder, then left the sickbay, hurrying toward the nearest lift. Giving him an opportunity to find out about Antosian medical techniques was not the only reason to include him in the landing party; Jim would want him there to keep an eye on Garth.

McCoy had no doubt that Garth was sane. Whether or not he still harbored his fear of transporters, Garth had managed to go to the transporter room and beam down to Antos IV. He had been down there for days, reporting regularly about the details of the arrangements for their arrival, and if that was taking longer than Jim had expected, that was only because Garth wanted to be certain that their diplomatic moves succeeded. McCoy had been observing the man during their short journey to this system. He had seen Garth practicing his fencing with Sulu, playing games of chess with Chekov, being voluble and at ease while dining with other crew members in the mess hall; he had noted the subtle way in which Garth had seemed to be in command of this mission while at the same time not usurping any of Jim's authority over the *Enterprise*'s standard operations. McCoy had done his best not to be too obvious, but he was certain that Garth knew he was being observed.

Garth's own behavior underlined the truth of the reports about him, that he was both physically and mentally sound. McCoy was well aware that it was only a legacy of medicine's dark ages that brought him a few passing doubts about Garth, doubts that he easily dismissed.

In the transporter room, Kirk had a moment of anxiety before he found himself with the other three members of his landing party in an open sunlit area that appeared to be a solarium. His anxiety was not for himself, but on Captain Garth's behalf; he was thinking of what it must have cost the other man to resume using the transporter. Garth had shown courage in allowing himself to beam down right at the onset of his mission to help prepare for the arrival of the *Enterprise* team.

Kirk's landing team included Mr. Spock, Dr. McCoy, and Yeoman Wodehouse; Kirk had left Mr. Scott in charge of the *Enterprise.* All of them carried tricorders and communicators, but Kirk had also brought a hand phaser, which was concealed inside his boot. With any luck, he would never have to use the weapon. The Antosians they were to meet now might be peaceful, but the rebel faction was not, and

Kirk did not want to leave his team without any protection. As it was, he hoped that he hadn't made a mistake by not bringing down anyone from security.

He also had to be prepared for the possibility that Garth might still lose his painfully won sanity, that being among the Antosians again might eventually unbalance him. Garth's actions after boarding the *Enterprise* were those of a sane, observant, and considerate man, but Kirk had to allow for a relapse. The concealed hand phaser was one safeguard, but there were other backups Kirk had arranged with Montgomery Scott. Scotty knew what he would have to do if the worst happened, and also that his primary duty was to the *Enterprise* and not to Kirk and his landing party.

Kirk glanced at the band of windows, which offered a view of a lake to the north and a ridge of mountains far to the west, then lifted a hand in greeting. Empynes and Gyneeses, clothed in long tunics and pants, stood with Captain Garth, who wore a long coat of a silklike fabric over his uniform; he had mentioned that the weather in this region could be cool.

"Welcome to Antos IV," Empynes said, nodded at Kirk, then pressed the palms of his long-fingered hands together. His black hair was clipped close to his head, while the shorter Gyneeses wore his light brown hair at collar length. Except for a slightly larger brain case, the Antosians were like most humanoids in having a wide range of skin tones, hair colors, eye colors, and body types.

"Thank you," Kirk replied. He quickly introduced the other members of his team, then said, "I am told that you hold the title of First Minister."

"Yes," Empynes said, "but I have never cared for titles—feel free to address me and Chief Adviser Gyneeses by our names." Gyneeses frowned, as if displeased by that remark, but Kirk told himself that maybe he was misinterpreting the Antosian's expression. "Please, let us sit down." He turned and led everyone toward the two rows of armchairs near the windows.

Gyneeses sat down first, with Empynes at his right. Kirk seated himself directly across from the two Antosians as Garth settled himself next to Empynes. Gyneeses gave Garth an impassive glance. What was the Chief Adviser thinking and feeling now? Kirk wondered. Garth had threatened the Antosians with destruction; what might Gyneeses be thinking when he looked at Garth's people? Representatives of a Federation that had also been threatened by the madman, but had somehow conveniently forgiven him his transgressions?

Kirk was only speculating; he was not yet familiar enough with this culture to be sure of anyone's thoughts. Still, there was something about Chief Adviser Gyneeses that troubled him. This entire mission had made him unduly suspicious. Why was Garth so subdued, even deferential, in the presence of the two Antosians?

Foolish of me, Kirk thought. Of course he would

be subdued; Garth would not want these people to glimpse anything that might remind them of his earlier grandiose self.

"We'd better get right down to our problem," Empynes began, "and be clear about exactly what it is that we're about to do. To put it directly, we are on the verge of a civil war over what future use we are to make of cellular metamorphosis. This ability, as you may know, was developed over time, from a possibility inherent in our larger brain cases. It once promoted our survival, though it is no longer necessary."

Kirk nodded, having been briefed by Garth on that point.

"We survive and have continued to thrive without exercising this talent other than in trivial ways," Empynes went on. "Many of us, a majority in fact, have felt for some time that we should give up this shape-changing ability, which can be troublesome and drains our energies when we do use it, as our children frequently do, but which now has no real use beyond that of play. But there are those among us who disagree. They see the political and military uses of the skill, especially when they look beyond our world to the larger sphere of the galaxy." He paused. "Some members of these factions, which comprise, I estimate, about ten percent of our people, have absented themselves from the rest of us—they've left this city, and continue to lay their plans against us at a distance." Empynes sighed. "But perhaps Gyneeses can finish the story of our growing discord, since I sometimes find it too painful to describe. It creates a knot in my mind that can become almost physically agonizing."

"Yes, of course, my friend," Gyneeses said in a low voice.

Empynes sat back in his chair. Gyneeses leaned forward. "If our people are to come and go freely among the intelligent races of the galaxy, the danger of collaboration in the service of martial ambitions may do great damage to the constructive impulses we have observed in your Federation's ideals."

"Exactly what precipitated the split among your people?" Kirk asked. "What made some members of your dissident factions decide to leave the city and rebel openly?"

"It was our proposal to genetically engineer the power of metamorphosis out of ourselves." Gyneeses looked regretful as he spoke. "The dissidents refused to consider that solution."

"But its medical uses show such great promise," Leonard McCoy cut in. "Look what you were able to do for Captain Garth. It'd be a damn shame not to have the benefit of such abilities."

"There would be benefits," Spock murmured, "but the same effect might be achieved in other ways."

"Exactly, Commander Spock," Empynes said as he sat up again. "Why should Antosian children be burdened with the temptations of such a talent, at an age when their judgment and self-control are just beginning to form? To control this ability, to rein in ourselves, we have lived under a series of centralized and authoritarian historical regimes—all of which, we now see, were shaped by the desire to control this one feature of our genetic inheritance and to keep it from corrupting us."

Spock said, "My own Vulcan people had to conquer the violent parts of their nature millennia ago. Those who were once our rebel faction became the founders of the Romulan Star Empire."

"Then you see what we must do, Commander Spock," Empynes responded. "Our renegades now propose, in effect, to give in to the temptations that we have so long been able to control. Our entire peaceful history and culture may come crashing down."

Empynes covered his eyes, clearly overcome by that prospect. Kirk almost expected him to break down and weep. The Antosian lowered his hand and looked up, seeming more composed, but it was obvious how much weight he carried on his shoulders. Now Kirk felt even more the necessity of Garth's mission to this world that he had helped to destabilize, and why Garth had pushed so hard for it.

The First Minister sighed, then continued, "Perhaps, Captain Kirk, you and your team could advise us on a matter of tactics. Our plan is to meet with the rebels personally. This has taken some time to arrange, but no other course is open to us, and they have agreed to such a meeting. We are a cautious people, however, and so our negotiating partners have asked that we approach the meeting place in full view, riding elleis—our native animal mounts. I for one do not expect any treachery, at least not until after the meeting."

"But you would like to have a plan," Kirk said, "that would guard against any eventualities." For a moment, he was puzzled about why Garth had not discussed possible tactics with the two Antosians, but perhaps the other man felt that such suggestions would carry more weight coming from Kirk.

Empynes nodded. "A number of important people must be risked to give this meeting credibility, so we need a plan to protect ourselves as we go to meet the rebels. I, as First Minister, have the final say on almost any important matter involving our people, and my advisers keep a close watch on those who work with them. It's a centralized system that has served to keep us at peace for millennia, but it only works because of the discipline we have imposed on ourselves, and it places a heavy load on the back of the First Minister. It also means that the rebels know that they have to deal with me to ensure any kind of settlement. Therefore, I must go talk to them myself, as must Gyneeses. Your presence, that of Captain Garth, and the three Starfleet personnel with you is part of an unspoken guarantee of sincerity on our part to the suspicious rebels. I am regretful that so much has to be risked."

"Without risk," Kirk said, "there is no progress."

"We'll have to leave the city and ride west," Empynes said. "This means crossing a long stretch of desert to reach the meeting place. Riding there on elleis, stopping at the oases along the way and allowing time to rest ourselves and our mounts, is a journey that will take at least two of our days. I wish there were some way to speed our travel, Captain, but we must make the approach to the meeting place on our mounts. Can you suggest anything?"

"Yes, I think I can," Kirk replied. He glanced at Spock, who nodded in his direction, and knew immediately that the Vulcan had thought of the same possibility. "Mr. Spock, please explain what we can do."

"To put it simply," Spock said, "we propose that we make use of our transporters to decrease our journey's duration. The *Enterprise* can easily beam us and our mounts from one place to another, enabling us to cross the desert and be at the meeting place in only a few hours."

Empynes clasped his hands together. "I had hoped you might be able to do something of that sort."

"And it has the advantage," Kirk said, "of getting us to the meeting place before the rebels expect us there."

"Are we then agreed that we'll begin our journey tomorrow?"

Kirk glanced at his companions, then said, "Agreed."

"We can hope this matter can be settled," Gyneeses said then, "but I have grave doubts about all this, whether it will be of any use." He turned toward Empynes. "I am Chief Adviser—I must tell you what I fear."

"And what do you foresee?" Garth asked softly.

"Civil war among ourselves, for a long time to come, ending only when one faction is victorious. I just cannot see any group willingly giving up what power it has, and any clear advantage it sees for itself."

Empynes sighed. "It will be as it will be, Gyneeses, but we must all take up our positions in this conflict and act according to our best judgment. I am not about to let our way of life die without doing everything I can to prevent it." The First Minister paused. "I propose to take all of you to our stable, so that you can see the mounts you'll be riding. After that, it would be best if we dine early, so that we're well rested for tomorrow. We've set aside quarters for you here in my compound, in the official residence, but you may return to your ship if you prefer to rest there."

"I'd prefer to stay here," Garth said, looking at Kirk.

"Then so will we," Kirk responded. The situation did not seem hopeful, he thought, as he suddenly imagined possible outcomes: a civil war with one victor; maybe an action by the Federation against rebellious and dangerous shape-shifters. As Kirk thought about it further, he also imagined an endless civil war, with no victor, the end of the peaceful Antosian culture, even the final extinction of the species.

Whatever happened, the powers the Antosians possessed could not be allowed to threaten the Federation, or to become the tools of the Federation's Klingon and Romulan enemies.

Chapter Five

McCoy breathed in the cool morning air, then draped his arms over the top of the wooden fence, watching the elleis as they milled around inside their pen. The four-footed, black-furred animals were roughly the size of horses, yet moved like cats on their padded paws; they seemed to him to be a cross between graceful equines and black panthers.

"They are beautiful, aren't they?" Wenallai said.

McCoy turned toward the Antosian woman. "Indeed they are."

Wenallai squinted at him, which seemed to be her equivalent of a smile. She was the bondpartner of Empynes and the owner and breeder of this particular herd of elleis, but she was also a healer, a fact McCoy had discovered last night during the dinner the Antosians had laid out for them.

"I wouldn't think there'd be much need for physicians here," McCoy had said to her after she had passed him a dish of delicately seasoned vegetables resembling ferns.

"Oh, but there is," Wenallai had replied. "Being able to use the art of cellular metamorphosis doesn't automatically turn one into a diagnostician. That's much of what I do: scan and mind-probe and give a detailed diagnosis, and then suggest the most efficient or least painful way to promote healing through cellular transformation. And with younger people, particularly children, I often have to guide them through the process of healing step by step."

"Were you one of those who healed Garth?" McCoy had asked.

"No, others healed him." A darker look crossed her face before she went on to speak of other matters. That the Antosians would have to change themselves somatically and genetically in order to give up their shape-changing abilities was probably necessary, but McCoy and she both worried that her people might become much more vulnerable to injury and disease if they gave up such talents altogether. Wenallai and other healers and biologists were already at work analyzing the Antosian genetic structure to see which of their abilities might be retained.

"If we could keep certain talents," she had continued, "the ability to, say, transform an ailing organ into a healthy one, or to mend a broken limb by reshaping it, most of us might be willing to give up our more comprehensive shape-changing skills. And we might also be able to help your people in time. That Garth was able to master cellular metamorphosis suggests that others of your people may have latent shape-changing abilities. Another hypothesis is that his transporter accident didn't only inflict deforming and life-threatening injuries on him, but also may have altered his neurological structures just enough for any latent shape-changing ability he had to be able to manifest itself."

"If that's the case, then Garth is an exception," McCoy said, "and possibly unique. Other non-Antosians may never be able to acquire his particular skill."

"But what may be true about Garth doesn't change anything for us," Wenallai said. "It seems that if we don't give up most of our shape-changing powers, we'll soon be at war. And if the dissidents win, they could become a threat to your people."

An ellei with its long tail held high padded over to McCoy and thrust a furry nose at him. He scratched the animal behind its pointed catlike ears; the ellei emitted a low humming sound that resembled a purr. The notion of riding one of these creatures for any length of time had not appealed to him at first; unlike the avid horseman Jim Kirk, McCoy did not consider himself much of a rider. But his visit to the pen yesterday had eased his mind considerably. The elleis were gentle, even affectionate, and were also surprisingly easy to ride. Empynes had taken them all on a short ride in a park near the stable and then along a trail toward the lake that bordered the city to the north, in order to get the offworlders used to their mounts, and McCoy had actually enjoyed the excursion. An ellei could slip forward like a cat and then race like a horse.

Wenallai patted the nose of another ellei, then turned to McCoy. "I worry about my bondpartner," she murmured. "Empynes has been under so much pressure. There are nights when he can't sleep, when he wanders the city and broods over what we may lose in the battle to come."

"Let's hope that we can avert that battle." McCoy thought of what Gyneeses had said about the prospect of civil war.

"I'm not thinking only of what your people mean by a battle, a fight with weapons. I am thinking of the struggle to save what is most valuable in our peaceful way of life—if anything can be saved." She leaned against the fence; her green eyes gazed past him.

McCoy had encountered her unexpectedly that morning. He had been up earlier than the others, and Wenallai was about to walk her young son Benaron to school; she had suggested that McCoy accompany them, since the school was near her stable. McCoy thought of how the little boy had rushed to join his schoolmates, of how they had played in the school gardens before disappearing behind the doors of the white building. The boy had transformed himself from a child with the black hair of his father Empynes into an elf with a shock of white hair, and then into a thinner and taller red-haired boy in a long black cloak. The other children had been shape-changing as swiftly, their hair and height and body types altering so rapidly that McCoy quickly lost track of which child was Wenallai's son. Even their garments did not remain the same; Benaron's black cloak had begun as a brown coat. Wenallai had explained that their shape-changing abilities made them able to alter the appearance of anything they were wearing, as though their clothes were a second skin. It was in fact easier for them than the flowing of living tissue.

McCoy had watched the mutable children flowing in and out of ever-changing humanoid shapes, laughing as they did so, and had found the sight moving and beautiful. How transitory everything is, he had thought as the children returned to themselves and hurried into the school. Such innocent shape-changing games were only one of the beauties the Antosians would have to sacrifice.

"The others will be here soon," Wenallai said, "and I must go to meet a few of my colleagues at our laboratory." She thrust her hands into the pockets of her long brown woolen coat. "Promise me that you and your comrades will watch over Empynes and do your best to keep him safe."

"Of course," McCoy replied.

"He is not used to fearing other Antosians, or having to deal with people who might want to harm him." Even as he watched her, Wenallai was changing, but very subtly, almost imperceptibly. Her reddish hair took on the sheen of copper; her green eyes grew larger and more lustrous; her olive skin acquired a golden glow. The quietly attractive female Antosian had transformed herself into a beauty, and McCoy began to see why, according to Garth, these people had a reputation for long and enduring pair bonds. Wenallai, he realized, could become whatever her bondpartner wanted her to be, and Empynes could transform himself for her. This private shape-changing between partners was perhaps another form of play that might forever be lost to their race.

"Farewell, Dr. McCoy. I wish you well." The coppery glow of her hair faded to a darker red as Wenallai walked away.

Kirk reined his ellei to a halt, then rose in his stirrups, gazing at the desert that lay ahead. The yellow sands joined the azure sky at what seemed to be a razor-clear line. He still wore the long brown coat that Empynes had given him at the stable; he had needed it against the cool morning air of the city, but the desert air was growing warmer. Beneath him, his ellei was very still, waiting for her rider's next command.

He had taken to the animal at once, guiding her

with the reins of a harness that resembled a horse's bridle, but which had no bit. His saddle had leather stirrups and a deep, reasonably comfortable seat; his mount's easy, flowing gait left him feeling unwinded even after nearly two hours of steady riding.

Kirk looked out over the desert and spotted a herd of wild elleis in the distance, sleek black creatures with a white-furred albino among them. Empynes had told him that the elleis were originally desert animals, and that untamed ones still roamed the desert that lay to the west of Pynesses; seeing an albino ellei was considered a sign of good fortune.

We could use some good luck, Kirk thought as he glanced at his companions. Spock, McCoy, and Lesley Wodehouse were also clothed in long brown coats, while Garth's coat was black. He sat his mount gracefully and moved easily with him, as if used to riding such animals. Garth was a skilled equestrian who had won every dressage competition at the Academy during his time as a cadet, and perhaps he had ridden elleis before during his time on Antos IV. Empynes and Gyneeses wore long black coats like Garth's; Empynes lifted an arm and shaded his eyes with one hand. The First Minister had looked tired, his face drawn, when Kirk had met him that morning, and had said almost nothing during their ride out of the city and over the grassy plain that bordered the desert.

Gyneeses had been equally quiet until Lesley Wodehouse had ridden closer to Kirk to speak to him.

"Captain, I hope this meeting succeeds," she had said, "but what will happen to the rebels if it doesn't? How will the peaceful Antosians be able to handle them?"

Gyneeses, riding in front of them, had turned around in his saddle, obviously having overheard the question. "You needn't worry about that, Yeoman Wodehouse," the Chief Adviser had replied. "We have discussed possible courses of action if we fail." His statement was reasonable enough, but the harder tone in his voice had bothered Kirk, and Gyneeses had not gone on to explain what he meant by possible courses of action.

"Ready?" Kirk called out to the others.

"Yes, Captain," Spock replied. Empynes nodded.

Kirk reached under his coat, flipped open his communicator, and said, "Kirk to Scott—you can prepare to move us now."

"Ready with your seven-league boots, Captain," Scott replied. The transporter room where the chief engineer was on duty could beam no more than six people at a time, so Wodehouse and McCoy had agreed to be beamed to their destination after the others.

"Is this truly necessary?" McCoy suddenly asked.

Kirk turned toward the physician. "If you would prefer to ride three hundred more kilometers across this desert, and then rest for the night at whatever oasis we find before going on . . ."

"We might as well have beamed there directly

from Pynesses," McCoy said, "instead of riding out. As it is, given how well-behaved these animals have been, maybe we'd be better off riding the distance than taking a chance on spooking the beasts with the transporter."

"Let me assure you that these elleis are very well trained," Empynes said, "and won't be easily frightened, now that they're used to their riders."

"Still—" McCoy began.

"Bones," Kirk interrupted, "it was requested that we arrive on elleis, and we agreed to that. The rebels want to be sure of our approach, and that we won't use our transporters offensively, or come armed in a shuttlecraft."

McCoy's ellei edged closer to Kirk. "They're being awfully damned fussy, if you ask me," McCoy muttered. "I don't know. Frankly, I'm starting to wonder if they're laying a trap for us."

"But we've taken that into account," Kirk said. "That's one reason for getting to the meeting place sooner by having ourselves beamed there."

"Unless by some chance that's what they're expecting us to do."

"Dr. McCoy," Garth said, and Kirk was relieved to hear his voice; Garth had been uncharacteristically subdued throughout last night's dinner and their ride into the desert. "Everything we can do to prevent a planetary civil war is something we must do. Riding in like this and using the transporter to speed our journey is a minor inconvenience. We will not give even the suggestion of being the aggressor here."

Kirk wondered if that was possible.

"A show of good faith," Empynes said, "requires that one do what one does not have to do."

McCoy sighed.

"Are you ready, Captain?" Scott's voice asked over the communicator.

"Proceed, Scotty," Kirk ordered.

The desert shimmered in his eyes—

—and was replaced by woodlands and green hills beyond the trees; west of the hills, a wall of mountains rose against a cloudless blue sky. He turned in time to see McCoy and Yeoman Wodehouse, along with their elleis, shimmer into solidity a few moments later.

Empynes trotted closer to Kirk. "I've camped out in this region before," he said, "when I was younger. Gyneeses and I will take the lead."

Kirk nodded; they were still at some distance from the designated meeting place. Empynes's ellei slipped forward, as if stalking creatures in the forest, followed by Gyneeses on his mount.

"Scotty," Kirk said into his communicator, "track us constantly. I'll report to you every two hours. If more than three hours go by without your hearing anything from me, beam me up along with the entire landing party and have security waiting."

"Aye, aye, Captain. Scott out."

Kirk glanced at Garth; the other captain looked pensive. "There's much to be done," Garth said, "and it won't be easy." His voice sounded weaker, without its usual timbre, as if Garth feared that they might fail in their mission.

As they rode slowly toward a virtual wall of trees, Kirk was struck by their awesome beauty. Massive trunks rose a hundred meters or more into the sky; smaller growths clustered around the titanic parent plants, perfect miniatures of the giants. The air was clear and fragrant with growing things, a mix of strangeness and familiarity that sang of refuge in the givens of nature, where one's skin would feel the air, sunlight, and water. It was, he thought, a siren song of the natural paradise from which all intelligent life was slowly exiling itself. That paradise had never truly existed, of course—nature was as cruel as any jealous god that might be imagined—but intelligence would survive as a gardener, a nurturer of beauty, a tamer of the beast within itself and custodian of nature's mirror world of necessary struggle.

They moved among the trees, the elleis prowling. Kirk found his thoughts drifting; he was reading an alien text, but it was beginning to reveal its beauties . . .

Suddenly the trees just ahead became humanoid figures.

"Halt!" a voice shouted. "Raise your arms very slowly, and be still!"

Kirk and his companions lifted their arms. Shadowy figures in cloaks and hoods came forward in the dusky light. Some were pointing spears in their direction, while others carried long knives.

"The First Minister has come to meet with you, as you asked," Gyneeses called out. "He has brought the offworlder Garth of Izar, along with the four Starfleet—"

"We know you," the stranger's deep voice interrupted. "Dismount from your elleis immediately, remove your coats, and don't try anything unless you'd like to feel the prick of a spearpoint."

Kirk dismounted, careful not to make any unnecessary moves, and draped his coat over the pommel of his saddle. His companions were being searched; four of the strangers grabbed at Lesley Wodehouse's tricorder and communicator. Spock was quickly relieved of his devices; two more men advanced on McCoy.

"I'm a physician," McCoy said, "a healer, and this is a medical tricorder. Can't you—" One of the hooded figures took the tricorder from him; the other jabbed at him with his long knife. McCoy took a step back and quickly handed over his communicator.

Kirk did not protest as he surrendered his equipment, thankful now that he and his team had not brought phaser pistols, but still conscious of the hand phaser strapped to his ankle inside his boot. If this was a trap, they had no choice but to wait until Scotty, after not hearing from Kirk, beamed them up to the *Enterprise.* He hoped that it would not come to that, or any chance for accomplishing their mission might be completely lost.

"We came here for a meeting," Empynes said. "We haven't even reached the site where the meeting is to be held, and—"

"You'll be taken there now," a voice said from the trees. "We mean you no harm." A tall hooded figure emerged, nodded at Empynes, then took a communicator from one of his comrades. "We know Empynes, and Gyneeses his adviser, and Garth the offworlder . . . Which one of you strangers is Captain James Kirk?"

Kirk took a step forward. "I am," he said, fearing that he would be searched more thoroughly.

The hooded Antosian handed him the communicator. "Then you may now assure your starship crew that you are in no danger."

"Is that true?" Kirk asked.

"I assure you that it is," the tall Antosian replied. "We mean you no harm. We are only trying to prevent any accidents by keeping you under restraint. Go ahead, contact your ship."

Kirk flipped open his communicator, wondering if this might be a trick. He and Scotty had set up a password system; he could order the engineer to beam them all up. But that would be a show of bad faith and would destroy any good that might come from this meeting. He would wait and see what developed, while putting Scotty on the alert to possible danger.

"Kirk to *Enterprise.*"

"Scott here," Scotty's voice answered.

"Scotty, routine check Aberdeen fourteen—"

The communicator was suddenly snatched from Kirk's hand. "No secret messages, please," the tall cloaked figure said.

But Scotty already had the essential message: a potentially perilous situation, stand by for further orders.

"We will now take you to the meeting place," the tall rebel said, dropping back his hood to reveal an angelic face with wide-set eyes and a head of thick gray hair.

"Heje-Illuss!" Gyneeses cried out, sounding surprised.

The gray-haired Antosian lifted his brows. "But surely you knew that I would be here."

"At the meeting place," Gyneeses said quickly, "not out here with these others." He looked around, as if expecting the rest to throw back their hoods and reveal themselves.

Garth turned to Kirk and murmured, "Heje-Illuss was one of those who saved my life by teaching me how to change shape."

"Captain Garth and I shared much," Heje-Illuss said. "I am pleased to see you well and among us again."

"I am well," Garth replied. Again Kirk noticed the lack of resonance in Garth's voice, the tired and almost defeated tone, but perhaps that was to be expected. This Antosian had been one of Garth's rescuers, and had been repaid for that by being infected with the mad Garth's dreams of power and conquest. Garth would be only too aware of that.

They made their way on foot through the forest

along what seemed to be a trail, leading their elleis by their reins, and soon came to a clearing. The rebels who brought them there took their elleis and led the animals to the far end of the clearing, where other elleis were tied to a long rope hanging between two large trees.

Kirk looked around the rebel camp, noting the campfire in the center of the clearing and the circle of tents and simple shelters made of tree branches thrown together; this was a meeting place ready to be abandoned at once. The Antosians who had led them here and the hooded figures huddled near the fire or standing near the shelters were no more than two dozen people, and there was not much room in the tents and makeshift shelters for many more.

A small group of rebels armed with spears and knives did not seem much of a threat. Yet Kirk had studied enough history to know that several successful revolutions in the past had begun with even less promise. The Antosians of Pynesses lived with a small-scale technology. Solar panels heated their homes, while elleis pulling carts and streetcars fueled by a natural gas were their primary means of urban transportation; only their biological sciences had been developed to a more advanced level. They were people who knew nothing of war; a determined band of rebels might be able to win control of their world.

The sky was becoming a darker blue. Heje-Illuss motioned to his visitors to sit down around the fire. Kirk sat down; even near the flames, he was grateful for the warmth of his coat, which Heje-Illuss and the others had allowed them to put back on.

"We have come here in good faith," Empynes began. "I do not see you as an enemy, Heje-Illuss." The Antosian leader glanced at Kirk. "He is a healer who used to work with my bondpartner Wenallai."

"I am not your enemy, Empynes." Heje-Illuss had stayed on his feet, and moved around the fire as he spoke. "I must tell all of you at once that there has been a schism in our group. Hala-Jyusa and her faction have left us and ridden into the mountains—exactly where, I do not know."

Empynes bowed his head. "When did this happen?" he asked with a sigh.

"As soon as this meeting was arranged. They feared an agreement, because they see any accord as giving up our strength or as a threat to it, especially if it might mean removing cellular metamorphosis from our inheritance."

"And how does your remaining group view the matter?" Empynes said.

Heje-Illuss stood still and held out his arms. "I am here to talk, as we promised, for as long as it takes to find a way to avoid the disaster that may come upon our world. But I already realize that we won't be able to please everyone among our people, and that whatever decision is reached may require that the prevailing faction restrain those who continue to disagree, using decisive force if necessary."

"I wonder if we're capable of that," Empynes said.

"If the majority seeks to restrain those who choose to retain shape-shifting, the struggle may well be impossible. Our only hope is persuasion, to rely on the inner restraint that has served us so well in the past."

"Restraint," Kirk heard Gyneeses mutter. "Self-restraint may not be enough for us anymore."

Kirk glanced around the camp, noting again how few people were here. How many had left with the Antosian called Hala-Jyusa?

"What can those who broke away from you do?" Kirk said to Heje-Illuss. "Can they raise an army?"

"In time, perhaps," the gray-haired Antosian rebel replied. "I do not underestimate Hala-Jyusa, Captain Kirk. She is a woman of strong emotions who was even more susceptible to the dreams of power roused in her by the offworlder Garth than was I." He offered Garth an unhappy look that seemed like a unspoken apology. "We must consider capturing and restraining her and her band. Would you be willing to help us?"

Kirk considered the request for a moment. "Not unless this is something you would plan to do yourself. There's a limit as to how much we can . . . interfere."

"Yes, Captain," Heje-Illuss said. "Garth has told us in the past of your Prime Directive. But how can noninterference be practical in this case, when doing nothing amounts to the same thing—standing idly by when some great war might be averted through action?"

"A sound argument," Spock said. "Reality often outruns the Prime Directive."

"But do you think this new splinter group has enough supporters to do more harm," Kirk said, "especially after they've broken with your group? And what do you think we should do—round them up and put them in some sort of prison?"

"Exactly that," Heje-Illuss said, "much as I regret that necessity."

"And your views?" Empynes asked. "What is the position that your group now takes, and how many more of you are there?"

"Our group?" Heje-Illuss waved a hand. "What you see here is our group, Empynes. We finally understand that renouncing metamorphosis would probably be the best course, but as you see, there are only thirty of us. The group that split off to follow Hala-Jyusa numbers a few hundred. I am counting only those involved directly in the struggle, of course; there are others still in Pynesses who sympathize with them, who are likely to rise up later."

Kirk suddenly imagined a pitched battle of shape-changers, confusing one another with continuous shifts of appearance as they wielded their spears and swords. A civil war on Antos IV would be bad enough, but with their lower level of technology and so much uninhabited land in which the rebels could set up bases, such a struggle would be a protracted one and would not soon be decisive for one side or the other. A third force might be needed to tip the balance, despite the Prime Directive. To do nothing would in itself be an action, as Heje-Illuss had correctly discerned, and inaction would benefit neither side.

And if the Federation did nothing, a third force—the Klingons, perhaps—might decide to intercede on Antos IV.

People were crouched outside their shelters, hoods thrown back from their cloaks, eating what looked like pieces of flat bread and drinking from water skins. They offered nothing to the visitors, not even to Empynes and Gyneeses, revealing that they probably had few provisions. A silence came over the forest, making Kirk uneasy; he was not used to the sounds of this world, but noticed now that the sounds of hooting and trilling birds had abruptly ceased. Maybe one hand phaser wasn't enough protection; his team should have come armed. He looked at Garth and saw him staring listlessly into the fire, as if all the life had gone out of him.

Kirk heard a mewling shriek. Heje-Illuss started. A series of short sharp shrieks followed.

"It's the elleis," Heje-Illuss said. "Trialla, go and calm them down." The mounts were flicking their tails and straining at the rope. A pale-haired woman strode toward the animals, followed by two men.

"Nobody move!" a familiar voice called out from the trees. "We have weapons aimed at you from all sides!"

Kirk jumped to his feet and looked around, but the

darkness beneath the trees surrounding the clearing seemed impenetrable. Several people outside the shelters grabbed spears and were about to hurl them toward the trees when other spears flew into the clearing. Two men dodged the lances as they stabbed into the ground; a woman quickly shimmered into a catlike form and slipped under a bush.

Kirk's vision of battling shape-changers was beginning to come to life.

"I warn you!" the voice from the woods shouted again. "Do not resist us!"

More spears flew out from the trees. A few people were fighting at the end of the clearing near the line of elleis; Kirk watched as they flowed into taller forms, shorter and more muscular forms, any shape that might give them a momentary advantage in the fight. One man threw another to the ground and pinned him, only to see his opponent slip out from under him in the shape of a long, impossibly thin biped. A woman stabbed at a man with a long knife; he feinted, blocked the blow with his own knife, then suddenly shrank into a short squat form before becoming himself again. They could not keep this up indefinitely; the morphing would drain them of too much energy, so much that the injured might lack the power later to heal themselves from their wounds.

Kirk was reaching for his hidden phaser when Empynes cried out, "Stop! Stop this fighting! Have we come to this?"

"Stop!" Heje-Illuss added. "I order all my people to lay down their arms. We cannot win this battle."

Spock was on his feet next to Heje-Illuss; McCoy and Wodehouse stood in front of Empynes and Gyneeses, to shield them from the fray. Several fighters suddenly dissolved into the hooded Antosians Kirk had seen earlier. Heje-Illuss's followers threw down their weapons and waited as other Antosians came out of the woods to pick up the spears, swords, and knives.

Perhaps he would not have to use his phaser after all, Kirk thought; these people were obviously not used to fighting or prolonged battles.

Garth still sat by the fire, as if unaware of everything around him.

A tall dark shadow moved out of the trees, crossed the clearing, and came into the light of the fire, and Kirk saw the mad Lord Garth smiling at him as he had done before, in the asylum on Elba II.

"Welcome, Captain Kirk!" The voice had the same commanding tone Kirk knew so well from his earlier encounter with the madman. "And Commander Spock, and of course the good Dr. McCoy! How good it is to see you again!" Garth bowed gracefully in the direction of Yeoman Wodehouse. "And I see that you've brought along your beautiful aide as well."

Kirk glanced at the other figure of Garth sitting by the fire, and saw him dissolve into the form of a fair-haired and muscular young male. The young Antosian looked up at Kirk with fear in his eyes, and Kirk understood why this Captain Garth had seemed so listless, so lacking in energy and charisma.

Kirk turned back to the remaining Garth and knew then that he was not speaking to his hero, to the rational captain who had traveled with him to this planet, but to the insane Lord Garth who had somehow reasserted himself in Garth's body.

Chapter Six

GARTH'S ANTOSIANS quickly secured the camp. They rounded up the small group in the camp, tied their wrists and ankles, then sat everyone down in the space between the fire and the shelters. At Garth's orders, the communicators and tricorders Heje-Illuss's people had confiscated earlier were seized. Antosians wearing black coats like Garth's stood over Heje-Illuss's followers with swords and spears.

Kirk and his landing party were herded unbound toward the fire, then told to sit down. Garth beckoned to the Antosian who had impersonated him. The young man got up and hurried toward the black-coated men who were guarding the camp's elleis.

"Garth," Kirk began.

"Lord Garth!"

"What's this all about . . . Lord Garth?" Kirk asked.

"Don't you know, Captain Kirk? Can you not guess? You have eyes, ears, presumably a brain—but you do not see!"

"Please explain it to me, Lord Garth." Kirk tried to keep a tone of sarcasm out of his voice.

"We're back to the beginning of the game we played some time back. Soon, when you fail to communicate with the *Enterprise,* we will all be beamed aboard. That was a great mistake on your part, Kirk. This time, the *Enterprise* will be mine, with an army of shape-changers to command. After we seize the nearest starbase, I will begin the construction of starships, using designs undreamed of by the Federation! What do you think I have been doing all this time? I have been planning and plotting and thinking!"

"Without a doubt." Kirk stared into the fire. He had accepted that Garth had recovered from his illness, that Donald Cory had not been mistaken in discharging him from his asylum, that the medical records were accurate, that the Garth who had traveled with him on the *Enterprise* was sane. But José Mendez had been prescient in allowing for a relapse, in planning that Garth be watched.

Kirk now saw that he might have made a mistake in letting Garth beam down to Antos IV ahead of the landing party; it was clear now that Garth's talk of Antosian sensibilities and the need for proper diplomatic arrangements with the First Minister had been part of a ruse. At some point Garth had been able to slip away from Pynesses and replace himself with an Antosian confederate, without Kirk ever suspecting that the image on his viewscreen and the voice on his comm during their brief conferences were not those of his fellow captain. Garth had just confessed that he had been laying his plans for some time before returning here.

No, Kirk thought to himself, he had not made a mistake in dealing with Garth at face value. Better to have drawn him out into the open, to have him reveal himself. He had allowed for that in his own plans.

"Bring that man here!" Garth shouted. Two of his followers pulled Heje-Illuss to his feet and dragged him by the arms toward the fire. Hobbled by the rope around his ankles, Heje-Illuss stumbled forward, but managed to stay on his feet. "I have a question for you."

"Ask it, then," Heje-Illuss said.

"Did you search Kirk and his people before bringing them into your camp?"

"Of course we did," Heje-Illuss replied. "Do you think I'm a fool?"

Garth raised an arm, as if about to strike the gray-haired Antosian, then let his arm fall. "And how was this search conducted?"

"They took off their coats, we searched them, and we took away the devices they carried."

Garth's eyes narrowed, and then he pointed at Kirk. "Take off your boots, all of you. Now!"

Kirk knew that it was pointless to resist; their captors would only remove his footwear by force. The boots of Spock, McCoy, and Wodehouse were quickly searched and handed back to them. Kirk took off his own, revealing the small holster tied above his ankle.

"Aha! I was right!" Garth smiled as he took the hand phaser out of the holster. "I thought you might try something like this, smuggling a weapon down here." He gave Kirk a mischievous look, then said, "Surely you understand that I can't let you keep this phaser."

Kirk sighed as he pulled on his boots, regretting bringing the hand phaser.

Heje-Illuss was led back to sit with the group of bound Antosians. Garth slipped the hand phaser under his belt, approached the fire with three of his comrades, then took out a communicator. As Kirk watched, Garth suddenly morphed into Captain James T. Kirk. His associates quickly shifted into the forms of the other three members of Kirk's team, all of them now wearing Starfleet uniforms and long brown coats.

"Now do you see?" Garth said with Kirk's voice. "Your ship will be mine, Captain Kirk." Kirk-Garth beckoned to others of his accomplices. "Take the captain and these other ineffectual wretches over there. They can watch as we're beamed up to the *Enterprise.* Once the ship is secured, I shall bring the rest of you aboard."

A spear point prodded Kirk in the back. With Spock, McCoy, and Wodehouse, he was herded to the edge of the clearing, near the elleis. He looked back and caught a glimpse of his own eyes. They were bright with firelight.

Kirk watched from the edge of the clearing as the doubles of his landing party stood together, waiting. Since Kirk had not checked in with Scotty for some time now, Garth would be expecting Scotty to beam up his team of impostors. The pseudo-Spock wore an appropriately impassive expression, Lesley Wodehouse's twin had the yeoman's reddish hair and round pretty face, and the false McCoy looked ready to mutter a mild but crotchety complaint about the increasingly cool night air.

They would pass initial inspection. But that was the least of it, Kirk thought. What Garth seemed to be counting on was that the transporter would focus on the communicators and tricorders now held by his team. But that seemed too slim a hope, all by itself, to rely on, he realized. There had to be something more.

"He's gone mad again," Yeoman Wodehouse whispered.

"You may be right," McCoy said in a low voice.

"Quiet!" Garth cried out with Kirk's voice.

They waited in silence. Scotty would have been beaming the landing party up to the *Enterprise* by now, but for Kirk's earlier coded warning to the engineer to stand by.

Spock's double frowned, looking annoyed; he fidgeted and tapped one booted foot impatiently.

"Lord Garth," Lesley Wodehouse's twin began in a voice slightly lower than the yeoman's, "I thought you said that—"

"Quiet, you cow!" The female Antosian shrank back. Kirk-Garth glared at Kirk. "We'll wait a few moments more."

They continued to wait. The clearing was silent except for a few coughs from the bound Antosian captives and occasional soft mewing sounds from the elleis. Kirk-Garth muttered something under his breath, then strode over to Kirk.

"What is wrong, Captain Kirk?" Garth spoke in the soft voice that had often been the mad Lord Garth's prelude to a screaming fit. "What can possibly be the matter with Lieutenant Commander Scott?"

Kirk did not answer.

"You changed the plan!" Kirk-Garth shrieked. "Back there!" He shook his fist, then spun around and walked toward the captive Antosians. "Heje-Illuss! Did you let that creature communicate with his ship?"

The gray-haired rebel leader did not reply.

"Answer me! Or one of your friends here will pay the price for your silence!"

Heje-Illuss pointed his chin at Garth. "I allowed the captain to tell his ship that he and his comrades were in no danger."

"Idiots! I am surrounded by imbeciles!" Kirk-Garth stomped back to Kirk, then halted, as if considering another tactic. Kirk stared into his own face. The match was uncanny, unsettling, bringing back the sense of unreasoning menace he had felt on Elba II, when he had first encountered the hero of his Starfleet cadet days only to see the great man degraded by mental illness.

The twin figure of Kirk suddenly reverted to Garth, and Kirk knew that the man was trying to conserve his energy.

Kirk said, "You're trying to re-create our confrontation on Elba II, when you failed to seize the *Enterprise.* But I've played this game before, Garth."

"Lord Garth!"

"And so has Scotty."

"Let me guess." Garth rubbed his chin. "You've changed the plan somehow," he said softly. "Of course you did, when Heje-Illuss allowed you to talk to him. How clever you are, Captain Kirk. You reversed it on your way here."

"I thought it wise to do so," Kirk said. "Surely you didn't think that simple possession of our gear would be enough to fool Scotty." He was bluffing, but his bluff might fool an unreasoning madman.

Garth grimaced, looking thoughtful and perfectly sane for a moment, then sighed. "Then I'll just have to play this hand out my way. You don't know how needlessly difficult you've made this." He smiled mirthlessly. "But then, how could you know?"

Garth again cloaked himself with Kirk's appearance and took out his communicator again. "Kirk to *Enterprise.*"

"Scott here, Captain."

"Scotty, beam up the landing party."

"On your signal, Captain."

Kirk-Garth scowled at the communicator, then reverted to Garth's form. "Doing your job, I see," he said in his own voice.

"Aye, Captain Garth," Scotty said.

"Lord Garth to you!"

There was a long silence. Kirk wondered if the frustrated Garth would now turn his anger against his captives.

"So that's how it is," Scotty's voice continued. *"We've been through this before. I'm sorry it turned out this way, but I had my suspicions. So did many of us."*

Garth looked thoughtful for a moment, then motioned to two of his men. "Seize the Vulcan." Garth bared his teeth. "That fellow there with the pointed ears." Two burly, black-coated Antosians hastened toward Kirk and his comrades, grabbed Spock by the arms and propelled him toward the fire. Garth studied the phaser in his hand, then slowly raised the weapon until it was aimed at Spock's chest.

"Beam us up, Mr. Scott," Garth said, "or we start by killing Spock."

The Vulcan lifted a brow. "Captain Garth—"

"Lord Garth!"

"As you wish," Spock said calmly. "Surely you know that a starship officer cannot be compelled to action by such threats."

"You should know that better than anyone, Cap-

tain Garth," Scotty's voice said from the communicator. *"You canna make me beam you aboard by threatening Mr. Spock."*

Garth laughed like a mad god. "Of course I can, Mr. Scott! I know full well the strong bonds that exist among you, Captain Kirk, Mr. Spock, and even the good doctor!" The madman circled behind Spock and struck him on the side of the head. Kirk tensed, but Spock stayed on his feet, seemingly uninjured by the blow.

"I say again," Garth continued, "that this phaser is no longer on stun—it's set to kill. Beam us aboard, Mr. Scott, or your precious first officer will be disintegrated into nonexistence! You do know I have a phaser, don't you?"

"Aye," Scotty said. *"I'm scanning it."*

Sorry, Scotty, Kirk thought.

"Now!" Garth cried.

"I have my orders," Scotty said.

Kirk thought: *Don't get into a debate with him, Scotty. Anything might trigger another of Garth's irrational outbursts.* He glanced at Wodehouse's staring hazel eyes and McCoy's rigid face, wishing even more fervently that he had not brought the hand phaser with him. Garth motioned with the weapon, and for a moment Kirk thought he saw a shadow of reluctance cross Garth's face, but that had to be a trick of the firelight.

"Let him go," Garth said to the Antosians holding Spock. They released him; Garth kept his phaser trained on the Vulcan. "You have only a moment, Mr. Scott. It's now or never. Beam us aboard, or Spock dies, and after him the pretty yeoman and the good doctor. And your captain can watch them die." He laughed again. "Shall I sing you the old so—"

Kirk did not hear the last word as the transporter seized him with what seemed a swift force greater than the usual scan cycle.

Scotty was pointing a phaser pistol at him. Kirk looked around and saw that the other transporter receiver plates were empty, then turned to face Scotty again. Next to the chief engineer were Ensign Chekov and a security detail of seven crew members, all armed with phaser pistols. Lieutenant Kyle was on duty at the transporter console, with Ensign Grinzo next to him at the controls.

"Good going, Scotty," Kirk said, "but what about—"

"Don't move." Scotty did not lower his phaser. "I picked you up blindly, along with Dr. McCoy, Mr. Spock, and Yeoman Wodehouse—and of course His Lordship. I'm fairly sure you're the captain, but I followed good old police procedure—when in doubt, arrest the lot, everyone in the area, and take them down to the station."

"You must know it's me," Kirk said.

"The sensor scan shows you are, and we were scanning you continuously for as long as possible after you gave me the Aberdeen signal, but appearances can be deceiving, especially on a planet of shape-changers."

"Where are the others?" Kirk asked.

"In transporter stasis. We're holding them there—I couldna take any chances, Captain. I'll have to bring them in one by one. If they're shape-changers, they shouldna be able to hold their forms during the cycle."

"You can't be sure of that," Kirk said.

"As I said, I canna take any chances, and I shan't." Scott turned and nodded at Kyle and Grinzo. Spock shimmered into existence on the plate next to Kirk's.

"Spock, is it you?" Kirk asked, doubting for a moment.

"I assure you that I am indeed Spock," the Vulcan replied in his familiar neutral tone.

Kirk took a deep breath, knowing it would not be so easy. The Antosian impersonating Spock had looked exactly like him. "I see Garth didn't have time to carry out his threat to execute you," he said despite his doubts.

"No," Spock said. "This is a curious fact, but I did observe that his phaser was set on stun only. I was apparently never in any danger."

"He was bluffing?" Kirk said.

"That would appear to be the case, Captain."

"Or else he was too irrational to notice that he hadn't set it properly," Kirk said.

"Possibly. But when Captain Garth struck me, his blow did not carry much force." Spock moved off his plate and took a step toward the edge of the platform.

"Stay where you are, Mr. Spock," Scotty said. "I still don't know it's you."

"I see." Spock stepped back onto his plate. "A wise precaution, Mr. Scott."

"And there are only two ways you can prove that we are ourselves," Kirk said. "The slow way and the quick way."

Scotty nodded. "I know. I wish we had time for the slow way, Captain."

He steadied himself, knowing what was about to happen. Scotty aimed his phaser and Kirk felt the darkness sweep over his mind as the engineer fired.

Kirk was lying on the hard surface of a floor. He opened his eyes and saw Spock and Scotty leaning over him.

"I set my phaser to the lowest setting," Scotty said as he and Spock helped Kirk to his feet, "but it still packed a wallop."

"You were right, Scotty." Kirk rubbed the back of his head. Strong and skilled as the Antosian shape-changers were, even they could not maintain forms that were not their own after being stunned by a phaser, but reverted immediately to their original selves. The encounter with Garth on Elba II had proved that.

"I can be sure of you and Mr. Spock," Scotty said. "He came to just a few minutes before you did. I suppose it's time to bring in another."

"Do it, Scotty." Kirk moved away from the transporter platform and waited with Chekov and the security detail.

Scotty signaled to Kyle and Grinzo. "Bring in the yeoman and the doctor, but leave Garth for last." The forms of McCoy and Wodehouse appeared on the transporter platform.

"Stay there," Scotty ordered as the security crew members near him took aim with their phasers.

McCoy frowned. "What the hell's going on? Have you all gone crazy?"

"I'm sorry, Bones," Kirk said. "We have to make sure you're you."

McCoy grimaced as he glanced at Wodehouse. The two crumpled to the floor as the phaser beams struck them.

Kirk's head still ached, but he was already feeling better. "You took a chance, Scotty, beaming us up like that."

"I know the safety of the ship had to come first, but I couldna let that madman kill the lot of you."

Kirk and Chekov went to the platform, where McCoy and Wodehouse were now regaining consciousness. McCoy sat up first, then eased the yeoman into a sitting position.

"I am sorry we had to do this," Chekov said.

"Remind me later," the physician muttered.

Kirk and Chekov helped the two to their feet. "Captain," Lesley Wodehouse said, "what happened to Garth?"

"He's in stasis hold."

"Who else is there?" McCoy asked.

"Our doubles," Kirk said. Empynes was still down in the camp, along with Gyneeses and Heje-Illuss's band of captive Antosians. None of them were likely to fare too well in the hands of Garth's followers, who had so abruptly had their leader snatched from them.

"Shall I bring in His Lordship now?" Scotty asked.

"He was holding a phaser," Kirk said. "We'd better be ready to grab it before he can fire it." He silently reproached himself again for having taken the phaser down to Antos IV. "Spock, stand behind that plate. Chekov, be ready to stun him."

"Aye, aye, Captain," Chekov said, raising his phaser pistol.

"Energize," Scotty said to Kyle and Grinzo.

Spock stood behind the plate that was to receive Garth. Kirk was saddened as he thought that the hero of his youth would again be brought low, and for the last time. A column shimmered above the plate and became the figure of Garth.

Spock was about to grab the phaser from behind, but Garth suddenly dropped the weapon to the floor.

"Well," Garth said calmly, "it certainly took you long enough."

Chapter Seven

KIRK STARED AT the man who had so recently been ranting at him. Even Spock, who was looking at Garth with upraised brows, seemed confused.

"You've done exactly what I was hoping you'd do," Garth went on. "I was counting on getting aboard, one way or another. It was part of my plan to help the Antosians."

"To rule them, you mean," Kirk said.

"You must believe me, Captain Kirk."

"Lord Garth, I can't believe you."

"Please—it's *Captain* Garth. Let me explain." Garth opened his arms. "Time is growing very short—you have to listen to me."

Though he spoke with an urgent intensity, Garth sounded rational. His blue eyes gazed at Kirk steadily. The madness he'd seen on Elba II—and in the clearing minutes earlier—was gone.

"Captain Garth," Kirk said at last, "I am placing you under arrest."

"But I can prove what I say."

"You'll have a chance to argue your case," Kirk said. "Ensign Chekov, take charge of this man, and see that he's restricted to quarters."

"Restrain me if you must," Garth said, "but at least listen to what I have to tell you first. There isn't much time—the lives of the Antosians we left behind are now in danger. What have you got to lose by hearing me out?"

"Very well." Kirk stepped back. "We'll listen to you, but you'll remain under guard." He turned to Scotty and said, "Bring the remaining doubles in from stasis and put them in the brig."

"Aye, Captain."

Garth was marched to the nearest briefing room. Chekov sat down next to him at the table, while two security guards stood behind Garth's chair, phasers at the ready. Kirk sat down across from Garth, with Scotty on his right and Spock on his left. Wodehouse was in the chair nearest the door.

McCoy quickly scanned Garth with the medical tricorder that had been brought to him in the transporter room. "No evidence of brain injury," McCoy said as he gazed at the readings. "No evidence of any injury, in fact." He looked up. "I'd conclude that he's sane, but I can't be absolutely certain until I confirm that diagnosis with a complete examination and workup in sickbay. The effects of shape-changing on his neurological functions, subtle damage that a quick scan might not pick up—all of that is possibly—"

"Doctor, let me assure you that I'm sane," Garth said.

"Maybe, maybe not." McCoy sat down. "But even being sane doesn't mean that you can't be duplicitous."

"Please." Garth folded his hands. "Listen to what I have to tell you before you judge me."

Kirk motioned with one arm. "Go ahead, Captain Garth."

"You've probably already deduced that a double traded places with me not long after I beamed down to Antos IV." Garth spoke in a measured tone. "Within a day after I was down there, Kellin—that young Antosian—had taken on my form. He's a strong youth, capable of holding shape for an extraordinary length of time, which is why I chose him. I coached him on how to act and advised him to keep to himself as much as possible, then rode out from Pynesses and went west to rejoin my followers, to assume my position as head of the rebellion once more."

"Head of the rebellion?" Scotty asked.

"Yes, Mr. Scott," Garth said. "I joined the rebellion—or, more properly, infiltrated it—more than a year ago, after my discharge from Elba II, when I stopped at Antos IV on my way back to Earth." He paused. "After arrangements were made by the rebels for a meeting with the First Minister and his Chief Adviser, I knew that you and my double would have to accompany them to the meeting place. Then, when you arrived there, I was counting on beaming up to the *Enterprise* under your automatic order, as we had planned, with the pretext of seizing the ship. My followers believed that was my intention, but once I was aboard the ship, my plan was to begin beaming up the rebel Antosians in groups in order to forward them to Acra, one of the islands in the eastern ocean, thus averting a civil war. All of you would have learned of my plan sooner, if Captain Kirk had not delayed me."

"Do you expect us to believe that?" Kirk asked.

"Acra is the northernmost of the Tiresian Islands, which are much like Earth's Hawaiian Islands, so no one would have suffered unduly by being confined there. But Acra is also an island from which there is no escape. One might be able to make it to one of the nearer Tiresian Islands to the south, but to reach the eastern coast of the continent of Anatossia by boat, assuming any such craft could be built, would take some days, and there would be no place to land anyway, since most of the eastern shore of the continent consists of extremely high, sheer, and rocky cliffs."

"So our preliminary sensor scans of the planet revealed," Spock said.

"I canna think," Scotty said, "that I wouldna have seen through your guise sooner or later, even if you had succeeded in getting aboard as the captain."

"I would have told you at once." Garth lifted his brows, then looked at Kirk. "And I would have brought you and your landing party out of danger as soon as it was feasible."

McCoy let out a breath. "Infiltrating the rebels. Beaming people to some island. It's ridiculous." He folded his arms and sat back. "Jim, it sounds to me like Garth is trying to re-create Elba II all over again."

Kirk studied Garth, but there was no madness in the other man's eyes, only a calm patience with children whom he had been forced to deceive.

"May I continue?" Garth asked.

Kirk nodded. "For the moment."

"It was my hope that in time, with the most recalcitrant of the rebels restrained, and the Antosians proceeding to rid themselves somatically and genetically of their morphing abilities, many if not most of the rebels would also agree to give up their shape-changing talents. Those who refused would remain imprisoned on Acra." He fell silent for a bit. "You are no doubt wondering why I kept all of this to myself."

"Of course I am," Kirk said.

"During my earlier visit to Antos IV, I fell into communication with several of the dissidents and managed to gain their trust. Given that a few of them were among those who had healed me and taught me the art of cellular metamorphosis, this wasn't difficult. Then I knew what I had to do." Garth gazed steadily across the table at Kirk. "The only sure way to stop a rebellion, especially one involving such powerful threats as genetic modification, is to take it over from within. Once this conflict erupted into the open, small groups would escape into the hinterlands and shape-shift forever, and they would also have time to gather new followers, people who might have second thoughts about giving up their skills." He leaned forward. "You made my task more difficult when you alerted Mr. Scott not to beam us up automatically. You might have derailed my whole plan." Weariness had crept into Garth's voice. "Maybe I was too clever for my own good, and should have told you, but I couldn't wait for permission from anyone to do what had to be done. I saw how things were in the higher circles of Starfleet Command. There were too many officers who wanted to force me into retirement for me to think that I would be able to get official sanction for my scheme in time to help the Antosians, and a good chance that I would never get such approval."

Garth sounded sincere, and his arguments, once his premises were granted, were plausible. Kirk felt shaken by the conviction in the other man's voice, but then said, "Captain Garth, a great man once said that extraordinary claims require extraordinary proof. Mr. Spock tells me that your phaser was set to stun and not disintegrate when you threatened him, and that you didn't deliver much of a blow to his head when you struck him, but that suggests only that you intended to bluff us into beaming you up, nothing more. If that is your proof of good intentions, it's not enough." He paused. "And another thing—I find it implausible that someone as intelligent as you hung so much of your plan on my backup arrangement for Scotty to automatically beam us all up."

"Unless he really is barmy," Scott muttered.

Garth glanced at Scotty. "Actually, I was counting on you to do something clever, Mr. Scott, since I had painted myself into a corner. You were my backup, just in case Captain Kirk altered his first plan without my knowledge. Luckily he'd brought a concealed phaser with him—I thought that he might have one, because sneaking one down is just what I would have done under those circumstances—and that weapon enabled me to add a lot of conviction to my bluffing and my threats. And happily I was able to rant and rave on long enough to give you time to figure out what to do."

Scotty had a dubious look on his face. "Let's assume that's true for a wee bit," the engineer said. "What would you have done if I hadn't acted?"

"Stunned Commander Spock with my phaser and started in on Dr. McCoy or Yeoman Wodehouse, hoping that they would be taken for dead. The rebels don't know much about phasers. It would have been the only course left to me, and then there would have been a chance, however slight, that Captain Kirk would have second thoughts and give you the order you required from him. And maybe that would have been enough to convince you that it would be the better course of valor to beam us all up."

"Lucky for you that I had my wits about me," Scotty said.

Garth focused on Kirk. "Sometimes you have to take things one step at a time, especially if you're in a corner, and see what develops."

Kirk found himself nodding in agreement. He knew the truth of that statement well, since he had followed the same course of action several times himself.

Garth continued, "One way or another, I was going to get myself and your doubles aboard."

"And what are we to accept now?" Kirk asked. "That the rebels will now believe that you've taken over the *Enterprise?*"

"That is exactly the plan," Garth said. "They will believe it, if I return to them. That I am here in your custody, that I wanted to be beamed up here with you, proves my point, that we are both on the same side. But time is short. Think of the lives that may be lost if this complex deception collapses."

"May I point out," Spock said calmly, "that you apparently intended to beam up with other shape-shifters to attack the *Enterprise.* Let us assume that this was your true intent, to take over the ship. Had Mr. Scott been taken in and believed you to be Captain Kirk, you might have succeeded. You would have been able to issue commands as the captain to others of our personnel, order them to beam down to the meeting site, and then replace them with more of your Antosian confederates."

"True, Mr. Spock, very true. But you'll note that I

avoided that circumstance. It was my decision that gave Mr. Scott his opportunity."

"Who else knows about this plot of yours?" Kirk asked, thinking of how subtle Garth's ability was to think and to act in a corner—if what he said was true. "I doubt that you could have carried it off entirely by yourself."

"Empynes and Gyneeses know parts of it," Garth said, "and I remind you that they are both prisoners right now."

"And what about Heje-Illuss and the other Antosian rebel leader who was mentioned, Hala-Jyusa?" Spock asked.

"They fell out from their own motives, after the meeting was arranged. I stayed with Hala-Jyusa, since she had the larger force. My purpose all along was to keep the rebels together in one large group, to make it easier to round them up." Garth smiled briefly. "I think Heje-Illuss had enough of my flamboyant ways, but as for the rest, I think Napoleonic posturings played very well."

Kirk shook his head. "This is still assuming that we can believe what you've just told us, and that this isn't a ploy of some other kind, or else a feeble attempt to worm your way out of a plot that's failed."

Garth stood up slowly. The security guards behind him stepped toward him; Kirk held up a hand and motioned them back.

"The only proof I can offer," Garth said, "is that you play out this scenario as I have sketched it. When the rebels are all confined on Acra, you'll know that I was telling the truth."

"Then this prison has been prepared," Spock murmured. "You would need Antosian cooperation for that."

"Who is your ally in this plot?" Kirk asked. "That person could confirm your story."

"Yes, he can." Garth sat down again. "But he won't."

"And why not?" Spock said.

"Because he is a traitor whom I have set to expose. He went along with my plans as far as setting up a place of exile on Acra. After the rebels were all gathered there, his intention was to equip and command his own private army, with the help of a starship, which I had promised to supply."

"I don't understand," Kirk said.

Garth sighed impatiently. "My plan coincides with that of my false ally's up to a point only. He has his own agenda and ambitions, and a backup plan in case he is unable to get a starship. If acquiring a starship fails, he plans to allow for a time of relative peace while he secretly arms the rebels on Acra, for use as his army some years from now, long after I am gone and the Federation's fears are presumably allayed. Once he is in control of the planet, he would, I suspect, plan for bigger things, although it's possible that all he wants is to rule Antos IV. In other words, he is planning to hijack my plan at some point."

"Who is he?" Kirk asked.

Garth replied, "We need him a bit longer. Who the

traitor is will become apparent. He'll reveal himself, and then you won't have to take my word for it."

Kirk studied Garth for a while in silence, then said, "One more thing. This explanation of yours still seems much too contrived and almost beyond proof. The return of the mad Lord Garth is a much simpler explanation for what's happened."

"I must say that I agree with you, Captain," Spock added.

Garth nodded. "But consider this—what have you to lose by believing me? I am your prisoner now. If you prevent my plan from going forward, there'll be a civil war down there sooner or later. Let me act according to plan, as if I have managed to take the *Enterprise.* Send me back down to Antos IV with a guard at my side—you, Captain Kirk—and I will prove the truth of what I've told you. You have everything to gain, and your shipmates will be on guard here. There's no danger of rebel Antosians taking over your ship without my help."

"Captain Garth," Spock said, "I must ask you another question. This solution of yours—namely, the imprisonment of the rebels on the island of Acra—is a drastic and cruel solution, is it not?"

"Yes, it is, Mr. Spock, and I am to blame. Once the lust for power entered Antosian culture through me, the choice of solutions became few. This is the only practical solution, while the number of rebels is still only a few hundred. They must be isolated from the vast majority of Antosians who have not been infected by their dreams of conquest, who may be ready to renounce shape-shifting for themselves and future generations in order to preserve their peaceful culture. We must help them to remove this unnecessary temptation by setting up new traditions."

"But to imprison them," Spock said. "The Prime Directive—"

"—does not apply in this case," Garth finished. "Mr. Spock, you saw how the Antosians live—in one city, with a First Minister whose authority is nearly absolute, because he can be trusted with such authority. Such centralization is all they know. They don't know how to deal with dissidents—they've never had rebels before. I did not propose to exile the rebels—that solution was put forward by Antosians. It is the only way they can think of to handle the problem. But as soon as I considered it, I knew that it was the only choice we had." He paused. "I remind you that there are still prisoners down there being held by the rebels. First Minister Empynes is a prisoner. I must get back there soon."

"Captain Garth," Kirk said in a low voice, "how can you claim to know all that you're telling us? How can you lay out such an elaborate plot and expect the reactions you hope for? Your scheme, from what you've said, can go wrong at any point, including right now, since it depends on whether we believe you or not."

"Yes, very true." Garth leaned back in his chair. "But I do have backups and alternatives, too many moves ahead of where we are at the moment to waste time in discussing them now."

Suddenly Kirk found himself being convinced by the hero of his youth, and he wondered whether he believed Garth because of the way circumstances, at least so far, seemed to confirm his story, or only because James Kirk wanted to believe it, rather than admit to and accept the mental collapse and failure of Garth.

"Mr. Spock," Kirk said, "what do you think of all this?"

"Improbable and exceedingly complex, Captain," Spock replied, "but self-consistent, and the complexity is plausible if we consider the complications of political power. The game of chess, even three-dimensional chess, is simplicity itself compared to a political game using pieces that can change their minds independently of other pieces." Spock looked thoughtful. "I am well aware that Captain Garth was a chess champion while a cadet at Starfleet Academy."

"There wasn't much he wasn't a prizewinner at," McCoy muttered. "You just don't know, do you, Spock? Admit it."

"Evidence is lacking in the extreme," Spock said.

"Still, there is some evidence in favor of Captain Garth," McCoy continued.

"And what evidence is that?" Kirk asked.

"Damn it, Jim, Captain Garth was cured of his neurological malfunctions, and my tricorder scan shows a healthy, functioning brain. There's no reason to think that a thorough workup wouldn't confirm that. As for his display of histrionics before Scotty beamed us all aboard, I can only say that he should have auditioned for the Starfleet Academy Dramatic Society—probably would have won a prize for acting, too. You certainly convinced me."

Garth said sadly, "Dr. McCoy, you did not have to confront me when I was truly mad—when I wasn't acting—as Captain Kirk and Mr. Spock did."

"And you assume that if I had, I'd have doubts now? Poppycock! I saw the medical reports, saw my own tricorder readings. I'd have to declare myself incompetent to deny the evidence of your recovery."

"We can't leave any room for doubt," Kirk said as he stood up. "Captain Garth, you'll accompany me and Dr. McCoy to sickbay, under guard. Bones, you'll give him every test you need to be certain that he's still sane, and then I'll decide what to do next."

"I agree." Garth got to his feet. "But quickly, Doctor, quickly."

Garth lay on a biobed, with his upper body raised nearly to a sitting position. Christine Chapel stood at his left, glancing from Garth to the readings on the display panel just above the bed; Chekov and the two security guards were on his right, phaser pistols in hand.

"Well?" Kirk said to McCoy.

"He's entirely sane and perfectly healthy by every test we can run, Jim. About the only advice I'd have for this patient is to get some rest."

"Doctor," Garth said, "time is short. I must—"

"Wouldn't hurt you to get a little rest while the

captain's making up his mind about what to do," McCoy cut in.

Garth closed his eyes as if grateful for the suggestion. Kirk looked at the suddenly composed face and knew that this visible extreme was part of an epic undertaking by the mind behind the mask. He wanted to believe it was something noble, but it was not yet time to excuse Garth from scrutiny.

Kirk motioned McCoy away from the biobed.

"Whatever he's doing," Kirk murmured, "we now know he's doing it with full knowledge and intent, and not as the puppet of a disability."

"That's exactly it," McCoy said in a low voice. "And if he's lying, he knows exactly what he's trying to do. He's entirely responsible for his actions. We can't get out of this by declaring him insane and shipping him back to Elba II."

"And if he's telling the truth about what's going to happen on Antos IV, then we can't let it happen. We have to do as he asks."

"Admiral Mendez gave you full authority to step in. It has to be your decision." McCoy offered Kirk a wry smile. "Sorry I couldn't give you a medical excuse for a way out of this mess."

Garth's medical examination had taken about an hour. Kirk knew that he could use some rest himself, but if the situation among the Antosian rebels was as grave as Garth had indicated, immediate action was necessary while it was still possible to exert control over events. Even the Prime Directive could offer him no guidance here, since it was clear that Federation interference, in the person of the injured and mad Garth, had precipitated the rebellion on Antos IV.

McCoy said, "It's your call, Jim. What will you do?"

"What I've often done," Kirk replied. "Take it one step at a time. There's no choice for me but to return to Antos IV with him, according to his plan, and letting him play out this game. But I'll watch him very closely."

"Madness in great ones must not unwatched go, if I'm remembering Shakespeare correctly. But why in blazes did he have to make this so complicated?"

"Because intelligent beings are complex, societies are even more so, and Garth had to choose a way equal to the task—a quick way." He was surprised at his own defense of Garth, but doubts still played their game in his mind, and he feared that Garth might be drawing them all into a labyrinth of illusion from which there would be no escape.

"We're too damned suspicious for our own good, is the problem," McCoy muttered. "Once trust is gone, it's almost impossible to restore it, but you seem willing to trust Garth."

"If he's telling the truth," Kirk said, more out of duty than conviction.

"Are you going to go armed?" the physician asked.

Kirk nodded. "Garth can't object, by everything he's told us." He would conceal his weapon, as he had before, and hope again that he would never have to use it—against any Antosians, or against Garth.

Kirk went back to Garth's bedside, McCoy right behind him. "Captain Garth?" Kirk said to the sleeping figure.

The other man was awake in an instant. "Yes, Captain Kirk?"

"I've decided that I am going to go planetside with you after all."

Garth sighed, looking relieved. "I'm glad to hear it." He sat up and swung his legs over the side of the bed as Chekov and the two security guards stepped aside. "We have to move fast."

"Exactly what am I supposed to do?" Kirk asked. "What role am I to play?"

Garth stood up. "Very simple, Captain. I'll explain it to you on our way to the transporter room. You are to be my accomplice, my co-conspirator if you will. You're going to join our cause."

Dawn was breaking. The sky above the clearing was lightening into a deep violet as Kirk and Garth materialized at the rebel campsite, both of them dressed in long black coats over their uniforms.

The Antosians on guard—two men and one woman who were sitting around the fire—jumped to their feet, clearly startled. They gazed at Kirk and Garth for a long moment in silence. Kirk looked past them and estimated that at least a hundred people were in the clearing, perhaps as many as two hundred. At last a muscular, fair-haired man stepped forward, and Kirk saw that he was Kellin, the youth who had impersonated Garth during the ride out from Pynesses.

"Lord Garth?" Kellin asked. "Can it truly be you? We had begun to doubt."

"Of course it is!" Garth cried out in his mad theatrical voice. A loud cheer went up from the Antosians; fists shook and spears rose above heads. "Lord Garth walks among you once again! Comrades—brothers and sisters in our coming battle—the *Enterprise* is ours!"

The massed Antosians cheered more loudly and stamped their feet. Kirk, standing just behind Garth, glanced surreptitiously around the clearing, but could see no sign of Empynes, Gyneeses, Heje-Illuss, or any of Heje-Illuss's followers. He felt a rush of dismay as his doubts assailed him once more. Garth might have deceived him. Something else entirely might be going on behind the scenes; luring him back to Antos IV might have been nothing more than a plan to trap him.

He quickly pushed such worries from his mind, reminding himself that the *Enterprise* was safely in the hands of Spock and Scotty. Security guards were on duty in every one of the transporter rooms; it would be impossible for any shape-changer to get aboard in another guise. The Antosians that he and Garth were planning to beam up, allegedly to a starship that was now under Garth's control, would not be permitted to materialize fully inside the *Enterprise,* but would immediately be forwarded to the island of Acra.

That was the plan. However much he turned it over

in his mind, Kirk could not see where there might be any possibility for treachery on Garth's part. Better to hold to his conviction that Garth was telling the truth and to do whatever he could to help resolve this situation. There were still too many points at which the complex scheme could fail.

"Lord Garth!" several Antosians shouted. "Lord Garth!" Others behind them took up the chant, and then they abruptly fell silent and backed away from the fire as another Antosian came striding toward Garth and Kirk.

She was a woman, tall and commanding, with long dark hair that was as black as the long coat she wore over a tunic and trousers. Her skin was a dark coppery color, while her pale eyes were golden; a sword and scabbard hung from her right shoulder. She stopped in front of them and stared for a while at Garth, then turned her attention to Kirk. Immediately he saw suspicion and resentment in her beautiful face, and suddenly guessed who she had to be: Hala-Jyusa, the rebel leader who had broken with Heje-Illuss.

"I greet you, Hala-Jyusa!" Garth called out, clasping the woman's hands.

Hala-Jyusa frowned, slipped her hands from Garth's, took a step back, then drew herself up again. "I am pleased to hear of your triumph, Lord Garth," she said in a resonant alto voice, "but how is it possible that you have taken control of the starship without any help from us?" She glanced around at the others.

"I arrived here with the rest of our followers only to be told that you had been taken from us, beamed up to the starship along with its Captain Kirk and the three who were with him, and with three of our fighters who were to take their places." She pressed her lips together in a thin line. "As brilliant as you are, my Lord Garth, I don't see how you could take over such a vessel with so little assistance so quickly."

"You are as discerning as always, Hala-Jyusa," Garth replied. "I did not need to take over the *Enterprise* that way. Captain Kirk has joined our cause!"

Kirk moved closer to Garth's side; the gathering grew silent. Garth had only had enough time in the transporter room to sketch out the kind of story Kirk should tell the rebels. He would have to ad-lib the details as he went along and hope that he was convincing.

Hala-Jyusa's eyes narrowed. "Is this true?" she said, still obviously doubtful. "He's come over to our side?"

"Of course it's true," Garth said loudly. "Kirk has always been my disciple."

Nice touch, Kirk thought. Next he'll declare me his heir apparent, as he did on Elba II.

Hala-Jyusa glared at Garth. Perhaps, Kirk thought, she resented the power Garth, the offworlder, held over her followers. "I did not pose the question to you, Lord Garth," she said, showing her teeth, "but to Captain Kirk."

"And I shall happily respond," Kirk said. The Antosians began to settle themselves on the ground or on the logs grouped around the fire. Hala-Jyusa kept near Garth, still with a wary look on her face.

"I have long been an admirer of Lord Garth," Kirk began, "ever since my days as a cadet. He's been one of my heroes for much of my life. I've always dreamed of serving with him, and then a time came, not long ago, when I learned that Garth—my hero, a legend, the officer I admired more than any who had ever served in Starfleet—had been confined to an asylum." All of that was true enough, and Kirk saw from the faces of the rebels nearest him that they believed him.

"They called him mad," Kirk continued, "and criminally insane, and perhaps he was, since he was then still recovering from the severe injuries he sustained after his first contact with your people. But his intellect was intact, his dreams of glory had not died, and when I realized that—"

"We know about all of that," Hala-Jyusa interrupted. "Tell us something we don't know."

"My dear Hala-Jyusa," Garth said softly, "our new ally Captain Kirk is speaking." His voice took on a harder tone. "Please show him the courtesy of hearing him out."

"Then let him tell us more convincingly why he's decided to join us," she said.

"That is what I am attempting to tell you, my lady and comrade." Kirk bowed in her direction; Hala-Jyusa gazed back at him coldly. "I well understand why you might have your doubts, but they are easily banished by facts." He paused. "I was given orders by Starfleet Command to bring Lord Garth back to Antos IV, supposedly to discuss with your leaders the possibility of your planet's becoming a part of the Federation. But I was certain that one so great as Garth, one who had once dreamed of greater glory, could not have allowed his dreams of conquest to die. I also suspected that he harbored some resentment against the Federation, and also against the officers who had mutinied and seized command of his starship and those who had sentenced him to Elba II. They called it a cure, locking him up there, but I saw it as trying to rein in a proud and noble spirit."

He had them now; he could see it in the upturned faces around the fire. Even Garth looked proud of his performance.

"I have my own grievances against the Federation and Starfleet Command," Kirk went on. "It is true that I have won command of a starship, but I have also been deprived of honors that might have been mine. Even though I was acquitted in the end, I have endured a court-martial as the result of false accusations against me. I did not reveal my resentments to Garth at first, but on our way here, I grew to know the officer I had so long admired. And when I followed him here, events soon showed me that his dreams were not unlike my own. I also well understand why you do not want to give up your biological heritage and the art of cellular metamorphosis that is so integral to your culture, for I value my own genetic heritage as much as you value yours, and would not willingly surrender it."

"Lord Garth was threatening you," Hala-Jyusa said. "I was told about that when I arrived here, that he was shouting that he would kill you and those with you if you did not allow him to board your ship immediately. What was that all about?"

"Lord Garth was not yet certain he could fully trust me or my crew," Kirk said smoothly, "and did not want to endanger your people—your followers—until he was sure of me. When we were beamed aboard, and I told him that I sympathized with him and would fight with him, he knew that he had an ally in this battle."

Garth was smiling as he looked around at the people in the clearing, but Hala-Jyusa still looked skeptical. "That's all very well, Captain Kirk," the Antosian woman said, "but what about the rest of your crew? Have they thrown in their lot with you and with us?"

Kirk thought quickly. "It is not necessary that all of them do so," he replied, "for they have but one imperative—to obey their captain. My authority over them is absolute." The Antosians would probably accept that, especially since they were used to being governed by a First Minister with such authority, but it wouldn't hurt to give them another convincer. "But as it happens, others among my officers have been moved to join our cause. Mr. Spock, my first officer, has also agreed to become one of us."

"The fellow with the pointed ears," Garth added with a big smile.

"Once his people, the Vulcans, were warriors," Kirk said, beginning to pace in front of his audience, "and Spock has long been an admirer of his ancestors and their accomplishments." It was similar to the truth, in any case, Kirk thought. "Another who has joined us is my chief engineer, whose people were once fierce warriors on our homeworld of Earth. And there are others who have a personal loyalty to me. Most of my officers and crew will follow me anywhere and won't question anything I do." He stopped pacing. "As for the rest—and they will be very few in number—they will obey my orders, or they can easily be put under restraint, as have those who tried to stand against you—Heje-Illuss and the First Minister and the others." He looked around. "By the way, where are they?"

"They are being held not far from here," Hala-Jyusa answered. "Why are you so interested in them, anyway?"

"Only because they might be useful as hostages," Kirk said, "and of course there is always the chance that they might give up their futile resistance to us. We should allow them the opportunity to do so."

"Captain Kirk is right," Garth said. "It would be foolish to harm people who might have their uses later on."

"They have not been harmed," Hala-Jyusa said, sounding angry. "My word on that should be enough for you, Lord Garth."

"Of course it is, my dear." Garth nodded his head in her direction. "But in order for the next stage of my plan—our plan—to succeed, we must all be gathered together. We must all take final control of the *Enterprise,* and quickly. Only three of our Antosian fighters are aboard at the moment, and most of Captain Kirk's crew is still unaware of our intentions. We mustn't give them time to entertain doubts about what we're up to and then to move against us out of fear, or perhaps to further their own interests." He took a breath. "We'll beam aboard in small groups. There will be no one in the transporter rooms except for one or two transporter officers, who can be easily overcome. Once we have control of those facilities, the rest of us will come aboard in a steady stream, but we have to move fast."

Garth was right about having to move fast, Kirk thought. The longer they talked and the more convoluted their tales became to cover any objections that were raised, the more chance that their subterfuge would unravel, that someone here, most likely Hala-Jyusa, would seize on some inconsistency in their improvised speeches.

"The power of a starship will be at our command!" Garth rose to his feet and thrust his arms upward. "We can secure the planet in a matter of hours!" He turned to Hala-Jyusa. "And you will be a co-commander of the *Enterprise* with us, my dear, fully equal in rank to Captain Kirk and myself." He bowed toward her. "You must beam up with the first group, my co-commander. We will have great need of your leadership aboard ship."

Hala-Jyusa smiled; her golden eyes filled with admiration as she looked up at Garth, but then her smile faded. "Lord Garth, you are moving too fast," she murmured as suspicion fired her eyes.

"But we must be quick if we are to succeed, my dear. Bring the prisoners you are holding to this site, in case we need them as hostages, and then we will begin beaming aboard the *Enterprise.*"

Hala-Jyusa stood up to face him. "I said that they were not far from here," she murmured. "When I saw you appear, and knew you had returned to us safely, I sent a man to them, to order that they be brought here. They'll be on their way to us now—they haven't far to ride." She glanced toward the forest to the east. "I see someone coming now."

The sky was light; morning had come to the clearing. Kirk saw the shadowy forms of people on foot and ellei riders amid the trees. As they emerged into the clearing, he saw that Gyneeses was among them. The Chief Adviser seemed unharmed. He felt relief and then noticed that Gyneeses was unbound and riding an ellei, while other Antosian captives were on foot with their arms tied behind them, being herded along by riders carrying spears.

"Victory will be ours!" Garth shouted to the newcomers as they dismounted and prodded their captives with their spears, forcing them forward. "The *Enterprise* will soon be in our hands!"

Another cheer went up from the assembled rebels. The prisoners sat down. Empynes was not among them, or Heje-Illuss, but only a dozen of the captives were present. Kirk hoped that the others would arrive soon, that Empynes had not been harmed.

"Lord Garth! Lord Garth! Lord Garth!" the rebels cried, shaking their weapons.

"And all hail our co-commander, Hala-Jyusa!" Garth responded, taking the Antosian woman's arm and holding it high in the air. "Hala-Jyusa will also lead us, along with our new brother, Captain James Kirk!" Hala-Jyusa lifted her head, accepting the homage, clearly proud of the power and position Garth was offering to her. Power, Kirk thought, was the greatest aphrodisiac, the greatest of temptations, and probably the greatest enemy of intelligent judgment.

Then Hala-Jyusa looked at Kirk, and he saw suspicion cloud her eyes once more. Gyneeses was walking toward them, looking as if he belonged at Garth's side. He's turned on Empynes, Kirk thought, realizing that Gyneeses was the traitor Garth had alluded to earlier.

"Greetings, Lord Garth," Gyneeses said as he came up to them. Hala-Jyusa's lip curled as she gave the Chief Adviser a look of contempt. "I am pleased to see that you are unharmed." He frowned at Kirk. "An excellent impersonation—I would never—"

"He is not an Antosian shape-changer," Garth said, "but Captain Kirk himself, who has decided to join our cause."

Gyneeses's frown became a scowl. Kirk stared back at the Chief Adviser, wondering if he could believe the story. Hala-Jyusa had fallen out with Heje-Illuss, and clearly bore Gyneeses ill will, while the Chief Adviser, according to Garth, was playing his own game. Garth would have to start beaming rebels aboard right away, before the whole complicated plot fell apart.

"Now we must seize the moment, my comrades," Garth continued. "The sooner we are aboard, the sooner our cause will triumph. With control of the starship, we can secure the planet in a matter of hours. We'll beam Hala-Jyusa aboard the *Enterprise* first, along with a few of her close comrades."

"Our transporter technicians are waiting," Kirk added, "and they will follow our orders."

"Then there is no reason to wait," Gyneeses said. "We—"

"We're moving too fast," Hala-Jyusa repeated. She turned to Garth. "Not that I object to your plan, Lord Garth, only the speed at which you wish to implement it."

"If we wait, we may lose, my co-commander and comrade," Garth said. "The *Enterprise* could be turned against us."

Gyneeses said, "I agree with Garth. We must—"

"Be silent," Hala-Jyusa said in a low voice. "You may be Chief Adviser, but your ancestors were still rounding up wild elleis while mine were masters of the healing arts." She turned her head toward Garth. "And I have no need of a title from an offworlder to tell me who I am. I am the true leader of this rebellion now, and however much I may honor you, Lord Garth, you would be wise not to overreach yourself. I will accept whatever aid we require from Gyneeses and this offworlder starship captain, but I do not yet completely trust them."

This was the moment, Kirk thought, at which the mad Lord Garth would throw a tantrum, if he was the insane Garth. But Garth's face was composed as he regarded the two Antosians.

"Time is of the essence, Hala-Jyusa," Garth said calmly. "We must, all of us, occupy the starship at once. Without it, we are nothing. The force that might be brought against us is beyond imagining, unless we move quickly!"

Gyneeses nodded eagerly. "Lord Garth is correct," he said. "We must act quickly."

"Captain Kirk will go with you," Garth said, "to aid you in securing command."

"No!" Hala-Jyusa shook her head. "You dare to order me in this way? My family is one of the oldest continuous lines on this planet, and one of the most skilled at shape-shifting, while you, great as you may be, are an offworlder. You may make a request of me, but you will not order me!"

"Of course, my dear lady." Garth tilted his head. "Forgive me. I respectfully request that you prepare to be beamed aboard the *Enterprise,* where you will command among equals."

But Garth's measured tones only seemed to anger the Antosian woman further. "First we were to beam aboard ourselves," she muttered, "take over the forms of members of the crew, then arrange to beam others aboard until the ship was ours and the offworlders under our control. Then Heje-Illuss weakened in his resolve, and broke with us, and now we have this Captain Kirk as an ally advising us, while Gyneeses grows ever more presumptuous."

The Antosian rebels near Kirk looked bewildered; he saw them murmuring among themselves, obviously dismayed by the bickering among their leaders. Garth was losing control of the situation.

"Now I find myself wondering," Hala-Jyusa continued, "who you are to involve yourself in our struggle, Lord Garth. I was one of those who helped you back to health, and taught you the art of shape-shifting, but why should you be here? Maybe you're here for some purpose of your own that is hidden from us." She paused and stepped back. "What is it? Does your Federation so fear us that they have some secret plan to disable us? Is our coming greatness a threat to them?" Her voice rose until she was shouting. "Why should we listen to offworlders? And where did this idea of altering our bodies and changing our genetic heritage come from?" She glowered at Garth, and for a moment Kirk imagined that the Klingon and Romulan empires might have begun in this way, from the realization that power could be wielded to fill a hunger without end.

"Calm yourself, Hala-Jyusa," Gyneeses said. "You are not speaking to enemies." His voice dropped to a whisper. "It would be better for us not to show our disagreements so visibly."

"Upstart!" the Antosian woman screamed. "Dung sweeper!" She seemed about to strike him, then let her arm fall. "I am only saying that whatever these offworlders promise, it is we who must be masters of this fight for our heritage." She was speaking softly again, but in an ominous way that made Kirk extremely uneasy. "And I must have time to consider this new plan for seizing the starship."

He had heard that voice before, Kirk realized, on Elba II, in the mad rantings of the insane Lord Garth. Hala-Jyusa had not only been attracted by the mad Garth's visions of glory, but had also been infected with his lusts.

She strode away from them toward the eastern edge of the clearing; a few of her followers trailed after her. Most of the rebels remained near the fire or outside the shelters, watching Garth and Gyneeses, clearly uncertain about what they should do, if anything.

And Kirk felt a sudden cold yet familiar calm. It came into him in moments of great danger, or when he couldn't see what was going to happen next.

Garth moved among the rebels, patting a few of the men on the back or gripping their shoulders for a moment, stopping occasionally to speak with a small group before going to the next.

Gyneeses watched Garth with narrowed eyes.

"He's telling them we have to board the starship now," Gyneeses muttered.

"Yes," Kirk said, wary of getting into any prolonged discussion with the Chief Adviser.

"Hala-Jyusa is too stubborn. She ought to listen to him." Gyneeses snorted. "But he'll bring her around."

Kirk nodded. Of course Gyneeses would want everyone beamed aboard as soon as possible. If what Garth had said was true, the Chief Adviser had plotted with him to have the rebels beamed to Acra, in accordance with his own plans to seize control of the rebellion later on. Perhaps he also planned to get rid of Hala-Jyusa.

If what Garth had told him was true . . . Kirk's doubts assailed him again.

Garth came back to Kirk and Gyneeses, then turned to face the Antosian rebels. "Have no fear, my brethren," Garth called out. "Better for us to bring up our small disagreements now, so that we can settle them before embarking on our next battle. I have only the greatest respect for Hala-Jyusa, my co-commander. Rest assured that when we board the *Enterprise,* we shall be united in our purpose—I, Hala-Jyusa, Gyneeses, and of course our new ally, Captain Kirk."

The rebels cheered, but not quite as loudly or as enthusiastically as they had earlier. They were losing them, Kirk thought.

Garth turned around quickly and walked toward Hala-Jyusa.

Kirk followed, trailed by Gyneeses. Hala-Jyusa folded her arms as they came up to her, still looking angry; her comrades hovered near her protectively. Garth suddenly held out his hands to her.

Garth was only stalling for time. In any case, Kirk had a sudden idea.

"Lady Hala-Jyusa," Kirk said, "please accept this tricorder as a pledge of our new comradeship." He held up his own tricorder. "With this instrument, you will be able to gather any information you require about your surroundings."

He scanned the clearing and the nearby forest quickly. The readings indicated that another group of Antosians on foot and on elleis was approaching the clearing. That was good to know, for it meant that Hala-Jyusa had not lied when she had said that the rest of the captives were on their way there.

Kirk slipped his communicator from his belt. "And with this communicator, you can speak to the *Enterprise.* But we must beam aboard quickly. My officers may already be worrying about me, and you do not want men in control of the power of a starship to wonder if ill fortune might have befallen their captain and to act precipitously against you. For another thing, your people are running short of provisions and must be fed—they should not have to wait here, growing weaker while we debate at length about our course of action."

"Which we should now settle among ourselves," Garth said softly.

The Antosian woman turned toward her close comrades. "Off with you!" she said. They hurried away to join the people around the fire.

"I should let my officers know that Garth and I are well," Kirk went on, "and that they must prepare themselves to greet you as our co-commander when we beam aboard."

Hala-Jyusa peered at the communicator in Kirk's hand. "Show me how you use this device," she said.

Kirk flipped his communicator open. "Kirk to *Enterprise.*"

Garth reached over and handed Hala-Jyusa his communicator. She flipped it open.

"Scott here," Scotty's voice said from her hand.

"Kirk here, reporting that Lord Garth and I are now in consultation with our allies Hala-Jyusa and Gyneeses. When we come aboard, you will treat Hala-Jyusa as if she were also a starship captain."

Hala-Jyusa allowed herself a smile.

"Aye, Captain," Scotty said.

"Stand by for further orders. Kirk out." He let his arm fall, but did not close the communicator. He wanted the channel open, so that Scotty and Spock would hear what was going on.

"It is not that I disagree with you," Hala-Jyusa said in a gentle voice to Garth, "it is only that I questioned the need for such haste." She gave him back his communicator.

"Of course, my dear," Garth said. "I understand."

Her smile widened. Kirk saw that she was ready to

go along with them now, and once she was out of the way, the rest of the rebels could be handled.

"We're wasting time," Gyneeses said. "We might have all been aboard the starship by now except for this bickering."

Hala-Jyusa stepped toward him, her face dark with fury. "I have heard enough from you—you, who were with Empynes, our weak First Minister. You went along with him and convinced him that we should give up our arts, and then you changed sides." Her voice was rising. "How can you be trusted? You turned on him too easily. What are you after? When will you turn on us?"

Her attention was fully on Gyneeses, her back to Kirk. He drew his communicator to his face and whispered, "Scotty, beam us up—me and the three with me."

And then he saw her hand reach over her shoulder and close around the hilt of her sword. Before he could move to stop her, she pulled it from the scabbard, pointed, and thrust.

The scene died in Kirk's eyes—

—and then he was suddenly in the transporter room, watching as Gyneeses took the blade in his chest.

Hala-Jyusa drew the blood-covered blade from him as he toppled forward. Scotty came toward them, phaser drawn, followed by two of the security guards.

"Get a medical team here from sickbay!" Kirk shouted at Ensign Somerville, the transporter officer on duty.

Somerville was already calling for help over the

ship's comm. "Dr. McCoy, we have a wounded man, sword through the chest," she said. Kirk knelt next to Gyneeses as Garth stepped toward them and took the sword from Hala-Jyusa's hand. She did not resist, but stared at him with confusion in her yellow-gold eyes. A look of compassion crossed Garth's face, and Kirk knew that he was blaming himself for the violence he had roused in her.

"Don't move, lassie," Scotty said, keeping his phaser pistol aimed at the Antosian woman. Gyneeses stared up at Kirk, his eyes wide with surprise. Blood was seeping through his tunic, but he did not seem to be bleeding as heavily as he should have been after such a wound. Kirk tried to block the flow with the flap of Gyneeses's coat; he remembered that Antosians could use their shape-changing skills to heal themselves, and wondered if Gyneeses had the strength left to do so.

The door to the transporter room opened; McCoy hurried through the entrance, followed by two men carrying a stretcher. He knelt next to Gyneeses, pulled the coat aside, tore the Antosian's tunic open to cover the wound with a bandage, made a quick scan of the injured man with his tricorder, then motioned to the two medical technicians with him. "He's failing fast," McCoy said. "Get him to sickbay."

"You cannot heal him. I cannot heal him. He cannot heal himself." Hala-Jyusa spoke in a toneless voice as the men laid the now unconscious Gyneeses on the stretcher and carried him from the transporter room; McCoy hurried after them.

Kirk motioned to the two security guards. "Keep her under guard."

The look of confusion on Hala-Jyusa's face turned to panic. "What is happening?" she shouted, her hand opening and closing as if grasping for her sword. "What does this mean? I am co-commander here!"

"Keep this woman under guard," Kirk repeated, "and don't let her out of sight for a moment. Don't forget—she's a shape-changer."

The guards took her by the arms. Hala-Jyusa suddenly became a twin of Ensign Somerville, then flowed into the form of an Antosian male Kirk had seen in the rebel camp, and then turned into a tall furred biped with long claws. She opened her jaws to show sharp pointed teeth and let out a long piercing screech, the sound of a cornered wild beast. Somehow the men holding her managed to keep a grip on her arms throughout all of her changes. At last she reverted to her own form and stood still, exhausted, fists clenched as the security men put wide cuffs around her wrists to restrain her, and Kirk saw that she finally understood.

"So I am to be a prisoner," she said. "We are not to command after all, and you are with our enemies."

"No," Garth said. "We are not your enemies, Hala-Jyusa."

"You're not an Antosian," she said. "You have no

right to interfere with our struggle. You were never with us."

"It is a struggle for only a few of your people," Garth said. "Most of them agree with Empynes, the First Minister. Even Heje-Illuss turned against the revolt."

"Heje-Illuss! A coward! He lost the will to fight on!" She hissed, and for a moment Kirk thought that she might morph again into something even more threatening than the furred creature he had seen. Then her shoulders sagged; she bowed her head in defeat. "You lied to us," Hala-Jyusa said sadly. "You lied to me."

Garth gazed at her, and then a look of such despair crossed his face that Kirk knew something had broken inside him. "Please believe me," he said in a choked voice. "I did not come here to betray you, I came to help. I came to repair the damage I caused."

"Liar! You came to rob us of our heritage."

Garth turned away from her, shaking his head.

"Keep her under restraint," Kirk said to the security men, "until further orders from me."

Hala-Jyusa was being led away when the entrance to the transporter room whisked open again, revealing Dr. McCoy.

McCoy came toward Kirk. "Gyneeses is dead," the physician said, but Kirk had already read that news in McCoy's solemn expression. "That sword ripped his heart to pieces and severely damaged one lung. There was too much brain damage from loss of blood and oxygen—I couldn't repair anything in time to prevent it."

McCoy looked back at Hala-Jyusa, who stood in the open entrance with her guards. Kirk expected to see a look of triumph on her face, now that her enemy was dead, but she was staring blankly in his direction, as if she no longer saw anything in the room. Then she disappeared behind the closing door.

Garth turned to face Kirk. "I am responsible for this," he said.

"But you couldn't—" McCoy began.

"I will not weep too much for Gyneeses. I suspect that even before I came to his world, he was a small and petty man, useful in sifting data and making recommendations to the First Minister, the most helpful of which were probably passed on to Gyneeses by his subordinates. Without me, he might have remained a petty but peaceful and harmless man. Perhaps my mad dream seduced him to lay his own plans, to betray the trust others had in him, yet it probably didn't change his underlying character. But Hala-Jyusa—" Garth let out a sigh of despair. "She is my creation. I know of her earlier reputation from others—she was a kind and compassionate woman, someone who felt that her long and ancient lineage also gave her a great responsibility to help others."

"Noblesse oblige," Kirk said.

"Yes, but more than that. She was kind and gentle, and when I was damaged and dying, she healed me. Heje-Illuss was also one of those who healed me, but it was Hala-Jyusa who found me, who insisted that those with her do everything they could to help me. And this is how I repaid her—with insane ambitions that have driven her mad."

"Captain Garth," Kirk said, "we have to get back to the rebel base."

"Yes, I know." Garth drew himself up. "They will be wondering what happened to us."

They stepped onto transporter plates. For a moment, Kirk reminded himself that, without a doubt, he and Garth were acting together, on the same side, in the just cause of restoring peace to Antos IV. If such a thing was possible.

"Energize," he said, resolved that he would make it possible.

Chapter Eight

AS KIRK AND GARTH reappeared before the massed rebels, a shout went up from the crowd in the clearing. At first Kirk thought that the cheer was for them, but then he saw that the Antosians were gathered in a half circle, watching a man being driven by spears across the empty space. Another cheer went up as an Antosian thrust a spear toward the man's feet.

The man tripped and sprawled into the dirt. His hood fell back, revealing his long white hair. It was Heje-Illuss. Another man was pushed into the space, spears prodding him forward, and Kirk recognized Empynes. The First Minister's black coat was in tatters; he seemed about to fall, then righted himself.

"Comrades!" Garth shouted in his most commanding voice.

The Antosians nearest them turned toward him and Kirk.

"You are safe, Lord Garth?" young Kellin called out.

"Of course I am safe!" Garth cried back.

The muscular young man came toward him as others cheered.

"I am greatly relieved to see you," Kellin said. "When you disappeared so suddenly—"

"Have no fear," Garth said, clapping a hand on the Antosian's shoulder. "We have control of the *Enterprise.* Hala-Jyusa and Gyneeses already command the bridge, while our allies wait to beam us all aboard." He gazed past Kellin at Empynes. "But this—this is beneath such brave men and women, to seek a petty revenge on Heje-Illuss and to show such disrespect to Empynes. However misguided he might be, he is still First Minister."

"For how long?" a dark-haired young man shouted.

Garth shot him an angry look; the young man and those standing near him shrank back, obviously intimidated.

"As I told you," Garth said in a soft but deadly voice, "these two, Empynes and Heje-Illuss, might be useful to us later on. But they'll be of no use at all if they're damaged." His voice was rising. "Now I say to all of you—prepare to board our great ship of justice and glory!"

"Glory enough after we kill those two!" a voice shouted back with a savage happiness that sent a chill through Kirk. He searched the crowd and saw a blond man shaking a spear. "Why keep them? Why waste food and water on them?"

"You fool!" Garth strode toward the man, who suddenly looked terrified. The Antosian dropped his spear and turned to run, but Garth grabbed him by one arm, swung him around in one swift movement, struck him hard in the chest, then threw him to the ground. "There is food and water aplenty aboard the *Enterprise,*" Garth continued, "and wine, and also the delicacies of many worlds to sate our appetites and fuel us for battle! There are brigs in which to hold our prisoners until they come around to our way of thinking, or until we find ways to use them in furthering our cause!" He grabbed the young man's collar and pulled him roughly to his feet.

The blond man gasped for breath. "Forgive me, Lord Garth."

Garth smiled broadly. "I am magnanimous, and I forgive you, comrade." He turned and walked back to Kirk. "Now bring those two misguided Antosians here."

Others in the group pushed Empynes and Heje-Illuss after Garth. "Heje-Illuss," Garth said as he turned around, "you should not have turned against my co-commander Hala-Jyusa. That was most shortsighted of you. But you were my comrade, and you did not betray Kellin to anyone when Kellin was impersonating me in your camp. So it pleases me to show you some mercy now."

Kirk wondered why Heje-Illuss had not said anything to him about Garth's double after they had arrived at the clearing, but kept silent. Heje-Illuss might have been waiting for the right moment to expose him, or he might simply have been too frightened of Garth to act. In any case, he had come around to share the view of Empynes, that the rebellion had to be stopped.

"And you," Garth said to Empynes, "can ponder the mistakes you have made and consider the wisdom of accepting the inevitable while you are our prisoner." He looked to the crowd. "Hear me, my comrades! When word spreads through the city of Pynesses that the First Minister is now our captive, fear will seize the minds and hearts of those who stand against us. We will win our first victory over them before we even have to fight!"

Heje-Illuss's eyes darted back and forth as he watched Garth. Empynes held himself erect, obviously refusing to be cowed.

"Bind their hands!" Garth commanded those standing near the two men.

The arms of Empynes and Heje-Illuss were quickly bound behind their backs.

"Captain Kirk," Garth ordered, "take them to that end of the clearing and have them beamed aboard to their imprisonment! And we will send those cowards who chose to follow Heje-Illuss after them!"

Garth's followers were already shoving their other bound captives in his direction.

Kirk accepted a spear from a man near him and

prodded Empynes and Heje-Illuss southward, away from the crowd, then reached for his communicator. "Kirk to Scott," he whispered, but did not wait for Scotty's reply. "Ready to beam two aboard. Make sure that they and the thirty who follow them end up at a different site from the rest, as far away from them as possible."

The First Minister glanced at him, but had the presence of mind not to react to what he had heard.

Kirk halted, then turned so the crowd could see him. "Hala-Jyusa," he shouted into his communicator, "I send you those who stood against you! Mr. Scott, beam them up!"

Empynes and Heje-Illuss dissolved in a shimmer.

"They are imprisoned!" Garth cried.

The captive Antosians who had given their loyalty to Heje-Illuss were now driven toward Kirk, all of them looking fearful and dismayed.

"Thirty more to beam up," Kirk said to Scotty.

"Aye, Captain," Scotty's voice replied. *"They'll go to the same place as the other two."*

"Stand in groups of six," Kirk ordered. The arms of the captives were still bound behind them, which was fortunate; the furious faces they showed to Kirk told him that they would have tried to resist if they could. One man muttered what might have been a curse; another spat on the ground. He was relieved to see how angry they were; it meant that his performance, and Garth's, had convinced them.

Heje-Illuss's followers stood together, whispering

among themselves, and then one group after another shimmered and was gone.

"We have secured our prisoners!" Garth shouted to the rebels. "Hala-Jyusa, my co-commander, awaits our arrival! Now to board the starship that will bring us victory!"

A woman stepped forward. "Lord Garth, I am ready to follow you, but why isn't Hala-Jyusa here to—"

"Silence!" Garth roared. The woman stepped back, but gripped her spear more tightly. "She is not here because she is in command of the *Enterprise.* Must she come back here to lead you aboard like children?"

The woman looked away.

"We have wasted enough time," Garth continued. "Come forward in groups of six."

Kirk waited, wondering if some of the rebels might resist from fear of the transporter technology.

But at last a few Antosians came forward toward Kirk. He motioned for them to stop in the clearing. As the transporter beam snatched them, another group of six took their place; they shimmered and disappeared. Some Antosians hung back, looking anxious and uncertain; they did not understand where they were going, or how they were being transported. Maybe a few of them were thinking of the accident that had befallen Garth when he had first come to their world.

"Do not hesitate," Garth called out. "You've seen me come and go without harm. You see Captain Kirk here. He has used the transporter hundreds of times without ill effect."

More Antosians came forward and disappeared. Garth nodded to each group reassuringly; but as the departures continued, Kirk saw warriors hesitate as they watched their comrades dissolve; from all that was visible to them, they might be going to their deaths. In a literal sense, Kirk thought, they were dying, as their atoms and physical structures were broken down, transmitted, stored, then sent on to the prison island of Acra. In those moments, all life ceased: death and resurrection, McCoy sometimes joked. It was death in a literal, trivial sense, and resurrection in the most important sense, since accidents, however improbable, were always possible. But for a moment it seemed strange to Kirk, despite the lessons of his years of command, that death should never be a trivial matter.

Group after group of sixes stepped into the area between Kirk and Garth; as they passed Garth, he spoke to them encouragingly or raised a fist in the air. The knot of tension inside Kirk began to ease as the rebels at the campsite thinned out; smaller numbers could be better controlled if any Antosians suddenly grew fearful. Martial figures came toward him, and dissolved in the glitter of the beam, until finally the clearing in the forest was empty, the throng of four hundred gone. Only the tents and shelters were left, and the softly mewing elleis tied up at the eastern edge of the clearing, and the pile of saddles near the animals, and the dying embers of the camp's fire.

Kirk and Garth scanned the campsite and the

nearby forest with their tricorders, but the readings showed that no humanoid life-forms were present.

Garth was silent as they walked toward the elleis, and Kirk wondered what he was thinking, if he was regretting the betrayal of those who had believed him to be their comrade and one of their leaders.

The elleis tied to the long rope mewed and pawed the ground as Kirk and Garth approached. "We'll have to let them go," Garth said.

"Can they survive?" Kirk asked.

"They'll feed on leaves and insects in the woods until they reach the desert, which is part of their natural habitat." There was a melancholy tone in Garth's voice. "They're nomadic—they wander the desert and find water at the oases and graze in the grassier lands bordering the desert. They'll survive. The Antosians say that there really is no such creature as a domesticated ellei, that however gentle they may seem, their gentleness is only a guise that cloaks a free spirit."

They walked along the rope, untying the mounts and removing their bridles. The animals slipped away through the forest. Kirk and Garth stood alone in the clearing and listened to the sighing of the wind in the trees.

"What will become of us," Hala-Jyusa asked, "now that you have turned against us?"

Garth replied, "I am not your enemy, Hala-Jyusa."

She gazed across the table at Garth and Kirk with a look of defeat. Two security guards stood at the doorway. She had killed a man, and was no doubt capable of killing others, but Kirk felt a little pity for Hala-Jyusa, who had the slumped posture and lifeless expression of someone who had lost everything.

"You had no right to interfere with our struggle," she said to Garth. "You know a little of our world, and thanks to Heje-Illuss and me, you have learned how to morph as we do, but you are not an Antosian. You will never be an Antosian."

"Heje-Illuss has turned against the revolt," Garth said. "Empynes is against it, and so are most Antosians."

"They don't understand." Her hands gripped the arms of her chair. "They don't know what will be asked of them. Their bodies and the bodies of their children will be robbed of our heritage, of an art—"

"—that is no longer needed," Garth said, "and might cause great harm, especially now that Antosians are beginning to look beyond their sky."

Hala-Jyusa shook her head. "Is there no other way?"

"Your planet could be put under quarantine," Kirk said, thinking of Talos IV, "but that would stunt the development and culture of your people. And there's much that others in the Federation could learn from you. Even with the little contact there has been so far between your people and offworlders, the Antosians have acquired a reputation for benevolence and peacefulness."

A wistful look passed over her face. "Oh, yes. We were kind, we were good. We could not bear to see the offworlder suffer, we could not leave him to struggle for breath as he lay dying at our feet, and we could not allow him to live on with the burden of deformities. We restored his body to what it was and taught him shape-changing, too, and he came back to our world to rob us of what we had given him." The gentleness in her face died and was replaced by a look of implacability. "So what now?"

"You and your followers will be confined on the island of Acra," Kirk said. "Your people will avoid a civil war, and many lives will be saved. You'll be given everything you need. You won't be locked up in a prison or punished, and Captain Garth tells me that Acra is a pleasant place. You'll talk to one another, and to Empynes and other Antosians who share his views, until agreements are reached that will keep the peace and allow you to join the Federation, if that is what you choose to do later on."

She laughed harshly. "What a fool you are, James Kirk." The glint of madness played in her golden eyes. "Do you think that the group you found with me are all of my followers? There are countless others, Antosians who sympathize with us and who will rise up if I call upon them to join my fighters."

"You have murdered a man," Garth said. "Do you love death so much that you wish to bring it to as many people as possible?"

"If I had not put my blade into Gyneeses, he would have thrust a knife through me sooner or later, and you know it."

Garth stood up. "Hala-Jyusa, you will leave the *Enterprise* now for Acra."

She looked at him coldly and said, "I go to the exile I deserve for ever having helped you, for ever believing that you were my comrade." She rose and stared at him until he looked away from her.

Kirk waited on a transporter plate. The transporter room disappeared—

—and he was standing on a hillside amid a profusion of green leafy shrubs and colorful flowering bushes that might have been a botanical garden. The trees that shaded them were unlike the tall trees he had seen at the rebel campsite; these trees had wide, flat green leaves and yellow and red orbs that looked like fruits. He heard a soft trilling, then the sound of sharp high squeaks. Several small birds with bright blue, green, and orange feathers suddenly flew out from the trees into the clear blue sky.

He glanced at Garth, then at Hala-Jyusa. The Antosian was looking around with wonderment; a fleeting smile crossed her face, but then she frowned again.

"So this is to be my new home," she said.

Garth nodded. Kirk moved down the slope, with Garth and Hala-Jyusa following him, until he came to a place where he could see what lay below.

The hill overlooked a horseshoe-shaped bay covered with white sand. The ocean to the west was a bright turquoise expanse with waves that gently lapped the shore below. Groups of rebels sat on the sand gazing out at the ocean, their coats lying beside them, while others wandered along the shoreline. Large birds with gray and white feathers and long broad wings swooped gracefully over the beach, alighted on the sand, then rose into the sky, gliding on the currents of the warm breezes. The Antosian dissidents would have a paradise for their prison, Kirk thought, and wondered if that would ease the anger inside them enough to allow them to give up their dreams of conquest and power.

"And what am I to do now?" Hala-Jyusa asked.

"The others will want to know you're safe," Garth said. "They'll know by now that they were tricked, and they'll be worrying about what's going to happen to them."

"They may think that I conspired with you," she said, "to bring them here."

Garth shook his head. "You were their leader. They will look to you. They'll listen to you. Reassure them."

"Reassure them about what?" Anger was in her eyes again. "What can I tell them?"

"That you'll be provided with ample provisions from our synthesizers," Kirk said, "and also with tools for building shelters and other structures, along with tents to use in the meantime. The *Enterprise* won't leave this system until you're all settled here, with everything you need to make a new life for yourselves."

"How magnanimous of you." Hala-Jyusa looked away from him. "I curse you, Captain Kirk. I curse you, Garth, my false friend." She spat at Garth's feet; he bowed his head. "May you someday suffer the pain I am feeling now." She gazed out at the beach, where a few of the rebels were now wandering toward the hill. "They will be cursing you now for what you did to us, but I must go to them. Perhaps they will lash out at me and vent their anger on me for what you've done, but I no longer care about myself."

She began to descend the hill. Kirk waited with Garth, wanting to make sure that she would be safe among them. More warriors were gathering at the bottom of the hill, but they had left their weapons on the beach. Kirk heard their voices.

"Hala-Jyusa! Hala-Jyusa!" People waved their arms and stamped their feet. "Hala-Jyusa!"

"We've been betrayed!" she cried out. "Lord Garth has plotted with First Minister Empynes and the offworlders to exile us to this island! And I am exiled here on Acra with you!"

A few Antosians climbed the hill toward her. She stopped and waited for them to reach her, and suddenly their arms were around her, embracing her. A man linked his arm through hers; she grasped the arm of another woman as they made their way down the slope.

"She'll be safe," Garth said, sounding relieved. "Perhaps this place will heal the madness inside her." He looked at Kirk, his blue eyes radiating sadness. "What would we have done if they had tried to harm her?"

Kirk gripped Garth by the shoulder for a moment,

wishing that there was something he could say that might console him, then pulled out his communicator. "Kirk to *Enterprise.*"

"Scott here."

"Beam us to the site where you sent Empynes and the others."

"Aye, Captain."

"We freed ourselves from our bonds and waited," Empynes said, "and then we made a meal for ourselves of the fruits and berries that grow here in such profusion, and then we slept after I assured everyone that you would arrive here soon. I hoped for that, at any rate, not knowing for certain if you would."

Kirk had come with Garth to a grassy inland area, about one hundred and fifty kilometers southeast of the beach to which Hala-Jyusa and her rebels had been transported. Heje-Illuss and his followers were sitting along the western bank of a stream that ran through this region. They had shed their capes and coats, and seemed to be deep in conversation. The air was as warm and pleasant here as it had been on the beach, although it lacked the slight scent of salt. Shrubs with purple and orange berries dotted the flat, grassy land. Empynes had come away from the group to greet Kirk and Garth.

"The rebels," Kirk said to him, "those who follow Hala-Jyusa, were set down near a beach to the west of this group. I am sorry to tell you that . . ." Kirk paused. "Gyneeses is dead. After Hala-Jyusa ran him through with her sword, we tried but were unable to save him."

"There is no need for apologies," Empynes murmured. "He was clearly planning to turn against me all along. I trusted Gyneeses, I made him my Chief Adviser, and yet he would have happily watched me die at the hands of those rebels if you had not beamed down in time to save me."

"He was plotting against me, too," Garth said, "perhaps not to do me harm, but to use me and the rebellion for his own ends. I don't think that my presence here, and my earlier madness, infected him as it did Hala-Jyusa and others, but I was the example that distorted his mind and brought him to act."

"You mustn't blame yourself too much for that," Empynes said. "After all, you came back here to help us. Now I am beginning to wonder if I should have listened to Gyneeses when he so vigorously argued in favor of isolating the rebel factions here on Acra, but it seemed we had no other choice then, and perhaps we still don't." The First Minister turned toward Kirk. "It would have been much more difficult to bring the rebels here without the help of your starship's technology. There is no region on the eastern shore of our continent of Anatossia suitable for a port—almost the entire shoreline is dominated by high rocky cliffs. We would have had to sail with our prisoners across Greblendon Lake, the lake you saw near Pynesses, east to a river that flows toward the ocean and then make the voyage east to Acra. Of course it is also the difficulties of such a voyage that make it nearly impossible for the rebels to escape. Even if they somehow managed to build a craft, they would have to sail far to the south to avoid the cliffs, or go north and risk icebergs and frigid air, in order to land far enough away from Pynesses, and I do not think they could carry enough food to survive such long journeys. This way, we can at least isolate them without subjecting them to mistreatment."

"We'll beam down food and other supplies," Kirk said, "enough to last them until they can take care of themselves. From what little I've seen of this island, they should be able to survive without difficulty."

Empynes made a motion with his hand, showing one palm to Kirk, that seemed to be a gesture of assent. "That's true. There are many varieties of fruit, land suitable for farming, and abundant fish in the streams and the ocean."

"And now that your people will have some contact with the Federation," Kirk went on, "we can arrange for a Starfleet vessel to come to your world every so often, to check on the Antosians here and beam down any other supplies they might need."

"Yes." Empynes was silent for a moment. "They can live here, as comfortably as we can make it for them, until our world changes, away from the ambitions that have grown in these hearts. It may be a long time." He gazed steadily at Kirk. "But from now on, this will have to be our problem. There should be no more help from your starship once you have finished beaming down the necessary supplies, and as little interference as possible after that."

"There may be other pockets of resistance," Garth said softly as he looked up at the vast blue sky, in which the Antosian sun burned like a hot jewel set in the gauzy cotton of a few clouds. "I only hope that their numbers do not increase."

"We'll have to talk to them," Empynes said, "and explain what we have done, and what's at stake."

Kirk, as he heard Empynes's words, was beginning to see this problem as akin to a series of boxes with weak bottoms. Each solution led to a breakthrough and a fall into the next box of problems. He suddenly doubted if bringing the rebels here would restore peace to this world and remedy the damage Garth had inadvertently caused. Others might rise up to fight against the somatic and genetic changes Empynes sought. Perhaps the infection, as Garth called it, had already spread too far to be contained by isolating the dissidents.

Heje-Illuss now stood up and walked toward them, trailed by another of his followers, a woman with hair nearly as white as his. They halted in front of Garth; Heje-Illuss seemed about to speak, then bowed his head.

"What is it?" Garth asked. "Say what you have to say."

"The First Minister told us," the white-haired man replied, "that all of the dissidents were to be imprisoned—kept here."

Empynes said, "That is so. I'd prefer that you call it exile, rather than imprisonment."

"It's a distinction without a difference to me," Heje-Illuss said. "Trialla and I"—he motioned at his companion—"were talking about that before, with the others. You must have been planning this even before you rode to our meeting."

"Yes, we were," Empynes said. "I'll admit that. But we did not come to the meeting to deceive you. We meant to give all of you, your group and Hala-Jyusa's, a chance to give up your rebellion, to agree to rejoin the rest of us. Had all of you done so, I would have agreed to allow you to resume your lives in Pynesses."

"So you knew what Garth was plotting," Trialla said.

Empynes waved a hand. "Only that he had a plan, not the details. As far as Captain Kirk and I knew, the man who rode with us to your camp was Captain Garth. I didn't know that Garth had infiltrated your movement, and when he came to the camp with Hala-Jyusa and her followers, I too believed that he had plotted against us."

"I had no choice," Garth said in a low voice. "It was the only way I could truly learn what was going on, find out which rebels might change and turn away from violence and which would never give up the cause. And when I realized that Hala-Jyusa and her group were set on fighting and gathering more adherents, I knew that I would have to find a way to disarm them and end their rebellion." He glanced at Empynes. "I am sorry that I had to deceive you as well, but I felt safer acting alone. Even Captain Kirk knew nothing of my intentions until later."

Empynes frowned. "You may have been wise, Captain Garth. Antosians are not used to rebellions and fighting. And had I known that Gyneeses believed he was working with you against me, I might have done something that would have upset your plans."

"Is that wretch going to be exiled here with the others?" Heje-Illuss asked.

"Gyneeses is dead," Kirk said. "Hala-Jyusa killed him."

"I'm not sorry." Heje-Illuss spat into the grass. "What's going to happen to us? The people with me, I mean."

Empynes sighed. "You were willing to give up your fight. All of you held firmly to that position even after Hala-Jyusa and her band made prisoners of you and threatened you. I think that you should be allowed to leave here and return to your homes and families in Pynesses."

"Some of us would want that," Heje-Illuss said, "maybe most of us. I'd want that myself, but I wonder if it's what we should do. We could go among the others here, talk to them. It's worth a try, anyway. Maybe we shouldn't give up on them yet if there's any hope at all."

Kirk was moved by the man's words. Heje-Illuss was now showing some of the patience, benevolence, and compassion for which the Antosians were known.

"I changed, didn't I?" the white-haired Antosian

continued. "I was so convinced that we had to fight, that we would be losing our chance for greatness if we didn't seize power over the rest of our people and then go on to other conquests. Something inside me seemed to come alive after Garth first came here, after we healed him and heard him rant about the power we could have and also the danger we posed to the universe, about how other worlds would be safe only if they acted against us before we could rise to glory. Even after he was gone, I dreamed of conquests, of the worlds that might be ours. It was such a new joy. And when Garth returned, I became convinced, with no help from him, that only through battle and conquest could we protect our own world from offworlders." Heje-Illuss wiped his forehead with one hand. "Now all of that seems a fevered delusion, a kind of madness." He glanced from Kirk to Garth and Empynes. "We'll have to give up our shape-changing abilities. I see that now—it'll remove that temptation. I'm not happy about that, but I can live with it if that will keep the peace. All of us can, and we're willing to stay here and see what we can do for the others."

"I only hope that we can convince Hala-Jyusa and her followers to make their peace with that choice," Trialla murmured.

"It may take years," Garth said, "maybe generations." He spoke with a heavy voice, and Kirk knew that his burden had not grown lighter.

"But better to isolate the dissidents than to allow

their ambitions to take root in other minds," Empynes added.

Kirk wondered about the isolation of groups, then of cultures, and the usefulness of a growing Federation, knowing that its ideal would have to be questioned and renewed repeatedly to succeed. Without a series of first contacts, one culture would remain ignorant of another's rise, and of the dangerous or constructive opportunities that might present themselves. The Klingons and the Romulans, he was convinced, despite their aggressiveness, were not as hostile as they might have been because they knew that they had neighbors. Isolation might be more dangerous than any other long-term condition of intelligent life, both to the isolate and to any being coming into a first contact with an isolated individual or group. "Better to have neighbors one does not like," a man named Clarke had written three hundred years ago, "than to be alone." First contact with Spock's homeworld of Vulcan had been a model of transitions, setting the stage for the formation of the Federation in the twenty-second century; first contact with the Klingons had been somewhat less so, fueling the distrust and suspicion that existed to this day between the Federation and the Klingon Empire.

What else waited out there that might be beyond peaceful contact? Kirk asked himself, and almost shuddered at the possibility of alienness that might live beyond all hope of conversation, beyond all understanding.

That was why he was here, Kirk reminded himself: to seek the unknown, to make contacts in a universe that was becoming aware of itself through intelligent life, that would benefit from learning that it was not alone in the great darkness. Suns lit the galaxies; intelligent life grew from the energy of these suns as they warmed planets and brought forth life upon them. These intelligences deserved to know other intelligences. That was why he was here with Garth, who had overcome so much within himself and was now trying to help the Antosians tame their own demons.

I should never have doubted him, Kirk thought.

"What are you going to do now?" Garth asked Empynes.

"I must return to Pynesses," the First Minister replied. "I am thinking that perhaps you should come there with me for a short time, Heje-Illuss. There will be people who will be wondering about the rebels. Relatives and family members of the rebels will want to know that their exile is necessary but won't be unduly harsh. You may be able to help in reassuring them."

"If you think that would do any good," Heje-Illuss said.

"It may. I have no Chief Adviser at the moment, and my other advisers don't know as much about the rebellion as you do. It may help if you meet with them, too."

Heje-Illuss turned to Trialla. "You'll have to take my place as leader until I return."

"Hala-Jyusa and her group don't know where you

are," Garth said, "or even that you're here. They are some one hundred and fifty kilometers northwest of you. So you should be safe until you're ready to contact them."

Perhaps by then the extremists would be ready to listen to this group, Kirk thought; or, maybe this was just another in the series of boxes with weak bottoms that would break and drop them all into the next set of problems.

He took out his communicator and flipped it open. "Kirk to *Enterprise,*" he said.

"Kyle here."

"Two Antosians, Empynes and Heje-Illuss, ready to be beamed to Pynesses. They're standing next to Garth. Set them down inside the First Minister's compound, and then we'll start beaming supplies down here."

"Aye, aye, sir."

Kirk stood on the hillside, looking down at the beach. McCoy and Uhura were walking toward the hill and being pointedly ignored by the Antosians they passed. In the wooded land bordering the sandy beach, under the trees, Hala-Jyusa's rebels had pitched the tents that would shelter them while they constructed more permanent dwellings with the tools beamed down to them from the *Enterprise.* They were still unloading the crates of food that would sustain them until they could grow and gather their own. There was enough food to last them for almost two of their years, which were nearly the same length as Earth's, and by then a Federation starship would have returned to Antos IV to see how well they were getting along.

Two of the large gray and white birds flew past Kirk. Earlier, he had seen others swooping down over the ocean and carrying off fish in their bills. The birds circled McCoy and Uhura as the two officers climbed toward Kirk, then flew on. Three days had passed, and whatever the rebels were thinking, they were going about the daily tasks of life, organizing their temporary dwellings and exploring their immediate surroundings. It was the same among the group of Antosians with Trialla. By the time the *Enterprise* left this system, the smaller group of rebels should have established some sort of peaceful contact with Hala-Jyusa's group, but if not, Kirk and Garth would have no choice but to beam them back to Pynesses. They could not leave Heje-Illuss's followers here, open to possible attack from those who had once been their comrades.

Hala-Jyusa's rebels would then be completely isolated. It was small comfort to know that a few communicators would be left with them. Their channels would be limited, and they would not be able to send messages to anyone except Empynes or a few of his closest advisers, but they would not be completely cut off, with no way to speak to the outside world. Kirk was sure that his crew had accounted for every necessity in the arrangements for the rebels, but he still worried about the wisdom of leaving them here on Acra.

"I didn't see you beam down, Jim," McCoy said as he approached. "How long have you been here?"

"Just a few minutes," Kirk said. "How is it going down there?"

"We showed them how to open the crates," Uhura said, "and I demonstrated how a communicator works, and after that it was obvious that they wanted to be left alone."

"Maybe that's just as well," McCoy said. "I'm not too anxious to be all that close to Hala-Jyusa, even if she isn't carrying a sword." He paused. "They're completely demoralized, to tell the truth."

"Garth spoke to me just before I beamed down," Kirk said. "He's still with the smaller group of rebels, and he says that they're just about settled. They'll be ready to have a delegation from their group beamed here in the next day or so to talk to Hala-Jyusa's group."

"I don't think the folks down there want to talk to anybody." McCoy sighed. "I hate to say it, Jim, but maybe Garth has interfered with the Antosians too much, even if he's not technically in violation of the Prime Directive. Maybe the best thing we can do is to leave them alone to work things out in their own way."

"That will happen, Doctor," Uhura said, "when we leave here."

"Yes," Kirk muttered, "but we can at least give them a realistic chance of working things out before we go."

On the hill above them, a pillar of air glittered and hummed, and then resolved itself into the form of Garth. "I thought you'd decided to keep away from here for a while," Kirk called out to him.

Garth descended the slope, carrying his long black coat over one arm. "I changed my mind," he said. "I've been thinking that it might be better for me to speak to Hala-Jyusa and her group before anyone else does. I am, after all, responsible."

"You're not responsible," McCoy objected. "You had no control over—"

"I have to do what I can."

"Seems to be you've done a fair amount already," McCoy said, in a tone that suggested that perhaps Garth had done too much.

Garth spread out his coat on the ground, then sat down next to a berry bush. "If I can get Hala-Jyusa to listen to me, then the rest of her followers will probably be willing to hear me out. Their exile can be a punishment, or it can become a time for healing and reflection, a time for them to—"

Kirk's communicator signaled to him; he flipped it open. "Kirk here."

"Spock here," his first officer replied. *"Captain, I have just received a communication from Wenallai, the bondpartner of First Minister Empynes. Her message came only a few moments after our sensors revealed that some two thousand Antosians are leaving the city of Pynesses and traveling east. Wenallai could tell me nothing about that, except that it seems*

to be some kind of protest, but she informed me that a group of some one hundred other Antosians have requested a meeting with the First Minister, and asked that he come alone."

"A meeting?" Kirk asked. McCoy raised his brows; Uhura frowned. "What about?"

"*Wenallai could not tell me that,*" Spock said, "*but she is very worried about her bondpartner's safety. When he first announced a day ago that all of the rebellious Antosians who threatened the peace of their world were to be exiled on Acra, it seemed that most of the people in Pynesses were in sympathy with the First Minister's decision. But since then Wenallai has heard rumors that many are angry about that decision, and that the relatives and friends of the exiles are especially enraged. It is some of those relatives who want to meet with the First Minister. At any rate, Empynes agreed to the meeting and is on his way there now. Wenallai said that he was to go to a northern suburb of the city to meet with them at an abandoned ellei pen.*"

Kirk did not like the sound of that. "Spock, get the coordinates of that meeting place and tell Mr. Scott to track Empynes."

"*We have already done so, Captain, and are tracking Empynes now. He went first to his bondpartner's stable to get a mount and is now riding toward the meeting place.*"

"Stand by, Spock. Kirk out."

"I'm worried," Garth said.

Kirk said, "So am I."

"Wenallai isn't the kind of person to panic easily," Garth continued. "If she's concerned about the safety of Empynes, we should be, too."

Kirk nodded. "I don't think he should be going to that meeting alone."

"Neither do I, Captain Kirk. I suggest that we beam to a spot near the meeting place and approach unseen."

"I was about to suggest the same thing," Kirk said.

"But we can't go there as ourselves." Garth stood up, then picked up his coat. "It will be nighttime in Pynesses now, so Antosian clothing should be enough of a disguise for you." He handed Kirk the coat. "Put this on—it'll hide your uniform. I'll morph if I have to."

"Can you hold another form long enough?" Kirk asked. "We don't know how long this meeting will take, and if we have to get him out of there—"

"I'll maintain my disguise, if it means preserving his life." Garth's eyes narrowed. "You'll see how much authority resides in Empynes, in anyone whom other Antosians regard as a leader. If anything happens to him, his advisers will be at a loss for some time, with no Chief Adviser to replace him right away and no other obvious successor. And while they're deciding how to handle that, along with having to face a situation without precedent in their history, we'll lose the best chance we have of restoring peace."

A series of weak-bottomed boxes, Kirk thought again. How many would there be?

He took out his communicator. "Kirk to *Enterprise*."

"Spock here."

"Patch me through to Scotty."

"Scott here," the engineer's voice said. *"Captain, someone else left the First Minister's compound right after he did, and now seems to be following his route."*

"Wenallai?" Kirk asked.

"No, Captain. She's still inside the compound with her son. I verified that just a moment ago. It's someone else, also mounted on one of those beasts—got one from the same stable Empynes went to and then rode after him."

Kirk gritted his teeth. "Scotty, beam Garth and me aboard and set us down near that meeting place."

"Aye, Captain. Scott out."

"Bones, you and Uhura stay here for now," Kirk ordered.

McCoy nodded. "Good luck, Jim."

Kirk took a deep breath and knew that he was standing directly on the weak bottom of the next box. The ghostly beam took the bright greenery of the hill from his eyes and restored him to his ship.

Kirk and Garth found themselves on a dirt road that led away from the northern edge of the city. They had beamed down near a rambling structure that seemed to be abandoned. On the distant western shore of Greblendon Lake, he saw the lights of houses and other buildings, but there were no structures near them, only flat grassy land and small flickering lights to the northeast.

Torches, Kirk thought as he gazed at the lights. That had to be the corral where Empynes had gone. He turned toward Garth, who was in the plain knee-length tunic and leggings of an Antosian laborer; he had made himself shorter and broader in the shoulders. Even in the darkness Kirk could make out the slightly larger head, thick mustache, and heavy eyebrows Garth had given himself.

They hurried toward the corral. Wheeled vehicles stood along the side of the road up ahead. Several elleis were tied to the wooden fence that surrounded the pen, near the crumbling wall of a building that might once have been a stable. Kirk crouched down and slipped into the shadows of the wall, followed by Garth. Smoky torches marked the perimeter of the rectangular enclosure. At least a hundred people were inside the corral, and Kirk could hear the anger in their voices.

Empynes stood at the center of the crowd, but he was not speaking. He lifted his hands, palms out, as if trying to ward off the other Antosians.

"You betrayed them!" one man shouted.

"You say that my son will be safe on Acra," a female voice cut in, "but how do I know that? Only a few ships have voyaged to the Tiresian Islands in my time—how can I be sure my boy is all right?"

"They are safe," Empynes said, in a surprisingly strong tone, "and they will live when they might have died—when many more of us might have died killing our brothers and sisters."

"Liar!" a woman called out. "We would have reached an accord with them."

"Criminal! You tricked us!" another man cried. "You plotted with that one there to trick the dissidents, and now you're lying to us about everything else!" Kirk was able to make out the man in the hazy yellow light of the torches; he was pointing at a dark shape that lay at Empynes's feet. "What was he, your spy?"

Empynes looked toward the speaker, his face pale and drawn. "Heje-Illuss was no spy," the First Minister said sadly. "He was an honest rebel who finally came to see how much violence and death civil war would bring to our world. He came to Pynesses at my request to meet with my advisers before returning to Acra to see what he could do to help the exiles who were once his comrades. He—"

"You were supposed to come here alone!" someone shouted from the far end of the corral.

"I came here alone," Empynes responded. "I didn't know Heje-Illuss had decided to follow me here. I believe he did so because he thought you might listen to him, that you might believe what he had to say. Maybe he also thought that I might need protection. I can't tell you what his intentions were, but I know that they had to be honorable. He was a good man who was led astray for only a little while, and a fine healer, and he was your brother, and you've killed him."

"We're too late," Garth whispered to Kirk.

Kirk pulled out his communicator and held it close to his lips. "Kirk to *Enterprise,*" he said very softly, "and keep your voice low."

"Scott here."

"Get a fix on Empynes. He's about six meters in front of me. There's a body at his feet—Heje-Illuss. Empynes says he's dead. We may have to—"

"Damned liar!" someone was shouting. "You'll imprison my child and then rob me of my heritage! You'll rob all of us of what we are! We should never have listened to you!"

Empynes suddenly cried out. Kirk looked up in time to see a spear strike the First Minister in the chest. Empynes staggered and fell backward.

"Scotty," Kirk said, "pick up Empynes and Heje-Illuss now." Heje-Illuss, he thought, might still be clinging to life. "Get them to sickbay and then beam Bones up there right away."

"Aye, Captain."

Garth was suddenly up and running toward the corral before Kirk could close his communicator. He was about to follow, then thought better of it. Garth climbed the fence, swung himself over it, and landed on his feet just inside the corral, then pushed his way through the crowd, still in the shape of a broad-shouldered Antosian laborer, until he came to the side of Empynes.

At once the fallen forms of Empynes and Heje-Illuss glittered and disappeared to the hum of the transporter. The Antosians who had been nearest them retreated a few paces.

"What have you done?" Garth cried, giving the words an Antosian accent.

"Who are you?" someone in the crowd yelled. "Another spy?"

Garth threw up his hands. "I carry no arms!"

Kirk's hand was inside his boot; he pulled out his hand phaser. Garth was reverting now, whether out of fear or inability to hold his shape, Kirk did not know. He flowed into his own shape and stood there in his captain's uniform, his arms up and his hands open.

"You all know me!" Garth continued. "I did not choose to become an Antosian, but your people healed me, you gave me back my life! I must use that life to remedy the damage I did to your culture, to avert the threat to your peaceful ways! I was not born of Antos, but this world is now as much my own as any planet! I accept being an Antosian, and sharing in whatever comes to pass among you now!"

Garth wanted them to see who he was, Kirk realized; he had reverted to his own form with a purpose. A few people shrank back, covering their faces. Kirk crept forward, keeping well away from the tied-up elleis at his left until he was near the fence, then stood up to peer over it. The expressions on the faces of many showed him that the crowd had not expected Garth, had not anticipated his words, and for a moment the Antosians and their stepbrother regarded one another silently in the dimming light of the torches.

Kirk gripped his phaser, set it on stun, then raised

his arm, aiming at the people nearest to Garth and alert for any sudden movements by others.

He waited, slowly realizing that Garth would not want him to use his weapon, because Garth was determined that matters would resolve themselves in a certain way or not at all . . . and that he would prefer to perish if he failed in his mission.

If Garth could not be a savior, he would become a martyr.

Kirk held his arm steady, prepared to shoot, even though he knew that once he used the phaser, nothing would go as Garth wished. His life might be saved, but it was likely that his soul, and the future of Antos IV, would be lost.

He waited, determined not to fire until he had no choice.

Garth stood his ground.

Kirk's muscles began to ache with tension. If the Antosians moved against him, if they tried to kill him, he would know that no offworlder influence would ever be trusted, that the Antosians would accept no help from outsiders, and that the planet would have to be left to its own history. There would either be a victor in the coming civil war, or a general debilitation, and a different culture would emerge, one that might one day threaten its neighbors and the Federation. But if the rebels stayed their hands now, it would be a sign of hope.

A woman in a long white tunic came toward Garth. Kirk set his phaser on her, then saw that she had no weapon in her hands.

"Offworlder," she said, "you call yourself an Antosian. Perhaps you see yourself as more than that. Perhaps you see yourself as our next First Minister. Perhaps that is why you infected the rebels with your dreams of power and the reason you returned here."

"I want no power on Antos IV," Garth said. "I only wanted to restore you to what you were before I came among you. That is all the Federation and Starfleet, whose uniform I wear, want from you. Our Prime Directive forbids us from interfering with the natural development of a civilization, and yet I unknowingly interfered with yours. All we want now is for your people to have back the peace and social order that were your culture's great accomplishments."

"By depriving us of our genetic heritage," the woman said. "That is how you would preserve our peace."

"That was not my solution, but that of Empynes," Garth answered. "He believed that the way to restore your culture was to remove the strong temptation to use your shape-changing powers for warfare and conquest." Kirk noticed that Garth was speaking of Empynes as though the Antosian leader were dead. "He thought that once you had changed yourselves, and given up that temptation, you would be more able to preserve what was best in yourselves. He argued that the alternative was dissention, civil war, perhaps a wider war, and that the Federation, forbidden to interfere, would have had no choice but to isolate this planet. In the long run, that isolation would damage your culture far more than any genetic and somatic alterations." Garth sighed. "Empynes came up with this solution, not I, but I saw that it might be the only answer, and the only way to open your culture to more contact with other civilizations, who will enrich your own and to whom you have much to offer. And most of you Antosians went along with your First Minister—it was only a few who threatened disorder."

"I thought the dissidents were wrong to rebel," the Antosian woman said. "I condemned them for breaking away and carrying weapons and saying that they would rather fight than give in to Empynes's solution." Some of the people near her were muttering among themselves, nodding their heads, and making other signs of assent. "And now I wonder if they might have been right to reject what the First Minister wanted for us." She held out her hands. "Why do we have to give up a part of ourselves? Isn't there any other way for us to reclaim our peaceful culture?"

"If there is," Garth replied, "Antosians must find it. I can do no more for you."

A silence fell over the crowd. Garth bowed his head. From behind the fence, Kirk gripped his phaser.

A bearded man came forward. "Leave us, off-worlder," the man shouted. "We do not want your blood, your counsel, or your advanced technology. We want nothing from you. Leave us and go to whatever hell you and Empynes have found for yourselves, and be damned. Leave us to find our own way." Kirk sensed both grief and a terrible despairing rage in the man's words.

The crowd began to break up into smaller groups. Knots of people moved in Kirk's direction. He retreated into the shadows as one man hurried to that side of the fence to open the gate, then reached for his communicator, ready to give the command to beam Garth and himself out of danger. Perhaps the people did not see him in the darkness, or maybe they thought him another Antosian. They passed with barely a glance in his direction and continued toward their vehicles. Others went to their elleis, untied them, and slowly rode away into the night. Garth watched them go, not moving, arms hanging stiffly at his sides.

When all of the Antosians were gone, Kirk hurried through the gate to Garth. "We've got to get out of here," Kirk said. "Some of them might come back. We're not safe here."

Garth stared at him in silence.

"Kirk to *Enterprise,*" he whispered into his communicator. "Get us both out of here, Scotty."

It seemed to be forever that he waited there with Garth in the middle of the empty corral.

Chapter Nine

THE TRANSPORTER BEAM sang to Kirk, and he breathed a sigh of relief. At his right, Garth stood in the transporter, looking at him wearily.

"You should have left me," Garth said.

"You might have died."

"That might have helped to end the conflict."

Kirk said, "No, it wouldn't have, and you know that as well as I do."

Lieutenant Kyle and Ensign Grinzo were watching them from behind the transporter console. The lieutenant seemed about to come around the console toward them, but as Kirk caught his eye, Kyle looked away. Kirk turned to Garth, saw the resignation in his face, and knew that the other man finally understood that his elaborate plan to help the Antosians was coming apart.

"How clever I was." Garth spoke with great bitterness. "What a master of tactics and improvisation. I wanted to help, and I only made things worse."

Kirk stepped off the transporter; after a moment, Garth followed him to the doorway. Kyle and Grinzo stood at attention as the door opened.

"So what now?" Kirk asked as they stepped into the corridor. "What do you think is going to happen down there?"

"The conflict will widen," Garth said as they walked down the hallway. "Friends and relatives of the exiled rebels will take up their cause. A leader will rise among them and they'll follow him, because the Antosians are adapted to that kind of central authority, and there may be no First Minister to oppose the new dissidents. They will fight, and win over others to their cause, or else they'll be defeated in a bloody battle, and there will probably be several such cycles of violence and even more factions led by charismatics rising up before it's over."

Garth halted and leaned against the wall. Kirk stood with him, waiting.

"They lack our advanced weapons systems," Garth continued, "but I fear that may only make the conflict even more protracted and violent. They'll be fighting with spears and knives and primitive explosives and simple projectile weapons and anything else they can use while riding into battle on elleis or in wheeled vehicles. They'll be doing most of their fighting hand-to-hand, and that will make their battles much more personal and the hatreds growing out of them more enduring. The cycles of violence will be costly, with accounts kept of the smallest wrong. My foremost aim on Antos IV was to stop a war. It got infinitely more complicated." He shook his head. "As if we could control and shape what goes on in a humanoid heart. Failing that, we justify lesser evils as the price of avoiding greater ones."

"Sometimes the price is worth paying," Kirk said.

"Sometimes."

Heje-Illuss was dead. McCoy informed Kirk and Garth of that while giving the two captains a quick med-scan in sickbay. The unfortunate Heje-Illuss had been dead even before being beamed aboard, probably only a few moments after he had been struck by the thrown spear and then stabbed repeatedly by knives.

Empynes was alive, but barely clinging to life. Kirk stood at the bedside of the unconscious Antosian, noting how pale and bloodless Empynes's face looked and how shallow his breathing was.

"I think we should bring his bondpartner aboard," McCoy said softly. "Antosian physiology is very similar to ours, but there are a few small differences. Wenallai's a healer. She might be able to help him. At least she'll have a chance to say her farewells." The doctor had an angry look in his eyes, as he so often did when speaking of death. "We should beam their son up with her."

"Yes," Garth said in a flat voice. "They may not be safe down there, with perhaps even more people turning against Empynes now."

McCoy looked sharply at Garth, then at Kirk. "Beam Wenallai and her son aboard," Kirk commanded, "as long as they're willing to come here. I'm going to the bridge." He waited for a moment, expecting that Garth would decide to come with him, but the other captain sank into a chair and sat there, shoulders slumped, his face sagging with defeat. Kirk left him there to keep his vigil at the side of the rapidly failing Empynes.

Kirk sat at his command station on the bridge, listening as Ensign Chekov reported to him from Acra. The ensign, along with Yeoman Wodehouse, was still with Heje-Illuss's band, who had just received the last of the supplies beamed down to them from the *Enterprise.*

"I told Trialla about the passing of Heje-Illuss," Chekov's voice was saying over the speakers, *"just after your last message, Captain. It was a blow to her. Hearing that Empynes is close to death was another blow. She tells me that she is not used to one Antosian striking down another in cold blood. She is saying that she must have been mad to think of fighting against others herself, that no cause is worth killing others of her people."*

"Is there anything more you and Yeoman Wodehouse have to do there?" Kirk asked.

"No, sir. These Antosians are more settled here now, and Trialla says that we have explained everything to them."

"Then prepare to beam aboard," Kirk said.

"Aye, aye, Captain. Chekov out."

Kirk sat at his station, thinking of the irony of the situation Trialla and her band now faced. They had chosen to stay on the island, instead of returning to their homes, in the hope of eventually persuading their fellow exiles to repudiate their rebellion and rejoin the rest of Antosian society. Now it was likely that Trialla and the rest of Heje-Illuss's followers were much safer on Acra than they would be in Pynesses; of course the same was true for Hala-Jyusa and her group.

He thumbed the intercom on the arm of his chair again. *"Enterprise* to Uhura."

"Uhura here."

"Anything new to report?" Kirk asked.

"No, sir," she said. *"It's another beautiful morning at the beach, and the Antosians below are still pointedly pretending that I'm not here even when I'm not keeping out of their sight. I'm getting a little lonely, being so ignored."* She paused. *"Excuse me, Captain. I do see something a little different."*

"What is it, Lieutenant?"

"Several people have gathered along the beach, near the edge of the water, and others are joining them." Uhura was silent for a few moments. *"Now they're just standing there, looking west. They're not moving at all. It's as if they're watching or listening*

for something, but there's nothing out there except the ocean and a few of those large shore birds."

Kirk frowned. "I was about to beam Chekov and Wodehouse aboard, but I'm going to station them there to keep watch with you instead. Beam out of there the second you feel you might be in any danger."

"Aye, sir. Uhura out."

Garth had still not come to the bridge. He was probably still in sickbay, brooding over the failure of his mission, perhaps feeling that he had once again been brought as low as he had been when he was confined on Elba II. But whatever the man's mistakes, Garth had made a noble effort. Whatever the flaws in his elaborate plan, Kirk was convinced that the situation on Antos IV would have been even worse in the long run if Garth had not tried to intervene.

"Captain," Spock suddenly said from his station aft, "our sensors indicate that more Antosians are now leaving Pynesses and traveling east. They seem to be following the same route taken by those who left the city earlier."

Kirk stood up and turned toward Spock. "How many are leaving?" he asked.

"Thousands," Spock said, looking up from his computer. "They have been moving northeast, as the earlier convoy did. It seems most likely that when they get to the river that flows east from Greblendon Lake, they will turn east, as their predecessors did, given that the river is too wide for them to cross without boats or other watercraft, and there are no bridges spanning that waterway."

"I want an image on the forward viewscreen," Kirk said to the ship's computer. "Show us what's happening around Pynesses, and then show us where the first group that left the city is right now."

"Yes, sir," the computer replied.

An image appeared, showing a mass of tiny shapes streaming from the northeastern outskirts of Pynesses. The image changed to reveal a long line of specks moving east along the southern side of the long river. Kirk estimated that the first group of Antosians would reach the eastern shore of the continent in less than a day, and that those in the second group would get there a day after that.

But why were they going east, when almost the entire eastern shore of the continent of Anatossia was sheer high rocky cliffs, with no access to the ocean except by ship through the deep channel cut by the river? What did they expect to do once they reached the cliffs?

"Mr. Spock," Kirk said, standing up, "maybe it's time we took a closer look at this mass migration. Stand by for my orders—I'm heading to sickbay."

McCoy shook his head at Kirk as he entered sickbay, indicating that Empynes was no better. Garth still sat in a chair not far from the biobed that held Empynes; a small dark-haired boy was sitting next to him. Wenallai was leaning over Empynes, her hands cradling his head. Too many seconds were passing between the rhythmic thrumming sound of Empynes's life sign readings. Kirk looked at the readings on the diagnostic panel above the bed and saw that they were almost flat.

He went to Garth. The boy next to him stood up. "I am Benaron," the child said.

"Then you must be the son of Empynes and Wenallai," Kirk said, seeing that the boy had his father's contemplative expression.

"Yes."

"I'm Captain Kirk."

Benaron's eyes glistened, as if he might cry. He bent his head toward Kirk, then went to his mother.

"Captain Garth," Kirk said, hoping to draw the other man out of his brooding, "our sensor readings now show that even more people are leaving Pynesses and heading east. Do you have any ideas about why they might be going there?"

Garth lifted his head and focused on Kirk; at least he was listening. "No, I don't."

Wenallai glanced toward them. "More are leaving the city?" she asked.

Kirk nodded. "They're traveling east, along the river that runs from Greblendon Lake to the sea." He went to her side; after a moment, Garth got up and followed him. Kirk gazed down at Empynes. "I am sorry that we didn't get to him in time."

"Heje-Illuss and I might have been able to save him together," Wenallai murmured. "I am trying to help him heal, trying to enable him to heal himself, but I sense resistance in him, almost as if he does not want to live after having other Antosians seek his death."

Kirk recalled that Garth had mentioned experiencing a technique similar to a Vulcan mind-meld when the Antosians were healing him. "You're using telepathy to help him?" Kirk asked.

"No, Captain Kirk, I would not call it telepathy. What I sense is much too tenuous for that. It is more like a natural sympathy or empathy with a fellow Antosian that we can sometimes feel." Wenallai cupped the pale, waxy face of Empynes in her hands. "I am losing him. And now his people are leaving Pynesses."

"Only some of them," Kirk said.

"I don't understand why any of them are leaving the city to go east," Wenallai said. "There's nothing there except cliffs and the ocean and far to the east, so far away that they cannot be seen from shore, the Tiresian Islands." Her green eyes widened slightly. "It is a protest, then. I guessed it might be. They must be going there to gaze in the direction of Acra, to demonstrate that they will not forget those exiled there. And perhaps more will join them, and then they may be moved to take up the cause of the exiles together. That's all it can mean. And perhaps they are not so wrong in wanting to retain our bodily heritage. Only shaping can help my bondpartner now, and even that art may not be enough to save his life."

Kirk stood with her for a moment, wishing there

were something he could say to console her. "I am sorry, Wenallai," Garth said next to him. "I brought him to this."

"You wanted to help us, Garth," Wenallai said. "You must not blame yourself for what happened to Empynes." She paused. "Death is only another shape-changing. That is what we have always believed. It is only another transformation. The dead are everywhere on our world, in the form of our trees and our rocks and our soil, still changing."

"Father," Benaron said. Wenallai slipped an arm around her son's shoulders.

Kirk crossed the room to where McCoy was studying a medical report on a small screen. "What are his chances?" Kirk whispered.

McCoy gestured at the readings on the screen, and Kirk saw the answer in the physician's scowl. He led Kirk toward his office; the door slid shut behind them.

"Jim," McCoy said as he sat down behind his desk, "there may be nothing more you can do for the Antosians now. Maybe we just have to isolate their planet for a while until the fever burns itself out. You and Garth tried, but maybe it's time to leave it alone."

Kirk sighed. "I don't know how well Garth would take the failure of this mission. At the very least, it would bring an end to any hope of reestablishing himself as a Starfleet officer, or possibly even of getting an honorable discharge. About the only hope he'd have of getting out of Starfleet without being disgraced is to prove that he was mentally impaired during this mission, that he had suffered a relapse."

McCoy shook his head. "And then I'd have to testify that he was mentally sound, and that my examinations showed no sign of any impairment."

"And if José Mendez needs to spread some of the blame around for Garth's failure," Kirk said, "I would also be on shaky ground. After all, I was assigned to be his watchdog. Not that I'd worry about that, as long as we could restore some kind of order to Antos IV."

He had trusted Garth, had gone along with him, had done his best to aid his plan. Maybe he would have to give up and admit failure, but this was not the time, not yet. His neck was out far enough as it was; he would see this mission through to the end. He could take a few more risks in the hope of aiding both the Antosians and the hero of his own youth.

Kirk pressed his hand against the communicator panel on McCoy's desk. "Kirk to Spock," he said.

"Spock here."

"Spock, you and Mr. Sulu are to go to the shuttlebay and take one of the shuttlecraft to the surface. I want you to take a closer look at those Antosians moving east. Don't get too close to them, and don't provoke them, just observe them and report back to me. I want them to know that we're still keeping an eye on them—that might prevent them from doing anything rash."

"Yes, Captain. We are on our way to the shuttlebay now. Spock out."

"Bones, I'm heading back to the bridge," Kirk said.

He left the office in time to see Benaron climb onto his father's bed and press his small form against the dying Empynes. As he watched, Benaron quickly flowed into the shape of a small furred creature and then curled up against his father's side, paws out, head down, as if the warmth of his furry body might somehow restore Empynes to life.

The forward viewports of the shuttlecraft *Galileo* opened as the vehicle entered the Antosian atmosphere. The shuttlecraft dived through wispy clouds toward the blue ribbon of the river, and Spock saw the line of tiny dots that was the procession of Antosians traveling east.

Lieutenant Sulu brought the shuttlecraft lower, then swooped toward the Antosians. Spock could see them clearly now. Several people on elleis, and others in open carts or covered wagons being pulled by pairs of elleis, led the procession. Others had stopped by the river, to water their elleis and get water for themselves. Still other Antosians, traveling in wheeled vehicles, had come to a halt and were opening solar panels on the roofs of their vehicles to recharge their solar fuel cells in the morning sunshine. But most were still on the move, pushing east over the flat green grassy plain that stretched before them.

Sulu flew east, made a long sweeping turn, then flew west, keeping several kilometers above the Antosians. A few people looked up at them, but most of the Antosians were ignoring the shuttlecraft. They were people of all ages, with many children among them, which indicated to Spock that they did not intend to return to Pynesses any time soon; otherwise, they would have left the elderly and their young in the city.

"Mr. Sulu," Spock said, "turn east again and follow them, but at a slower speed."

"Yes, sir." Sulu peered at his instruments, then lifted his gaze to the center viewport. "They don't seem too worried about us."

"No, they do not," Spock said. They stood in orderly rows along the riverbank, waiting, looking to the east. Sulu circled them until they mounted their elleis or climbed back into their vehicles and were on the move once more.

Spock opened a channel to the *Enterprise.*

"Kirk here. See anything interesting down there?"

"The Antosians who left the city are still traveling east," Spock said. "They are people of all ages, including children and the old, and they do not seem to be armed—in any case, I have seen no weapons. Some of them stopped to rest and get water for themselves and their animals, and then they moved on. I have also noticed that there appears to be little interaction among them."

"What do you mean?"

"They do not gather to converse with one another or to share a meal. Instead, they seem intent on their purpose, whatever that may be, almost as if they are in a kind of trance."

"As if something outside themselves is holding them all together," Sulu added. "Could something else be controlling them?"

"I don't know, but . . ." Captain Kirk fell silent for a few seconds. *"Welcome back to the bridge, Captain Garth."*

"I just overheard your exchange with Commander Spock and Lieutenant Sulu," said the voice of Garth. *"I don't think those Antosians are either in a trance or being controlled."*

"Then what do you suspect?" Spock asked.

"They know that relatives and friends are now exiled on Acra," Garth replied, *"and that knowledge is impelling them to go east as a protest. It has created a bond of sympathy among them. As Wenallai explained to Captain Kirk before, her people aren't telepathic, but they do share a kind of deep empathy at times. That may be why those Antosians seem to be entranced—they are, in their own way, a very suggestible race. Otherwise, those who became rebels wouldn't have been quite so susceptible to my mad ideas."*

"In other words," Spock said, "their minds and their thoughts can, under certain conditions, change shape as easily as their physical selves do when they are changing shape."

"That's one way to put it," Garth said, *"even if the reality is somewhat more subtle and complex. It's why Empynes believed that the only way to put a stop to the rebellion and prevent widespread bloodshed*

was to isolate the dissidents at Acra, and also why Gyneeses felt that he could control the rebels for his own purposes once they were exiled. It means that a more forceful mind, or a more powerful will, can impose itself on other Antosians by drawing on that natural empathy."

Sulu had flown their shuttlecraft ahead of the procession. Spock considered what Garth had told him, then said, "I think that Mr. Sulu and I should remain here and observe these people a while longer. I propose that we continue on to the cliffs, land a short distance from the Antosians, and then wait to see what they will do next."

"My prediction," Garth said, *"is that they'll stay there for a while and then either turn back to the city or go off on their own to start their own rebellion. There won't be much you can do in either case, Commander."*

"Stay there as long as you feel it's necessary," Kirk added, *"but don't interfere."*

"I intend only to observe," Spock said.

Garth approached the captain's station. Kirk looked up at his fellow captain, who had been followed to the bridge by McCoy.

Garth drew himself up. He seemed steadier now, ready to resume an officer's duties. Lieutenant Farley Longstreet had taken over at Sulu's helmsman's station, while Ensign Enrico Carulli was at the navigator's post usually occupied by Chekov.

"Perhaps you can take over Spock's bridge duties," Kirk said. He might have ordered Garth to do so, but he would observe the courtesy of treating the other captain as his equal as long as the man seemed up to the responsibility.

"Of course." Garth went to the science officer's station and sat down.

McCoy came toward Kirk and stood at his left. "There's nothing more I can do for Empynes," the physician murmured. "His life signs are just about flat. I left him in Ilsa Soong's care, but it's largely up to Wenallai now, and I don't know how much even she can do for him."

"I'm sorry, Bones."

"I'm damned sorry myself."

Kirk studied the latest sensor readings on the viewscreen. The second group of Antosians to leave Pynesses was gaining on the first group, and a third group was massing in the northeastern end of the city, as if preparing to follow the first two. He wondered how many more would join the protest, how many more might decide to carry on the fight that the exiles had begun.

Sulu had set the *Galileo* down near the edge of the cliffs. Spock stood with the lieutenant near the edge of one precipice. Ahead of them, to the east, stretched the vast calm expanse of the Antosian ocean, a blue-green sea with gentle swells. Nearly a kilometer below them, at the bottom of the high sheer scarp, waves lapped against a shoreline of black sand and flat black rocks.

Spock turned away from the view and looked northwest. On the horizon, he could just make out the tiny forms of riders on elleis. The Antosians in vehicles fanned out from the riders, moving southeast across the flat plain of grass.

"It looks," Sulu said, "as though they're getting ready to spread out in a long row along the edge of the cliffs."

"A reasonable assumption, Mr. Sulu," Spock said. "I suggest that we fly farther south, so as to keep our distance from them. We do not want them to feel threatened by our presence."

More Antosians appeared on the horizon, in carts and on elleis, moving steadily east as Spock and Sulu hurried toward the *Galileo*.

On the beach below, Hala-Jyusa was striding up and down in front of the massed Antosian rebels. Uhura watched from the hillside as the Antosian woman opened her arms, gestured at two of the large shore birds as they flew overhead, then turned to point to the late afternoon sun in the west. Hala-Jyusa was speaking to her comrades, but Uhura was too far away to hear what she was saying.

"I wonder what they're doing," Yeoman Wodehouse said next to her.

Chekov squatted at Uhura's left. "It looks as though she is making some sort of speech," he murmured.

Uhura reached for her communicator, wanting to be ready in case they had to beam out of there quickly. Another Antosian, a tall man with blond hair, went to Hala-Jyusa's side and lifted a hand; he seemed to be pleading with her. Hala-Jyusa shook her head at him; the man took a step back. Then the Antosians on the beach began to line up along the shoreline in three rows, still gazing to the west.

Suddenly the Antosians were changing, their bodies flowing. "They are morphing," Chekov said as he stood up.

Uhura quickly got to her feet.

The necks of the people below were lengthening. Their clothing vanished as feathers sprouted from their bodies. She heard a high-pitched, almost hysterical shriek coming from the morphing Antosians. The human figures were gone, and hundreds of tall, gray-feathered birds covered the white sand.

"Uhura to *Enterprise.*"

"Kirk here."

"Captain, the Antosians on the beach have taken on the form of large birds. They—"

Uhura broke off as the birds nearest the water line extended their wings and then lifted, flying out over the sea. Others flapped their wings and quickly took off after them.

"They're flying west, over the ocean," Uhura finished.

"They're trying to escape," Kirk's voice said.

More birds lifted out across the ocean. Far over the

water, a swarm of winged creatures was flying sunward. A chill passed through Uhura; the sight reminded her of a Dürer engraving depicting the escape of devils from hell. The western sky was filled with fliers emitting a piercing sound, like laughter. Below, on the beach, a few Antosians had taken on humanoid form once more. They looked up as the last of the large gray birds took off after the swarm.

"They can't make it, Captain Kirk," Garth said from the science officer's station aft. "They won't have enough strength to keep that shape long enough to reach the coast, much less to carry their own greater weight. They're too far away from the continent to make the flight."

Kirk realized that the escaping Antosians had also taken on the forms of birds much smaller than themselves. A morphing Antosian could not decrease his own mass, which would be too great to keep him aloft for long.

"What can we do?" McCoy asked.

"A shuttlecraft," Kirk said. "We might be able to turn them back." He pressed a panel next to the comm at his station. "Kirk to Spock."

"Spock here," the Vulcan replied. *"Captain, the Antosians are lining up about a third of a kilometer to the north of us. They are standing near the edge of the cliff, looking east across the ocean, as though they are expecting—"*

"Are they morphing?" Kirk asked, thinking that

some of those Antosians might also begin to change shape and transform themselves into birds.

"No, Captain."

"The Antosian exiles at the beach on Acra have morphed into birds," Kirk said, "and they're flying in your direction. You and Sulu are to take off immediately. Fly toward those birds as fast as you can and try to make them turn back." Kirk turned aft. "Captain Garth, come with me to the shuttlebay. We'll take the *Columbus* down and see if we can herd them back to Acra."

"Of course, Captain," Garth said as he headed toward the lift.

"And I'm coming with you," McCoy said as Kirk stood up. "Those fliers will be burning up every bit of energy they have. You might need a doctor there."

Uhura hurried down the hillside and thrashed her way through a thicket of shrubs, Chekov and Wodehouse at her heels. On the darkening beach, the few remaining Antosians milled around nervously before the breakers, still looking out across the sea toward their invisible homeland five hundred kilometers away. Over the ocean, the cloud of fliers grew smaller. A dark-skinned man suddenly morphed into a large bird and lofted, flying after the distant cloud.

"Stop!" Uhura cried. "Turn back!" The other Antosians backed away from her and then fled up the beach.

"Don't they know they can't make it?" Wodehouse asked. "Are they suicidal?"

"That is why some of them stayed behind," Chekov said.

The winged fliers were now a swarm of insects against the glow of the setting sun. Uhura searched the sky for some sign of the *Columbus,* even though she knew it was still too soon to see it. A suicide flight, she realized, meant despair among Hala-Jyusa and her followers, and the end of all hope. She wondered at the depths of their feelings, of the desolation they must have felt at the coming defeat of their cause, and at the threatened loss of part of their physical heritage. The dream of flight, Uhura thought, the wish to escape on wings, was about to end in a nightmare of death.

But somehow she could not accept that this was a mass suicide. Most of the fliers had to believe they would make it, despite the expenditure of energy required to keep their avian shapes, despite the added mass, regardless of the distance that had to be covered. Maybe they would make it, she told herself, silently cheering for them.

Sulu was at the controls. Spock gazed through the *Galileo*'s three forward viewports at the distant flock of fliers as the shuttlecraft flew over the wrinkled blue surface of the ocean. He still thought that the Antosians who were gathered along the cliffs far behind them had left Pynesses to protest the exile of their fellows, and were keeping a vigil along the eastern coast as a prelude to their own rebellion.

Now Spock hypothesized that somehow, perhaps unconsciously, the Antosians on the cliffs had sensed that the exiles were going to attempt an act of desperation.

Ahead of the shuttlecraft, the cloud of fliers began to resolve into individual figures. "Maybe they'll turn back," Sulu said, "now that they've seen us."

"Perhaps," Spock said. He saw the flying Antosians clearly now; a few of them were losing altitude. Others seemed to be weakening, dropping lower until they were only a few meters above the ocean surface. Still they continued their flight; he saw that they were not about to turn back.

Sulu banked to the left in order to avoid them, then circled the fliers in a wide arc. The sun was low in the west; a long golden band bisected the dark blue surface of the sea. Above, Spock noticed a small black object in the sky.

"Kirk to Spock," the captain's voice said from the comm.

"Spock here."

"I'm just above you, at the controls of the Columbus," Kirk said. *"Stay near them."*

"Aye, aye, sir," Sulu said.

"They are not turning back," Spock said, "and they are showing no signs that they will."

"Get in front of them," Kirk ordered. *"We'll try some bird herding."*

* * *

Kirk piloted the *Columbus* toward the cloud of flyers. The feathers of the Antosian birds were silver-gray in the light of the evening sun. He brought the shuttlecraft down directly behind them, then dropped below them. He saw now that several were flying perilously close to the surface of the water.

At his right, Garth said, "They're weakening."

The *Columbus* shot westward until it was under the flock. The shuttlecraft's sensors indicated that the *Galileo* was north of them, also flying under the Antosians. Kirk slowed his shuttlecraft until he was matching the speed of the birds.

There was a thud from overhead, as if something had struck the *Columbus.*

"One of them has landed on top of us," Garth said; he was studying the sensor readings on the console in front of him. "The instruments confirm that. They're tiring."

Kirk glanced at the sensor readings on his console as another thud sounded from above; a second flier had landed on their craft. Suddenly a body dropped past the viewport; he caught a glimpse of what looked like a human body with wide feathered wings for arms.

Icarus had fallen into the sea, he thought, and wondered how many others would follow.

Garth took a deep breath. "It's begun," he said. Kirk looked toward the other captain and saw the expression of pain and horror on Garth's face. "Some of them are already losing their strength. Only a few will make it to the mainland."

"Maybe none of them will," McCoy said behind them in an anguished voice. "Isn't there anything else we can do?"

Kirk looked up through the forward viewports at the dark shadow of the fliers, and realized that to turn the flock back would be difficult at best and would only tire the Antosians more quickly, unsuited as was their size to staying aloft long enough to cover either the long distance ahead, or even the distance back to the island of Acra. The point of no return might have already been passed, given the physical energy that was being expended with every moment spent in flight.

Kirk opened a channel on his comm. "Kirk to Spock."

"Spock here."

"The fliers are getting weaker," Kirk said. "At least two have landed on our craft, and one's fallen into the ocean. Any ideas?"

"It would appear to be hopeless, Captain, unless they turn back. But there is no sign that they intend to return to Acra." Spock paused. *"Two fliers have just fallen from the top of our shuttlecraft. We could slow down even more, and perhaps a few would be able to land on either the* Galileo *or the* Columbus *and hang on, but we would be unable to rescue more than a few that way—perhaps two dozen at most."*

If the Antosians could not make it to the mainland, Kirk thought, they seemed determined to die in the attempt. It was a suicidal gesture; only a few of them could still be deluding themselves that they would make it to the coast of Anatossia. There was a thud from above; another flier was desperately clinging to life.

The Antosians who had remained behind on Acra huddled together on the beach, keeping their distance from Uhura and her comrades. She slowly walked toward them, with Wodehouse at her right and Chekov at her left. They shrank away from her as she approached, and she thought that they might suddenly flee up the hill or into the tropical forest that bordered the beach, but they remained where they were, and then she saw the tears on their faces.

"We won't hurt you," Uhura called out. She held out her hands, to show that she was holding no weapons.

"They will not make it," a brown-haired woman said as Uhura and her shipmates halted near the group. "I was going to go with them, I wanted to go, I felt myself changing, but then I grew afraid."

"Something is wrong," a bearded man said. "I feel it, I sense it. I believe that some of our comrades are already lost."

"Hala-Jyusa told us that it was our only chance," a short, broad-shouldered man murmured. "She said that if we made ourselves into fliers, if we could cross the ocean and make it to the eastern cliffs of Anatossia, that our people would finally realize that we could not be defeated, that our cause was just.

She mocked those who thought that we could be bound by the limits of this island, that we would be content to live here passively with no resistance at all, without trying to reclaim our rightful destiny." As the man spoke, his dark eyes grew lighter until they were golden yellow; his gaze was that of a fanatic, or of Hala-Jyusa herself. Then he looked away and bowed his head. "They cannot reach Anatossia. I have come to understand it. The sea will claim them."

"Captain Kirk will do everything he can to save the others," Chekov said. But Uhura doubted there was anything anyone could do for them now.

Kirk heard the sound of another flier drop onto the roof of the *Columbus* and knew that there was something else he would have to try, as desperate a measure as it was.

"Kirk to Spock," he said into the comm.

"Spock here."

"Stand by, Mr. Spock. Kirk to *Enterprise.*"

"Scott here."

"We're still below the flock of shape-changers," Kirk said, "and we've lost a few already. Can you use the ship's transporters to pluck them out of the air?"

"It's risky, Captain. Trying to capture a moving object with a transporter beam risks severe damage to the subject. I could try to track several fliers, so as to keep the beam steady relative to their motion, but it

would be extremely chancy. I'd have to allow for the ship's motion, and we'd need all the transporter rooms even to—"

"Do it," Kirk said. "Save as many as you can."

"We will lose some of them, Captain," Spock's voice said.

"It's too risky," McCoy said from his seat aft.

"It's either that or their certain deaths," Kirk said.

"We'll not like some of what we rematerialize," Scott said ominously. Kirk glanced at Garth and knew that the other man was remembering his own transporter accident.

"We have no choice, Scotty," Kirk said. "How long?"

"Fifteen minutes to program the computers and get a crew on duty in every transporter room. You and the Galileo *will need to fly well ahead of the rest of the flock for a wee bit, until I can get a fix on them. I'll start picking them up from the rear, using your shuttlecraft as a primary coordinate fix."*

"Acknowledged. Kirk out." He increased speed and flew out from under the flock, feeling as though both he and the Antosian birds were chasing the setting sun. "Garth, how many have we lost?"

"The sensors say four. There are three hanging on top, and two on the *Galileo.*" Garth paused. "They're brave. Insanely brave. They have more strength than I thought possible, but they'll never make it to the shore."

* * *

Sulu stayed ahead of the flock, flying only slightly faster. "*Columbus* to *Galileo,*" Kirk's voice said over the comm.

"Sulu here."

"Mr. Scott has the data he needed. You can let the flock catch up with you now."

"Aye, aye, sir," Sulu said, and Spock soon saw from the sensor readings that the fliers in the lead had caught up with their shuttlecraft and were now above them.

"Remain at this altitude, Mr. Sulu," Spock said. "We are just enough of a distance below them for some of them to be able to land on top of our craft safely when they lose their strength."

"But there isn't room for more than a few of them," Sulu said.

"I am aware of that." Spock was silent for a moment. "Exactly how much are you able to slow down the speed of this craft while still keeping us aloft?"

"Almost to a hover, Mr. Spock."

"At such a speed, can we open our side exit and still fly safely?"

"Of course," Sulu replied.

"*Galileo* to *Columbus,*" Spock said into his comm. "Captain Kirk, Mr. Sulu is slowing our speed so that I can open our side exit. If we are moving slowly enough, it may be possible for more exhausted flyers to land safely on our craft and remain there. It may even be possible to—"

"I'm ahead of you," Kirk interrupted. *"We're*

slowing down, too, and we'll do what we can to get at least a few of the Antosians inside."

Spock quickly rose from his seat and moved aft toward the side exit.

McCoy was pressing the panel that would open the *Columbus*'s side exit when Garth got up from his station next to Kirk. Garth was holding himself together, doing what had to be done, but McCoy saw that it was costing the man every bit of psychological strength he possessed.

The side door slid open slowly. McCoy heard the air rushing past the opening. He looked east and saw transporter beams capture several of the large birds. "Scotty's doing it, Jim!" he called out. "I see fliers disappearing behind us."

A hand caught his arm. "Be careful, Doctor," Garth said.

McCoy took a step back from the opening. Gray feathered fliers were working furiously to stay in the air. Heads turned toward him and Garth, then stretched on long necks toward the setting sun once more; he glimpsed fear and panic in the black eyes of the birds. One bird glided closer to the shuttlecraft; fatigue showed in the slow flapping of its wide wings, and McCoy knew that this Antosian was suddenly desperate to reach the haven of the *Columbus.*

He motioned with his arms. "Over here!" McCoy shouted. At first, the Antosian seemed to drift closer, but then pulled away.

To the rear of the flock, other fliers disappeared, caught by the *Enterprise*'s transporter beams. Scotty was doing his job, but the interval between each capture of fliers was long, and over three hundred remained to be plucked from the air. He would do it safely or not at all, McCoy knew; Scotty was a careful engineer. He would save as many as he could, but even the chief engineer and all of the *Enterprise*'s technology could not save them all.

A thump sounded from above. Another flier had found safety, but perhaps only a temporary haven, on top of the *Columbus*.

The sun had set. Spock watched from the open side of the *Galileo* as shimmering transporter beams cut through the darkness.

"We've got six Antosians on top of our craft," Sulu called out from the pilot's station. They had, Spock knew, been there for some time now. Holding on tightly to one side of the exit with his hands, he leaned out of the opening into the wind as another beam caught a few of the birds.

"Come inside!" Spock shouted to the flock. But the Antosians flew on, clinging to their irrational pride, ignoring him. He saw two shadowy shapes fall toward the black waters of the sea.

At the controls of the *Columbus*, the sensor readings showed Kirk that there were seven Antosians on top of his craft. A small screen on his pilot's console gave him a view aft, capturing the gray-winged images of fliers. Scotty and the transporter crews still picked off the tired fliers behind them. As Kirk watched each blip disappear on his sensor readout, each gray form vanish from the small viewscreen, he felt a fleeting moment of relief. One more Antosian saved. One more who would not fall into the sea.

"Another one just dropped into the ocean," Garth called out from the shuttlecraft opening. "And the ones still flying refuse to enter our craft."

"Kirk to *Enterprise.*"

"Scott here."

"Can you save any of the ones in the water?"

"We just picked up two from the rear of the flock as they fell," Scotty replied, *"but to try for the ones in the ocean—"*

"Try, Scotty."

"We're trying, Captain, but they're hard to get a fix on, and we canna risk losing more of the ones who are still aloft."

Kirk watched the blips on his small screen disappearing slowly, and knew that time would run out, that the task of moving objects with transporter scanners and beams was laborious and fraught with danger. Again he thought of Garth's transporter accident.

"Scotty," Kirk said, "I'm almost afraid to ask, but how is it going?"

"It's going well, but it's slow work. We have only forty-six so far."

"Any damaged people?" Kirk asked.

"Not yet, Captain, but we canna pick them up at a faster rate, and then it's a statistical certainty that we'll have a damaged one sooner or later. Chaotic indeterminacies haven't yet kicked in."

The Antosians on the beach had made a fire for themselves, using deadwood brought down from the hillside and some dry driftwood farther up the beach. Uhura sat with Chekov and Wodehouse several paces away from the Antosians, finishing a meal of rations. The Antosians had gathered their wood listlessly and had been sitting by their fire ever since night had fallen, staring into the flames.

Uhura had spoken through her communicator to the other band of Antosians on Acra, telling Trialla that most of Hala-Jyusa's group had transformed themselves into birds to make their escape to the west. Trialla was so silent after hearing the news that Uhura had begun to wonder if the Antosian had accidentally closed the channel.

"They've flown away?" Trialla had said at last. *"But they won't make it to land."*

"I know," Uhura replied. "Captain Kirk is out there now, with our shuttlecraft, trying to rescue as many of them as he can. A few stayed behind, on the beach."

Trialla had sighed after that, and then signed off.

The Antosians around the fire had said nothing to one another since sitting down; not one of them had gone up to their tents to fetch food. Suddenly Uhura heard a strange sound from overhead, a long low note that reminded her of the honk of a goose.

A flock of large birds landed on the beach, only a few paces from the Antosians. Uhura jumped to her feet and watched their wings become arms and their feathers disappear.

Trialla stood there in the light of the fire, the other members of her band around her, having flown the short distance from their own encampment on Acra. They gazed at the other group for a few moments, then went to them. A few sat down by the fire; others embraced their fellow Antosians, as if trying to console them. Uhura thought of what Wodehouse had told her about the landing party's experiences. Trialla and her comrades had been captured and threatened by those whom they were now trying to comfort, yet they were reaching out to them. Maybe there was still some hope for the Antosians.

The birds flying alongside the *Galileo* emitted high-pitched cries and shrieks. Observing the fliers closest to the shuttlecraft, Spock saw that they were tiring. They had lost altitude; if they dropped any lower, the *Galileo* would have to skim along the top of the ocean to stay below them.

One bird swooped near the opening, fluttering one wing. Still hanging on to the side of the opening with his right hand, Spock grabbed the flyer by the wing with his left and pulled the Antosian into the shuttlecraft. The bird quickly flowed into the shape of a brown-skinned woman with blond hair. "Save them," she gasped. "Save the others."

"I am endeavoring to do just that," Spock said. Another bird flew near; Spock managed to pull that flier into the craft. The flier morphed into the form of young Kellin.

"Mr. Spock," the young Antosian gasped, "I . . . I . . ." The effort he had made showed in his drawn, agonized face. He lay on the floor, obviously unable to move, looking as though he had aged several years.

If Kellin, who had possessed the strength to hold Garth's form for days, was so drained of energy, Spock was certain that most of the other fliers would soon fail.

He extended his arm and pulled another flier into the craft.

McCoy and Garth stayed at the *Columbus*'s exit for most of the night, rescuing those who flew near enough for them to reach out and pull them inside. They took turns leaving the opening, in order to help those who could still walk to seats and to carry those who were still too exhausted to get themselves well away from the open exit. McCoy had managed to give each of the fifteen Antosians they had so far rescued a cursory scan with his medical tricorder, and had not liked what the readings showed: severe muscular strain, muscle atrophy, hearts damaged by the strain, dehydration, mineral levels so low that it was clear the fliers had used up all of their caloric reserves to stay aloft.

Fifteen, McCoy thought, and six on top of their shuttlecraft. Sulu had spoken to Kirk only a few minutes ago, saying that there were eleven Antosians inside the *Galileo* and five hanging on top. Even as the transporter beams searched through the sky to save a few more fliers, others were falling into the sea.

McCoy clung to the side of the opening, then beckoned to another flier. The salty sea air rushing past his face felt a bit warmer. His eyes felt gritty from lack of sleep; he squinted against the wind and caught the soft glow of light in the east. Dawn was coming, he realized, and then watched helplessly as yet another flier fell, spiraling into the sea.

A bird suddenly fell toward him, keening a high-pitched whine. McCoy reached for a wing and pulled the flier inside; it fell, slapping its wings against the floor, still keening. The bird's cry did not sound like one of agony to McCoy, but of despair. In another moment, the shape-changer lost control of the bird form. An Antosian woman with long black hair lay prone on the deck of the *Columbus*.

McCoy knelt at her side and gently eased her onto her back. The yellowish eyes of Hala-Jyusa stared sightlessly up at him; her eyes were red from broken blood vessels, and she was barely breathing. He reached for his medical tricorder.

Garth was watching from the opening, a look of horror on his face. "Beam her up!" He looked toward the forward end of the craft. "Beam her up!" he repeated. "Kirk, it's Hala-Jyusa, and she's dying. Beam her up to sickbay!"

Kirk shot Garth a quick look from his pilot's station, then turned back to the controls. "Kirk to *Enterprise.* Scotty, one to beam up—just inside the opening, next to McCoy. Get a fix on her and—"

"I canna do it, Captain." Scotty's voice sounded faint and far away, but McCoy was able to make out his words. *"Every transporter beam is occupied. I would have to break in on a precision program, and then there's no telling how many I might lose."*

"Try!" Garth cried out.

McCoy looked at his tricorder readings and knew then that they had lost the Antosian. "It's no use, Garth, even if we got her up to the ship. Her heart is burst beyond repair, with massive arterial and pulmonary damage." He reached down and closed her bulging, bloodshot eyes. "She flew her heart out."

Garth came toward them and seemed to shiver in the sea air coming in through the entrance. He looked down at the lifeless form of Hala-Jyusa, then covered his face with one hand and wept.

The *Galileo* and the *Columbus* crept ahead of the rapidly shrinking flock toward the coast of Anatossia. Kirk sat at his pilot's station, watching the sensor readout. The blips he saw there were of two kinds: the ones that vanished quickly, and those that plummeted into the sea, still visible but rapidly fading.

He glanced to his right as Garth sat down next to him. "We have twenty-two Antosians aboard," he said in a weary voice. "We could squeeze in some more, but the ones still flying aren't even trying to get inside."

Kirk studied another sensor reading. The six fliers who had found safety on top of the *Columbus* were still there, but had to be tiring. More fliers fell into the sea; the last of the blips disappeared from the screen of data readouts.

Kirk looked up; through the viewport, in the distance, he could now barely make out the high rocky wall of the Anatossian eastern coast.

"Kirk to *Enterprise.*"

"Scott here."

"How many did we pick up, Scotty?"

"Two hundred, Captain. There are no more coming in now, and it's drained our energy. We'll have to shut down for a bit."

"We've got more than twenty," Kirk said, "and the *Galileo* picked up about as many." He turned his head toward Garth. "Most of them, Garth. Do you hear? We managed to save most of them."

Garth nodded at him listlessly. "Yes, Captain, most of them."

"Bones," Kirk called out, "better get away from the exit. I'm going to close it now."

"Wait a minute, Jim!" McCoy shouted from the opening. "I see a school of large fish, about twenty of them, heading for the coast."

Up ahead, Kirk saw the tiny forms of Antosians at

the top of the coastal cliffs, thousands of them, gazing out at the sea. He brought the *Columbus* lower until the craft was almost skimming the surface of the water. On the screen, the readout now showed twenty-one blips below them, swimming westward.

McCoy saw the aquatic life-forms clearly now, swimming just below the surface. He had thought that they were large fish, but they bore a closer resemblance to porpoises or dolphins, and McCoy knew them for what they actually were: Antosian shape-changers who had fallen into the sea.

"Some of our brothers and sisters," a voice said near him. McCoy turned and noticed that a tall man was standing near him, looking down at the swimmers. "More of us will live."

But only a few more, McCoy thought. Most of those who had struck the water would have been far too weak to make this last transformation. Even as he watched, one swimmer morphed into a pale-haired woman and disappeared beneath the waves.

"Sit down," McCoy said to the Antosian next to him. "You're still recovering." The man made his way back to a seat. North of the *Columbus,* the *Galileo* was also flying close to the sea, following the swimmers.

"If they can't make it as birds," Garth said from his forward station, "then they will succeed as fish." His voice had regained its former resonance; McCoy heard him over the sound of the rushing wind.

They flew on after the fish. As the *Columbus* neared the sheer cliffside, the shuttlecraft began to turn slowly to the south in a long curve. McCoy caught a glimpse of two humanoid figures as they stumbled from the water and fell forward on the black sand just before the shuttlecraft's door slid shut.

Chapter Ten

THE SUN HAD JUST risen out of the ocean. Sulu brought the *Galileo* in about fifteen meters away from the *Columbus*. Both shuttlecraft were now about half a kilometer south of the Antosian multitude gathered along the cliffside overlooking the ocean.

"Kirk to *Enterprise,*" Kirk said.

"Scott here."

"What's the current status of those Antosians you rescued?"

"About a hundred and twenty of them are already back on Acra," Scotty replied. *"We beamed the strongest of them there, the ones who needed no medical care, although it'll be a while before they regain all their strength. There's a security detail with them for the time being, but I canna think any of them are*

going to try to escape again. Another sixty are resting here under guard until they're well enough to leave." The engineer paused. *"We lost twelve Antosians, Captain. Five died just after they came through—accordin' to Dr. Soong, their poor hearts couldna take the strain. The other seven came through scrambled too badly to be saved. And there's about eighteen of them still in sickbay."*

"More transporter accidents?" McCoy said from behind Kirk.

"Dr. Soong said that some of them had suffered strokes, and that the hearts of others were too damaged for them to be moved right now. All of our medical personnel are on duty in sickbay, and Wenallai is helping them with her healing techniques."

Kirk was about to ask how Empynes was faring, but kept silent. If Wenallai was trying to help other Antosians, then Empynes no longer needed her aid. That might mean either that her bondpartner had recovered, or else that he was dead.

"Stay where you are," McCoy was saying to the Antosians aboard their shuttlecraft, some of whom were in seats but most of whom were now stretched out on the floor. "You're all in a greatly weakened state. We'll get food to you as soon as we can, but the best thing you can do right now is rest and give yourselves time to recover."

"Stand by, Scotty," Kirk said. "You may need to beam some more Antosians up to the ship soon." He got up and made his way past the seated Antosians to

McCoy; he wanted to get the physician's assessment of which of their passengers might require some time in sickbay.

"Captain Kirk," Garth suddenly called out, "the sensor readings are showing—" Garth jumped to his feet. "People are diving off the cliffs!"

Kirk slapped the panel near the exit; the doorway slid open. He was out of the shuttlecraft in an instant, leaping to the ground and then running across the plain of grass. Garth jumped out right behind him and soon caught up with him.

Kirk picked up his stride, keeping pace with Garth. Now he could see, in the distance, what looked like people in capes hurling themselves from the edges of the cliffs, and then he noticed that the capes were wings.

The Antosians had morphed into birds; others were changing shape even as Kirk and Garth ran toward them.

"Stop!" Kirk shouted, but no one even glanced in his direction. He slowed his pace as he neared them. A woman who had begun to flow into the form of a bird suddenly reverted to her own shape again and turned toward him and Garth.

Kirk approached her cautiously. Garth was at his back, ready to cover him, and as he glanced south, Kirk saw that Spock had left the *Galileo* and was running toward them across the grass. Kirk turned toward the Antosian woman, who held out her hands, palms out.

She shook back her long dark hair, then gazed from him to Garth in silence before pointing to the east. Kirk moved cautiously to the edge of the cliff and looked down in time to see two birds alight on the black sand below and then revert to the shape of humanoids. Other tiny forms crouched over bodies that were stretched out on the sand or on the flat rocks near the waterline. Several Antosians were helping to pull another man out of the water. What he had taken to be the start of a mass suicide was in fact a rescue mission.

"Some among us are healers," the woman was saying to Kirk. "They have flown down to try to help the survivors who made it to shore, and then we will have to find a way to get them all back up here when they're strong enough to be moved."

Other Antosians were gathering near her as she spoke; those farther away from them watched from a distance.

Kirk said, "Our starship's transporters can beam them up here almost instantly."

"Why did you come here?" Garth abruptly asked the woman. "Why did you leave the city? What brought all of you out of Pynesses to this place?"

A bearded man stepped forward. "At first it was our despair, and a feeling that we could not stay in our homes while others we knew and cared about were condemned to exile on Acra. That's what I recall, anyway, but most of us were not thinking all that clearly. Then, when we left the city, many of us were already beginning to feel that we had to come here, that something was drawing us to these cliffs, almost compelling us to travel to this place. I cannot explain it any more clearly than that."

"I understand," Garth said.

"We had to come," the dark-haired woman said. "The closer we came, the more I felt that something was about to happen. And we were right to feel that way, I knew it as soon as I saw that flock of birds flying toward us. Yet only a few of our friends and kindred made it to these shores."

"We saved as many as we could," Kirk said. "We rescued some two hundred of them, and there are others—"

"Too many were lost," the man said, and Kirk saw his grief reflected in the faces of others.

Kirk stood in silence with Garth until Spock reached them, then said, "I'll ask my crew to start beaming those below up to safety as soon as you give the word."

"What will happen?" the woman said plaintively. "What will happen to them now?"

"We've been sending the strongest back to Acra, at least for now," Kirk replied, "but what becomes of them later on will have to be decided by your people."

"We've done everything we can to remedy the damage I caused," Garth said, "but we can do little more without violating Starfleet directives, and perhaps there are some who will say that we bent our own rules too much as it is. In any case, the fate of your culture and your world is in your hands." His voice had regained its former resonance, but there was a subdued quality to its timbre. "You will have to decide what measures to take to restore the peaceful life you once knew."

"But what can we do?" the woman asked. She regarded Spock for a long moment, as if the Vulcan might have some wisdom to offer, then turned back to Kirk and Garth. "We have no First Minister now, not even a Chief Adviser to step into his place. Worse yet, a few among us raised their hands in violence against the First Minister when he came to meet with us, and killed a man who came with him to protect him, and others of us stood by and did nothing to prevent that evil deed." It was as if she were saying that all of the Antosians, having known sin, could never be cleansed again. "And some of us were lured by dreams of glory, and turned against the rest of our race. Our world has been torn apart, and never can be mended."

Garth said, "I refuse to believe it."

"Captain," Spock said, looking back to the shuttlecraft.

Kirk turned around and saw four Antosians outside the *Columbus,* along with McCoy. Sulu stood with them, with a tall, fair-haired man at his side. One of the Antosians handed what looked like a large wrapped bundle to the Antosian next to Sulu, and then the group started to walk in Kirk's direction.

Kirk and those with him watched them stride across the grassy expanse. As they came closer, Kirk recognized Kellin, the young man who had impersonated Garth. Kellin was still carrying the bundle that had been handed to him, and now Kirk saw the long black hair that hung from one end of Kellin's burden.

Garth let out a sigh as they approached. Kirk glanced at him and caught the look of pain and loss in his pale eyes as he stepped forward and took Kellin's burden from him. The body had been wrapped in a cloak; part of the garment fell back, revealing the face of Hala-Jyusa, her eyes closed, looking as though she were finally at peace. Garth held her in his arms, trembling slightly, biting his lips, and Kirk saw what it was costing him to control himself.

Garth turned to face the crowds of Antosians again, still holding Hala-Jyusa. "This is what the lust for power brings," he called out. "This is the reward for dreaming of conquest and glory and forcing one's own violent will upon others."

Kirk saw that the Antosians nearest to them were murmuring to others, passing Garth's words along to those who were farther back in the multitude.

"This woman, Hala-Jyusa, was one of those who healed me," Garth continued. "She was a kind and gentle soul before dreams of glory corrupted her. The art which brought beauty and grace to your culture and use in healing, became a weapon in Hala-Jyusa's hands, and wielding that weapon brought her death."

He knelt and lay the Antosian's body gently on the ground.

"I give up my dreams of glory!" Kellin cried out

then. "I must turn away from what I became, and I am convinced that all of my comrades will do the same. What happens to us, whether we must stay on Acra or be allowed to rejoin the rest of our people, will have to be decided by others. I do not blame Garth for what I became, for some other offworlder might have come here and turned me against everything we are taught. At least this man came back to try to remedy the damage."

Kellin helped Garth to his feet, then stumbled a little. McCoy gripped Kellin by the arm, helping him to stay on his feet.

Kirk looked around at the Antosians near him, then took out his communicator. "Kirk to *Enterprise.*"

"Scott here." The eyes of two children standing with the Antosians widened with surprise at the sound of the engineer's voice.

"Prepare to beam up the Antosians from the beach below this cliff," Kirk said.

"Aye, Captain, but first there's someone I have to beam down. He insists, and I'll keep a fix on him in case we have to bring him back aboard quickly. He's in a transporter room now, and Kyle will set him down right next to you."

A translucent glittering column had already appeared at Kirk's right. Several in the crowd gasped as the particles of light resolved themselves into the form of Empynes.

More gasps went up from the Antosians. At least a few in this crowd had to have been at the corral where

Heje-Illuss had died and Empynes had been struck down; the woman who had first spoken had admitted that. Kirk suddenly feared for the First Minister, even while knowing that Kyle would be scanning them continuously, prepared to beam the Antosian back aboard if trouble threatened.

But the Antosians in the front of the crowd were staring at Empynes with awe, even with expressions of joy.

"You are alive!" a gray-haired man said. "Our First Minister has returned to us!"

Empynes gave his people a solemn look, then glanced down at the lifeless body of Hala-Jyusa.

"I am sorry it had to come to this," he said in a low but strong voice. "I had hoped that Hala-Jyusa would be given time to reconsider, to heal, to become as she once was." He lifted his head. "But it is not too late for the rest of us. I must forgive you for what you have done, for I too have made many mistakes, and cannot find it within myself to condemn others for reacting with anger or fear to unforeseen events that we never expected to face, and which we lacked the experience to handle. What is done is past. We can gain nothing by allowing it to poison our future."

"What are we to do?" a man cried out from the crowd. His cry was quickly taken up by others.

"What shall we do?" a woman said.

"What will happen to us now?"

"Will we have to give up flowing forever?"

"What will become of our brothers and sisters on Acra?"

Empynes lifted his arms, and gradually the Antosians fell silent. "I do not know," the First Minister replied, his voice betraying the strain that recovery had placed on him. "That remains for us to decide, when we have returned to Pynesses."

The Antosians were whispering among themselves, passing on word of the return of Empynes and what he had said. Kirk realized that Empynes was now safe among his people, chastened and mournful as they were about the fate of Hala-Jyusa and so many of her comrades.

Kirk stepped back, then held his communicator to his face. "Kirk to *Enterprise,*" he said softly. "Scotty, you can beam the Antosians at the foot of the cliff up here now."

"Aye, Captain."

All along the cliffside, Antosians began to take down their tents and prepare their elleis for the return to the city.

Kirk was apprehensive as he entered the meeting room. All of the officers most involved in the mission to Antos IV had recorded and filed their reports, but he had decided to limit the number of crew members at this meeting to Spock, McCoy, Garth, and himself.

He was the last one to arrive; the others were already seated around the table.

"The purpose of this meeting," Kirk began as he sat down, "is to record our thoughts about what has happened, so as to give Admiral José Mendez a basis for deciding whether this mission has succeeded or failed. I have already collected and stored the reports of all officers and crew involved in various aspects of the mission, since Admiral Mendez may ask for them later." He paused. "Let the record show that First Officer Spock, Chief Medical Officer Leonard McCoy, Fleet Captain Garth of Izar, and I, Captain James T. Kirk, are all present to certify to the best of our knowledge and understanding what has happened. We are here to attempt, at least, to agree on the facts."

McCoy leaned forward and rested his elbows on the tabletop. "I know this is being recorded, Jim, but do we have to be so damned formal?"

Kirk shook his head. "Not at all, Bones. Be as informal as you wish, if that will help us."

"Captain," Spock asked, "will you also be providing the relevant passages from your captain's log to Admiral Mendez?"

"No, at least not yet," Kirk replied. "At first I thought we might all transmit our reports to him, and that is still an option." He gazed at Garth, who sat with his head bowed, not looking at anyone. "I think it's best that we all know what is said here, and record it under the assumption that Admiral Mendez may want to listen to it, unless at the end of this session we decide that transmitting it to him isn't necessary. I believe that this will offer the best chance of fairness in any judgment about the decisions that Captain Garth made."

McCoy sighed. "What have we done here? What

did we imagine we were doing? Sure, Scotty was able to get most of the Antosian rebels beamed aboard safely, without accidents, and maybe that proves he's the engineer we all know he is, or else maybe it's just luck. There were still too many dead, and some of them are still washing up on that black-sanded beach."

"Dr. McCoy," Garth said, "consider how many would have died in the coming civil war."

"Is that so clear?" McCoy objected.

"Yes, Doctor, it is," Garth said.

"Really?" McCoy sat back and folded his arms. "You made mistakes, Garth, you didn't anticipate certain events. For all we know, the rebels, left to their own devices, might have settled for the occasional relatively harmless guerrilla foray into Pynesses, or gone off to play at rebellion on their own. Maybe most of the other Antosians would have ignored them after a while."

Garth fixed his gaze on McCoy. "You're wrong. You saw how desperate the fliers were. You saw the thousands who found themselves impelled somehow to leave Pynesses and travel to the eastern cliffs. Had Empynes died instead of returning to them, they would have become another band of rebels, a larger one, capable of carrying on a fight to free the exiles. Do you think—"

"You're not what you were," McCoy interrupted.

"You mean I'm not deranged," Garth cut in.

"Yes!" McCoy snapped. "But what's really worrying me now is how easily you enlisted us all in your complicated plan."

"I understand, Doctor," Garth said. "But I saw no other way, and still don't, despite the number of dead and the greater number who have suffered to one degree or another. Believe me, I am not callous about the degree to which things went wrong."

"Went wrong? That's putting it mildly!"

"To have let matters develop without any intervention," Garth said, "would have led to no resolution at all. The Antosian culture was already fragmenting. Dissident groups would have proliferated, each with its own central figure and suggestible followers. There would have been more violence, and more dislocation. I remind you that contact with the Federation, through me, began this chain of events. In medical terms, Doctor, I infected Antos. And it was up to us to heal the sick and provide some sort of vaccine against another outbreak."

Spock said, "Captain Garth, as a matter of pure logic, I would contend that your influence on the politics and society of Antos IV was that of a proximate cause, not that of the underlying one."

Garth nodded at the Vulcan. "Thank you, Commander Spock, but it does not console me."

"Then what in all damnation are you defending?" McCoy demanded.

In the silence that ensued, Kirk wondered whether this meeting would accomplish anything at all. Maybe private reports from each of them would give

Admiral Mendez a more honest picture of the mission. Too much was still unsettled, with possible resolutions still uncertain. Uhura, Chekov, and the other *Enterprise* personnel who had been with the remaining exiles on Acra, including the security detail, were back aboard ship, but the Antosian rebels, including all of the survivors of the attempted escape, remained there. Empynes had spent the past days in long meetings with his advisers and in consultations with various groups of citizens, risking his health and a possible relapse, but Kirk did not know what decisions, if any, had been made.

"When cultures meet," Spock said at last, "there will always be unexpected results."

"And yet we cannot avoid meeting others," Kirk added, "and reaching out, hoping to bridge whatever may separate us from one another."

Spock shrugged. "Meetings might be delayed."

Kirk stood up. "Gentlemen, I suspected that we might want someone else to join this discussion. I now see that we must hear from him."

He went to the door; it slid open.

Empynes stood outside, with Christine Chapel at his side.

"Please come in," Kirk said.

The First Minister entered the room. The other men rose to their feet; McCoy seemed about to come around the table to assist Empynes.

"Please sit," the Antosian said. "I need to do so myself." His face was tight with fatigue, and he leaned heavily against Chapel as she guided him to a seat, but his dark eyes were alert.

"Are you well enough to be here?" McCoy asked. "I told you that, when you were back in Pynesses, you would need a lot of rest for some time."

"Rest enough in the grave, Doctor," Empynes murmured. "There was much work to be done, and I believe that we've found a solution to our present dilemma."

Chapel stepped back and seemed about to leave the room, but Kirk motioned to her to sit down. The others sat down again as Kirk seated himself. "I remind you," he said to Empynes, "that we're recording this meeting for our superior at Starfleet Command."

Empynes nodded. "I understand." He took a breath. "First, I must tell you that it's now clear to nearly all Antosians that the disagreement that divided us was a false dilemma. Our choices are not whether to retain shape-changing and all its risks, or eliminating the ability. Elimination goes too far. There is a third way."

McCoy nodded. "I've been leaning in that direction myself."

"I listened to my Chief Adviser, Gyneeses," Empynes continued, "and his advice seemed sound to me. I didn't know that he was deliberately misleading me. The issue was drawn by him as being between two choices, while, unknown to me, he was seeking personal power. Round up the rebels and exile them, eliminate our flowing skills—it was all part of his plan to make the rebels into a fighting force of his own, and leave the rest of us with less power to resist them."

Garth said, "My madness infected him, too."

Empynes looked at Garth. "You blame yourself for too much, Captain Garth. Your presence did awaken certain . . . ambitions among us. But those might have developed in any case, even if we had never been contacted by your Federation. Why? Because all intelligent life tends to run through its long repertoire of behavioral possibilities. They are always there, waiting, in the nature of a creative universe."

Garth said, "But I agreed to the plan that Gyneeses proposed, and must now face the fact that the exile of the rebels on Acra was a most inadequate solution. Worse still, it led to the deaths of too many of them."

The Antosian held up a hand. "Nevertheless, your agreeing with that solution and going along with it helped us avoid a much wider conflict, and stopped Gyneeses from misleading our people and furthering his own ambitions. Without your intervention, without your improvised plan, I seriously doubt that we would have discovered what he was up to until too late. Gyneeses might have been vastly more successful than we can imagine. He would have been able to exploit the simple fact that an organism will resist giving up any of its versatility, which is what the elimination of our shape-changing skill threatened. Such a change must come from inner conviction, not compulsion from outside."

"So where do matters now stand?" Kirk asked,

glimpsing for a moment the possibility that the Federation might withdraw and leave the people of Antos IV to solve their own problems.

Empynes said, "I have met with many Antosians over the past days, and had communications from many more. The eloquent horror of the escape from Acra, the tragedy of so many deaths, has led to a new insight, to a cultural rather than a biological change among my people. I do not know if this is of any comfort to you, Garth, but perhaps poor Hala-Jyusa, by leading her followers on their futile flight, has made some sort of reconciliation possible for the rest of us."

"Then you won't seek to eliminate your shape-changing ability?" Garth asked.

"Any solution to the misuses of that ability," Empynes responded, "must be a long-term one. Perhaps in time our descendants may choose to eliminate it, and perhaps they will not. But any solution we find will lead to greater self-control, and to more productive uses of our talent."

"More medical uses," Christine Chapel murmured.

"Yes, Nurse Chapel," Empynes said. "The tragedy has brought home to us the dangers of unchecked power and the misuse of our arts." He gazed across the table at Garth. "We might easily have torn ourselves apart, Captain Garth. Through your actions, and aided by Captain Kirk, you faced us with the alternatives."

Garth said, "You are giving me too much credit."

"And you are giving yourself too little." Empynes

smiled slightly. "Consider—we now understand that the menace of shape-changing is in fact a very limited one. It may be a useful and sometimes good tactical weapon, but hardly decisive. This skill, we have reason to believe, developed in us as a means for quick escape from danger, as a form of camouflage. The more civilized among us long ago learned to use it for pleasure, for play, to bring a bit of beauty into our world, and later for healing. Then some of us began to imagine that it might be used for political and criminal purposes. But the exercise of this ability is a very costly one in bodily energy, and cannot be used wildly, as the escape from Acra proved."

"Gyneeses was laying his own plans," Garth said, "before I returned to Antos IV on this mission. He was hoping to extend the applications of metamorphosis after he came to power. When I learned this, I knew he had to be stopped, and so I tempted him with the possibility of seizing a starship. But my own plan disturbed me when I set it in motion, and even now. Much went wrong, and even more might have gone wrong."

"But your plan did bring the rebels together in one place," Empynes said, "and forced us all to face their example, along with the consequences of their attempts to gain power. Even the survivors on Acra are wrestling with the consequences of their deeds. I have spoken to them in recent days through the communicators your people left them. They have renounced their rebellion, and seek a restoration of the peace we once had."

"But how plausible is that renunciation?" Garth asked.

"I trust them," Empynes said, and Kirk found himself wondering about this wise and kindly Antosian's possible gullibility. How could anyone ever be certain that the goodwill of the present would not again drift into mad ambition?

Kirk noticed then that Empynes was gazing directly at him. "I see the doubts in your eyes, Captain Kirk," the Antosian went on, "and also in your expression, Captain Garth."

Kirk nodded. "Suspicion builds its own endless bureaucracy of questions and doubts."

"And only the unfolding of time will tell the tale," Empynes said. "No individual, and no culture, can settle any complex question for all time."

"Antos IV and the Federation have no quarrel," Kirk began, "so there is no reason—"

"Except for me," Garth said. "I tried to destroy Antos IV."

"When you were not yourself, Captain Garth," Empynes said, "and after Antosian healers had treated you in ignorance of certain details of human physiology. Had they known more about your kind, if we'd had more contact with other races in the past, perhaps they would have been able to heal you and restore your form without causing your derangement."

"It was Heje-Illuss and Hala-Jyusa who did the most in saving my life," Garth said, "and their reward for that was death."

Empynes watched Garth in silence for a few moments, then said, "Before Captain Kirk requested my presence at this meeting, I was about to ask him to beam me to Acra, and to ask both him and you, Captain Garth, to accompany me there. I intend to speak to the exiles face to face, and to offer them the opportunity to rejoin the rest of us in Pynesses."

"But are you sure enough of them to do that?" Kirk objected.

"You yourself said that the fate of the exiles would have to be our decision," Empynes said.

Spock lifted a brow as he glanced at Kirk. "The First Minister recalls correctly, Captain."

"Will you and Captain Garth come with me to Acra now?" the Antosian asked. "If there is to be friendship between our world and the Federation, then perhaps you should be present when I speak to the exiles."

"Very well." Kirk stood up. "I'll come with you."

Garth slowly rose to his feet. "And so will I."

The white-sanded beach stretched before them. Kirk looked to his right to see groups of Antosians gathered outside their tents and in front of what looked like the walls of more permanent structures. They were beginning to build homes for themselves here; he wondered what they would say to Empynes's offer.

Empynes, still weak, was leaning against Garth as the three of them walked among the exiles. Two men came forward and ushered them toward the trunk of a felled tree, offering them all a place to sit. The Antosians settled themselves around them.

"I said that I wanted to speak to all of you," Empynes began, "and Captains Kirk and Garth agreed to come with me, now that there is to be friendship and more contact between us and the Federation. There is much we can gain from such an association, but the Federation will not interfere in our affairs or any decisions we must make for ourselves."

The Antosians were watching them all, Kirk noticed, with contemplative but also apprehensive expressions. Empynes searched the crowd, then gestured at Trialla and those near her.

"Trialla," the First Minister continued, "there is no reason for you and your comrades to remain here in exile. You gave up your rebellion, and tried to protect me when I was held captive with you. Your leader and friend Heje-Illuss gave up his life while trying to guard mine. I came here to tell you that you may return to Pynesses, and that the *Enterprise*'s transporters will take you there whenever you are ready to leave Acra." He paused. "But I also wish to tell the rest of you that, now that you have renounced your rebellion, you may also return to your homes and families and former lives. I know from what you've said to me through the communicator channels that the experience of the attempted flight has marked and changed you. If there is to be peace among us, then there must be trust, and my coming here is a demonstration of my trust in you. If we are to mend what has been torn apart, we must come together once more."

There were no cheers at this announcement, and no applause, only silence and what looked to Kirk like puzzled stares.

"I am sincere in what I say," Empynes said at last, breaking the silence. "You will be welcomed back to Pynesses, and perhaps then—"

A hand was thrust up from the middle of the crowd. Kellin stood up and came forward. "May I speak, First Minister?" he asked.

Empynes held up a hand. "Of course."

"We thought that you might make such an offer," the young man said. "Some of us have spoken to friends and family during the past days, and they told us that there was much sentiment favoring forgiveness and a pardon for us. But—" He looked down. "We have all agreed on what I must say. We think we need more time here, more time to understand what we've done and to come to terms with it. We do not know if we're ready yet to rejoin the rest of you."

Empynes seemed about to object, and then Trialla stood up. "The people with me have also been considering what we should do. We concluded that we should stay on Acra with our former comrades, in order to keep them from becoming too isolated from other Antosians. Some of our friends and kindred in Pynesses have told us that they would willingly come to live here as well, if you will permit them to do so."

"We would all rather go home," Kellin added. "We would prefer to return and take up our old lives as if nothing had happened, but that doesn't seem right somehow."

"May I say something?" Kirk asked.

Empynes nodded, then held up a hand.

Kirk said, "There is no quarrel between the Federation and Antos IV, and there will not be one tomorrow, or next month, or next year. We must go forward on that basis, and help our friendship grow. After hearing what you have to say, I have every reason to think that it will be a long and lasting friendship."

Empynes seemed to be smiling. Garth stood up then and beckoned to Kirk. "The First Minister should have a few moments to consult with his people," Garth said, then turned toward Empynes. "We'll stay here until you are ready to return to Pynesses."

"Thank you, Captain Garth," Empynes replied.

Garth led Kirk away from the others and along the beach until they were walking along the water's edge, the waves lapping at their feet. A few of the large gray shore birds flew overhead, skimmed the ocean, and then flew on; Garth gazed after them for a moment, and Kirk knew that he was thinking of Hala-Jyusa and her followers.

"They're choosing to stay here," Garth said as they came to a halt. "As beautiful as this island is, that will be hard for them, much harder for an Antosian than it would be for one of us."

"The Federation will be able to establish ties with

this world now," Kirk said. "Starfleet will be sending starships here regularly. No one will have to remain an exile on Acra permanently."

"Young Kellin was right about one thing." Garth folded his arms as he stared out at the blue-green ocean. "They cannot simply take up their old lives as if nothing had happened. And neither can I."

"What do you mean?" Kirk asked. "Are you thinking of resigning your commission?"

"I may not have to resign it. Admiral Mendez and Starfleet Command may decide that I don't deserve it."

Kirk shook his head. "But your mission here was successful. Even if you insist on resigning, you might get a commendation for your service here. The Antosians are at peace, a civil war has been averted, and we have every reason to hope that Antos IV will eventually be a member in good standing of the Federation."

"I still took too many chances. I made too many mistakes, and they cost lives."

Garth seemed to change subtly as Kirk looked at him; his hair was grayer, his face more lined and leathery in the bright sunlight, his body a bit more stooped and aged. Then he straightened, growing slightly taller and more erect, and the lines around his eyes and mouth slowly faded.

"I feel like a kind of exile myself, Captain Kirk," he continued. "There is still a residue of fear in me, however unwarranted and unreasonable, that I might lose my sanity again. I can tell myself that when I was mad, I wasn't responsible for my deeds, but I did threaten the Antosian people, and I committed my share of cruel deeds while I was an inmate on Elba II. Something in me feels that I haven't atoned properly for that. Since returning here, I feel that I am not quite human anymore, and yet I'm not an Antosian, either. I don't know if there is any place for me, but if there is, I do not think it's in Starfleet."

"Then that will be Starfleet's great loss," Kirk said.

A smile briefly flickered across Garth's face. "It is kind of you to say so."

"Captain Garth!" a voice called out behind them. "Captain Kirk!"

Kirk turned to see Empynes coming toward them, supported on either side by Trialla and Kellin and trailed by a number of Antosians.

Kirk and Garth went to meet them.

"I have something more to say," Empynes said, "something most important, and then you will beam me back home, where Wenallai is going to insist that I rest and do absolutely nothing for at least a few days." He paused. "You spoke of friendship between our world and your Federation, Captain Kirk, and to that end, I have one last request to make, one that I've discussed with my council of advisers, with delegations of citizens, and with the people here. I would like to request that Captain Garth be appointed the Federation's ambassador to Antos IV. We will be most pleased to welcome him and to provide a suitable residence."

Kirk saw the sudden flood of feeling that came

into Garth's face; his pale eyes glistened, and for a moment he thought that Garth might break down. But Garth held himself in check as he murmured, "I would be honored to accept." He turned toward Kirk. "That is, if no one in the Federation diplomatic corps or in Starfleet Command objects."

"They won't dare to object," Kirk replied. "I'll see to that, Captain Garth. You have my word. I'll do everything possible to secure that appointment, and so will my officers." But once again, he realized, he had thrown his hat over a cliff and was about to dive after it. He could keep his promise to fight for Garth, but did not know if José Mendez would agree to back him up. He might only be setting Garth up for further disappointment and sorrow.

But Garth was smiling as he gripped Kirk's shoulder. "Thank you . . . Jim," he said softly, "for having some faith in me. You don't know how much that means to me."

Kirk swallowed hard and tried to remain composed as his feelings raged through him. His Academy hero had thanked him. It was as though King Arthur had knighted him. Yet Kirk feared that he might yet fail him.

Chapter Eleven

"SO THERE you have it, sir," Kirk said to Admiral Mendez from the desk in his quarters. "You've seen the record of our meeting, all of the relevant entries in my captain's log, and the reports from my officers that you asked to see. You know everything."

"You've given me an abundance of data, Captain, but it's far from everything." José Mendez's image gazed up at him from the viewscreen. *"Only a little bit seems to show of the most important and crucial parts."*

Kirk was silent.

"I think I grasp what you intended to do," Mendez went on, *"and even if it wasn't exactly by the book, one has to say that you and Garth succeeded in your mission. Whether or not you deserve a commendation for it is another matter. Even worse, some might*

easily argue that you both overstepped the bounds, and that Garth in particular still shows signs of instability, to put it mildly. And there's the Prime Directive. You two may not have violated it, but you certainly stretched it somewhat. Garth may have affected the Antosian culture more than he or you realize. You may have removed the greatest threats to amicable relations with the Antosians, but the future of the Federation's relationship with them remains uncertain."

Kirk felt a moment of irritation. "The same thing can be said of a number of other worlds that are Federation members in good standing."

"You know what I think, Jim?" Mendez asked, smiling.

"What?"

"I think you learned just about everything you know from Fleet Captain Garth."

Kirk grimaced. "I choose to take that as a compliment, Admiral."

"I suspected you would. Like him, you're always improvising, stretching regulations, overstepping procedures when you think you're right. Garth was that way long before his illness, which only distorted his abilities, temporarily making him almost a caricature of himself." Mendez leaned forward. *"Part of me wants to urge that you both be given a commendation for this mission, and the other part is wondering if it might be better to reprimand you and ask Garth for his resignation."*

"He doesn't deserve that."

"I can try to see that he gets an honorable discharge."

"He wouldn't want to leave Starfleet that way," Kirk said, "honorable discharge or not."

"You mean that it would wound him psychologically."

"I mean that he deserves better than that for what he's done, and for the years of brilliant service he gave to Starfleet before his mental collapse." Kirk leaned back in his chair. "May I say something else, Admiral?" He knew that he would have to speak as frankly as possible, to take every chance at getting Garth the ambassadorship that had been offered to him.

"Permission to speak freely, Jim," Mendez replied.

"Procedures and rules too often try to mechanize what may be too complex to make orderly. Extreme cases call for extraordinary measures."

"Quite right," Mendez said. *"So we have people like you, and we talk to them off the record. A very dangerous creativity lives in people like you and Garth, Jim. Meditate on that."*

"I do, often," Kirk said. "There were a number of moments when I might have pulled back, restrained Garth, decided that events were getting out of hand. But had I done so, instead of following his lead and my own instincts, or taking extraordinary measures, I believe our mission would have failed, or something worse would have happened."

"But there's more, isn't there?" Mendez said. *"You felt for Garth."*

Kirk nodded. "There's an old story, 'The Secret Sharer' by Joseph Conrad, in which a sea captain rescues a sympathetic soul and feels a kinship with him."

"I know the story. The captain sets him free."

"It's something like that, as if I were looking at the universe through another set of eyes."

Mendez smiled. *"I thought it might be like that. Now I know I was right to send you with Garth to Antos IV."*

"And what now?" Kirk asked.

Mendez was silent, staring at him from the small screen. The admiral knew that the Antosians, through their First Minister and his advisers, had formally requested that a Federation embassy be opened in Pynesses, and that Fleet Captain Garth of Izar was the ambassador they preferred. Garth was more familiar with their culture than any outsider, and was largely responsible for bringing about the possibility of more contact and exchanges with other races and worlds. But if Starfleet Command demanded Garth's resignation from Starfleet, there was almost no chance that the diplomatic service would approve his appointment as an ambassador. He would be tainted; too many doubts would again be raised about his sanity and his judgment. Even Mendez was probably wondering if Garth had a diplomat's temperament.

"Would Garth be welcome on Antos IV," Mendez

said then, *"if he was forced to resign his commission and chose to stay there as a private citizen?"*

"Yes, sir, he would. I have no doubt of that." Kirk had to admit the truth. *Here it comes,* he thought. Mendez would seize on that and convince himself that he could ask Garth to resign without denying him a chance to live out his life among the Antosians. Kirk found himself seeing through Garth's eyes again, living on Antos IV as an exile with a clouded reputation, with no true role to play in either Federation or Antosian affairs, and no way to atone for his past mistakes. For a proud spirit like Garth's, such a life, however pleasant and comfortable, would be a slow death.

Mendez looked down for a moment, as if considering what to say.

"Admiral Mendez," Kirk said, "I was at Garth's side throughout much of this mission. I saw what he had to overcome to accomplish his task. Frankly, I think he deserves a commendation, and I know how valuable he'd be as our first ambassador to Antos IV. If you insist on recommending to Starfleet Command that they demand his resignation, I'll file a protest and demand a hearing for Garth, and I can promise that I'll offer a deposition in his defense if that's what I have to do."

"Regardless of the possible consequences."

"Yes, sir."

"I expected you to say something like that." Mendez sighed. *"Very well, Jim, Garth will get his*

commendation, and can retire from Starfleet when he so chooses with honor, and he'll be ambassador to Antos IV—my recommendation will guarantee that. And I hope that history doesn't make fools of us." The admiral smiled, then said, *"Jim, I'll be truthful with you. I looked in my tool chest for what was available. I knew you. You knew Garth. That made you the best intermediary between Starfleet and Garth."*

"And Garth the best intermediary between Antos IV and the Federation."

"Most definitely. Good work, Jim. Mendez out."

The screen went blank. Kirk let out a sigh of relief. He had dreaded having to disappoint Garth.

His door sounded. "Come in," Kirk said.

It slid open and Spock entered. Kirk motioned to a seat. Spock sat down. "So you couldn't stand the suspense, either."

The Vulcan nodded. "It was disconcerting."

"Yes, it was. Garth pretty much put it all on the line with what he did on Antos IV."

"And you with him, Captain. I surmise that you put even more on the line, as you say, during your conference with the admiral, that you informed him that you supported Garth's appointment as ambassador and would fight for it regardless of the consequences to yourself and your career."

"You surmise correctly, Mr. Spock," Kirk said with a small smile. "Still, Garth won't be just an ambassador, but also an exile. He feels not quite Antosian or human, you know, but something in between."

"In other words, a perfect ambassador," Spock said.

Kirk stood up. "We must tell him at once."

"That would be indicated, Captain."

Chapter Twelve

GARTH STOOD ALONE by the road that ran past his residence and gazed north toward Greblendon Lake. His guests of the past days were riding away on their elleis. At the lake, they would turn east along the shore until they reached the river that flowed to the coast. As he watched the six riders, Garth saw Kellin turn around in his saddle and lift his hand in farewell.

Kellin and Trialla and four other Antosians from Acra had visited Garth after meeting with Empynes and his advisers, and were now on their way home. At the coast, they would board their glider and the gentle winds would carry them home to Acra.

Small ships now sailed to the Tiresian Islands with goods and people who wished to stay on Acra for a while, and then returned with exiles who had decided to come home at last; but the gliders were becoming more popular among the Antosians. They were light aircraft, each able to carry five or six people; they were powered by sun and wind and were relatively easy to pilot. The gliders enabled the travelers to avoid the inconveniences and dangers of the sea voyage, which required sailing to the southeast from a northern port through icy waters often crowded with floes and icebergs, thus avoiding the cliff-lined eastern shore of Anatossia where no ships could be launched or safely land.

Garth had helped in designing the gliders, and recalled the pleasure he had felt when he had seen the first one swoop over the plain to the west of the city. The exiles of Acra would again be airborne, carried safely over the ocean to their island.

Since then, more Antosians were traveling between Acra and Pynesses, and the place of exile had become a settlement. Many were already planning to build new communities on the other Tiresian Islands, since ships could easily sail the short distances separating them. The ties between the former rebels and the rest of their people had been renewed, but Garth also felt that something new and valuable to the rest of Antosian society would eventually grow from Acra. The island settlers were the first Antosians in the recorded history of their people to live apart from the rest of their race, to break away from the highly centralized community that had always constituted their society. They would remain connected to the rest of their people, but in time they would diverge, however gradually and subtly, and that divergence would enrich the rest of their culture.

The residence in which he had been living for some years was at the northern edge of Pynesses. The official embassy building, now staffed by four Antosians and two human diplomatic aides sent there recently by the Federation, was adjacent to the First Minister's compound, but Empynes had offered Garth this house.

It was a square stone building with two floors and large, spacious rooms suitable for diplomatic receptions; massive trees grew in the grounds around the residence, shading the building with their leafy boughs. Once, this house had belonged to Hala-Jyusa and her family, but her brother and sister had left it after her death and had been among the first to join the exiles on Acra. Garth had been reluctant to live here at first, and had often slept in the embassy building instead, but the house had become a comfort to him, a link with the past. Hala-Jyusa was buried here, next to the path of flat white stones that led to the front door. A slender tree now grew from her grave.

Death, Garth thought, was only another shape-changing.

He stood there in the late afternoon, as he had so often done, looking at the trees that surrounded his house. The trees were vast tenements of life, reaching down into the soil and bedrock, and into the heavens toward the stars that waited beyond the brightness of the sky.

His understanding of the Antosian way of life had grown with the years. Cellular flowing was the primal link between the Antosians and their planet, a closeness beyond words or thought. It was a musical stream of feeling that sometimes became a torrent of emotion. It was a solidarity with a library of life; it was the center of their life. He gazed up at the trees and felt his bond with all the life here.

Birds sang in the high branches of the trees.

Garth stood still and opened his arms to the sunlight that shone through the boughs—

—and became a small tree among the giants.

As the solar warmth spread through him, he listened to the planet's ancient music. It sang to him across time, from the first cells to the multi-organisms of today, and through his body.

He had been an intruder.

Then a student.

But now he was home.

Afterword

This is in many ways a long-cherished wish, to write about this character. Among the many actors who brought Star Trek characters to life, Steve Ihnat was probably the most unusual. As "Lord Garth," the tall, blond, blue-eyed devil out of Starfleet's past, he presented a noble, tragic figure of Shakespearean proportions. Only Ricardo Montalban's Khan Noonien Singh, featured in the episode "Space Seed" and the movie *Star Trek II: The Wrath of Khan,* is a worthy rival. One may wonder whether, if Steve Ihnat had not died prematurely, he might have been the character who would have been developed as Kirk's antagonist for the second feature film instead of Khan.

Our novel represents a youthful wish to have seen that happen. The wish stayed with us, and here it is.

—Pamela Sargent & George Zebrowski

About the Authors

Pamela Sargent and **George Zebrowski** have been watching *Star Trek* since the 1960s, when they were students at the State University of New York at Binghamton.

Pamela Sargent sold her first story during her senior year in college and has been a writer ever since. She has won a Nebula Award and a Locus Award, and has been a finalist for the Hugo Award; her work has been translated into twelve languages. Her epic novel *Venus of Dreams* was listed as one of the one hundred best science-fiction novels by *Library Journal. Earthseed,* her first novel for young adults, was chosen as a 1983 Best Book by the American Library Association. Her other acclaimed science-fiction novels include *Cloned Lives, The Sudden Star, Watchstar, The Golden Space, The Alien Upstairs, The Shore of*

Women, and *Venus of Shadows.* The *Washington Post Book World* has called her "one of the genre's best writers."

Sargent is also the author of *Ruler of the Sky,* a historical novel about Genghis Khan, which *Booklist* called "an impressive novel from a veteran writer," and best-selling author Gary Jennings described as "formidably researched and exquisitely written." She has also published *Climb the Wind: A Novel of Another America,* a finalist for the 1999 Sidewise Award for Alternate History, which Gahan Wilson called "a most enjoyable and entertaining new alternate history adventure which brings . . . a new dimension to the form." Among the anthologies she has edited are *Women of Wonder: The Classic Years* and *Women of Wonder: The Contemporary Years,* which *Publishers Weekly* praised as "essential reading for any serious sf fan." Her latest novel, *Child of Venus,* came out from Eos/HarperCollins in 2001; two collections, *Behind the Eyes of Dreamers and Other Short Novels* (Thorndike Press) and *The Mountain Cage and Other Stories* (Meisha Merlin), were published in 2002.

George Zebrowski's thirty-five books include novels, short fiction collections, anthologies, and a book of essays. His short stories have been nominated for the Nebula Award and the Theodore Sturgeon Memorial Award. Noted science-fiction writer Greg Bear calls him "one of those rare speculators who bases his dreams on science as well as inspiration," and the late Terry Carr, one of the most influential science-fiction editors of recent years, described him as "an authority in the field."

Zebrowski has published more than seventy-five works of short fiction and over a hundred articles and essays, including reviews for the *Washington Post Book World* and articles on science for *Nature* and *Omni* magazine. One of his best-known novels is *Macrolife,* selected by *Library Journal* as one of the one hundred best novels of science fiction; Arthur C. Clarke described *Macrolife* as "a worthy successor to Olaf Stapledon's *Star Maker.* It's been years since I was so impressed. One of the few books I intend to read again." He is also the author of *The Omega Point Trilogy* and *The Sunspacers Trilogy,* and his novel *Stranger Suns* was a *New York Times* Notable Book of the Year.

With scientist/author Charles Pellegrino, Zebrowski is the author of *The Killing Star,* which the *New York Times Book Review* called "a novel of such conceptual ferocity and scientific plausibility that it amounts to a reinvention of that old Wellsian staple: Invading Monsters From Outer Space." *Booklist* commented: "Pellegrino and Zebrowski are working territory not too far removed from Arthur C. Clarke's, and anywhere Clarke is popular, this book should be, too." Zebrowski and Pellegrino also collaborated on *Dyson Sphere,* a *Star Trek: The Next Generation* novel.

Zebrowski's most recent novels are *Brute Or-*

bits, published in 1998 by HarperPrism, which was honored with the John W. Campbell Award for best science-fiction novel of the year, and *Cave of Stars,* a novel that is part of the Macrolife mosaic, published by HarperPrism in 1999. A collection of his short fiction, *Swift Thoughts* (Golden Gryphon Press), came out in 2002.

Sargent and Zebrowski are also the authors of *Star Trek: The Next Generation: A Fury Scorned, Star Trek: Heart of the Sun,* and *Star Trek: Across the Universe.* They live in upstate New York.

Look for STAR TREK fiction from Pocket Books

Star Trek®

Enterprise: The First Adventure • Vonda N. McIntyre
Strangers From the Sky • Margaret Wander Bonanno
Final Frontier • Diane Carey
Spock's World • Diane Duane
The Lost Years • J.M. Dillard
Prime Directive • Judith and Garfield Reeves-Stevens
Probe • Margaret Wander Bonanno
Best Destiny • Diane Carey
Shadows on the Sun • Michael Jan Friedman
Sarek • A.C. Crispin
Federation • Judith and Garfield Reeves-Stevens
Vulcan's Forge • Josepha Sherman & Susan Shwartz
Mission to Horatius • Mack Reynolds
Vulcan's Heart • Josepha Sherman & Susan Shwartz
The Eugenics Wars: The Rise and Fall of Khan Noonien Singh, Books One and *Two* • Greg Cox
The Last Round-Up • Christie Golden
Gemini • Mike W. Barr
Garth of Izar • Pamela Sargent & George Zebrowski

Novelizations

Star Trek: The Motion Picture • Gene Roddenberry
Star Trek II: The Wrath of Khan • Vonda N. McIntyre
Star Trek III: The Search for Spock • Vonda N. McIntyre
Star Trek IV: The Voyage Home • Vonda N. McIntyre
Star Trek V: The Final Frontier • J.M. Dillard
Star Trek VI: The Undiscovered Country • J.M. Dillard
Star Trek Generations • J.M. Dillard
Starfleet Academy • Diane Carey

Star Trek books by William Shatner with Judith and Garfield Reeves-Stevens

The Ashes of Eden
The Return
Avenger
Star Trek: Odyssey (contains *The Ashes of Eden*, *The Return*, and *Avenger)*
Spectre
Dark Victory
Preserver
Captain's Peril

#1 • *Star Trek: The Motion Picture* • Gene Roddenberry
#2 • *The Entropy Effect* • Vonda N. McIntyre
#3 • *The Klingon Gambit* • Robert E. Vardeman

#4 • *The Covenant of the Crown* • Howard Weinstein
#5 • *The Prometheus Design* • Sondra Marshak & Myrna Culbreath
#6 • *The Abode of Life* • Lee Correy
#7 • *Star Trek II: The Wrath of Khan* • Vonda N. McIntyre
#8 • *Black Fire* • Sonni Cooper
#9 • *Triangle* • Sondra Marshak & Myrna Culbreath
#10 • *Web of the Romulans* • M.S. Murdock
#11 • *Yesterday's Son* • A.C. Crispin
#12 • *Mutiny on the Enterprise* • Robert E. Vardeman
#13 • *The Wounded Sky* • Diane Duane
#14 • *The Trellisane Confrontation* • David Dvorkin
#15 • *Corona* • Greg Bear
#16 • *The Final Reflection* • John M. Ford
#17 • *Star Trek III: The Search for Spock* • Vonda N. McIntyre
#18 • *My Enemy, My Ally* • Diane Duane
#19 • *The Tears of the Singers* • Melinda Snodgrass
#20 • *The Vulcan Academy Murders* • Jean Lorrah
#21 • *Uhura's Song* • Janet Kagan
#22 • *Shadow Lord* • Laurence Yep
#23 • *Ishmael* • Barbara Hambly
#24 • *Killing Time* • Della Van Hise
#25 • *Dwellers in the Crucible* • Margaret Wander Bonanno
#26 • *Pawns and Symbols* • Majliss Larson
#27 • *Mindshadow* • J.M. Dillard
#28 • *Crisis on Centaurus* • Brad Ferguson
#29 • *Dreadnought!* • Diane Carey
#30 • *Demons* • J.M. Dillard
#31 • *Battlestations!* • Diane Carey
#32 • *Chain of Attack* • Gene DeWeese
#33 • *Deep Domain* • Howard Weinstein
#34 • *Dreams of the Raven* • Carmen Carter
#35 • *The Romulan Way* • Diane Duane & Peter Morwood
#36 • *How Much for Just the Planet?* • John M. Ford
#37 • *Bloodthirst* • J.M. Dillard
#38 • *The IDIC Epidemic* • Jean Lorrah
#39 • *Time for Yesterday* • A.C. Crispin
#40 • *Timetrap* • David Dvorkin
#41 • *The Three-Minute Universe* • Barbara Paul
#42 • *Memory Prime* • Gar and Judith Reeves-Stevens
#43 • *The Final Nexus* • Gene DeWeese
#44 • *Vulcan's Glory* • D.C. Fontana
#45 • *Double, Double* • Michael Jan Friedman
#46 • *The Cry of the Onlies* • Judy Klass
#47 • *The Kobayashi Maru* • Julia Ecklar
#48 • *Rules of Engagement* • Peter Morwood

#49 • *The Pandora Principle* • Carolyn Clowes
#50 • *Doctor's Orders* • Diane Duane
#51 • *Enemy Unseen* • V.E. Mitchell
#52 • *Home Is the Hunter* • Dana Kramer-Rolls
#53 • *Ghost-Walker* • Barbara Hambly
#54 • *A Flag Full of Stars* • Brad Ferguson
#55 • *Renegade* • Gene DeWeese
#56 • *Legacy* • Michael Jan Friedman
#57 • *The Rift* • Peter David
#58 • *Faces of Fire* • Michael Jan Friedman
#59 • *The Disinherited* • Peter David, Michael Jan Friedman, Robert Greenberger
#60 • *Ice Trap* • L.A. Graf
#61 • *Sanctuary* • John Vornholt
#62 • *Death Count* • L.A. Graf
#63 • *Shell Game* • Melissa Crandall
#64 • *The Starship Trap* • Mel Gilden
#65 • *Windows on a Lost World* • V.E. Mitchell
#66 • *From the Depths* • Victor Milan
#67 • *The Great Starship Race* • Diane Carey
#68 • *Firestorm* • L.A. Graf
#69 • *The Patrian Transgression* • Simon Hawke
#70 • *Traitor Winds* • L.A. Graf
#71 • *Crossroad* • Barbara Hambly
#72 • *The Better Man* • Howard Weinstein
#73 • *Recovery* • J.M. Dillard
#74 • *The Fearful Summons* • Denny Martin Flinn
#75 • *First Frontier* • Diane Carey & Dr. James I. Kirkland
#76 • *The Captain's Daughter* • Peter David
#77 • *Twilight's End* • Jerry Oltion
#78 • *The Rings of Tautee* • Dean Wesley Smith & Kristine Kathryn Rusch
#79 • *Invasion!* #1: *First Strike* • Diane Carey
#80 • *The Joy Machine* • James Gunn
#81 • *Mudd in Your Eye* • Jerry Oltion
#82 • *Mind Meld* • John Vornholt
#83 • *Heart of the Sun* • Pamela Sargent & George Zebrowski
#84 • *Assignment: Eternity* • Greg Cox
#85-87 • *My Brother's Keeper* • Michael Jan Friedman
    #85 • *Republic*
    #86 • *Constitution*
    #87 • *Enterprise*
#88 • *Across the Universe* • Pamela Sargent & George Zebrowski
#89-94 • *New Earth*
    #89 • *Wagon Train to the Stars* • Diane Carey
    #90 • *Belle Terre* • Dean Wesley Smith with Diane Carey

#91 • *Rough Trails* • L.A. Graf
#92 • *The Flaming Arrow* • Kathy and Jerry Oltion
#93 • *Thin Air* • Kristine Kathryn Rusch & Dean Wesley Smith
#94 • *Challenger* • Diane Carey
#95-96 • *Rihannsu* • Diane Duane
#95 • *Swordhunt*
#96 • *Honor Blade*
#97 • *In the Name of Honor* • Dayton Ward

Star Trek®: The Original Series

The Janus Gate • L.A. Graf
#1 • *Present Tense*
#2 • *Future Imperfect*
#3 • *Past Prologue*
Errand of Vengeance • Kevin Ryan
#1 • *The Edge of the Sword*
#2 • *Killing Blow*
#3 • *River of Blood*

Star Trek: The Next Generation®

Metamorphosis • Jean Lorrah
Vendetta • Peter David
Reunion • Michael Jan Friedman
Imzadi • Peter David
The Devil's Heart • Carmen Carter
Dark Mirror • Diane Duane
Q-Squared • Peter David
Crossover • Michael Jan Friedman
Kahless • Michael Jan Friedman
Ship of the Line • Diane Carey
The Best and the Brightest • Susan Wright
Planet X • Michael Jan Friedman
Imzadi II: Triangle • Peter David
I, Q • John de Lancie & Peter David
The Valiant • Michael Jan Friedman
The Genesis Wave, Books One, Two, and *Three* • John Vornholt
Immortal Coil • Jeffrey Lang
A Hard Rain • Dean Wesley Smith
The Battle of Betazed • Charlotte Douglas & Susan Kearney
Novelizations
Encounter at Farpoint • David Gerrold
Unification • Jeri Taylor
Relics • Michael Jan Friedman
Descent • Diane Carey

All Good Things... • Michael Jan Friedman
Star Trek: Klingon • Dean Wesley Smith & Kristine Kathryn Rusch
Star Trek Generations • J.M. Dillard
Star Trek: First Contact • J.M. Dillard
Star Trek: Insurrection • J.M. Dillard
Star Trek: Nemesis • J.M. Dillard

#1 • *Ghost Ship* • Diane Carey
#2 • *The Peacekeepers* • Gene DeWeese
#3 • *The Children of Hamlin* • Carmen Carter
#4 • *Survivors* • Jean Lorrah
#5 • *Strike Zone* • Peter David
#6 • *Power Hungry* • Howard Weinstein
#7 • *Masks* • John Vornholt
#8 • *The Captain's Honor* • David & Daniel Dvorkin
#9 • *A Call to Darkness* • Michael Jan Friedman
#10 • *A Rock and a Hard Place* • Peter David
#11 • *Gulliver's Fugitives* • Keith Sharee
#12 • *Doomsday World* • Carter, David, Friedman & Greenberger
#13 • *The Eyes of the Beholders* • A.C. Crispin
#14 • *Exiles* • Howard Weinstein
#15 • *Fortune's Light* • Michael Jan Friedman
#16 • *Contamination* • John Vornholt
#17 • *Boogeymen* • Mel Gilden
#18 • *Q-in-Law* • Peter David
#19 • *Perchance to Dream* • Howard Weinstein
#20 • *Spartacus* • T.L. Mancour
#21 • *Chains of Command* • W.A. McCay & E.L. Flood
#22 • *Imbalance* • V.E. Mitchell
#23 • *War Drums* • John Vornholt
#24 • *Nightshade* • Laurell K. Hamilton
#25 • *Grounded* • David Bischoff
#26 • *The Romulan Prize* • Simon Hawke
#27 • *Guises of the Mind* • Rebecca Neason
#28 • *Here There Be Dragons* • John Peel
#29 • *Sins of Commission* • Susan Wright
#30 • *Debtor's Planet* • W.R. Thompson
#31 • *Foreign Foes* • Dave Galanter & Greg Brodeur
#32 • *Requiem* • Michael Jan Friedman & Kevin Ryan
#33 • *Balance of Power* • Dafydd ab Hugh
#34 • *Blaze of Glory* • Simon Hawke
#35 • *The Romulan Stratagem* • Robert Greenberger
#36 • *Into the Nebula* • Gene DeWeese
#37 • *The Last Stand* • Brad Ferguson
#38 • *Dragon's Honor* • Kij Johnson & Greg Cox
#39 • *Rogue Saucer* • John Vornholt

#40 • *Possession* • J.M. Dillard & Kathleen O'Malley
#41 • *Invasion! #2: The Soldiers of Fear* • Dean Wesley Smith & Kristine Kathryn Rusch
#42 • *Infiltrator* • W.R. Thompson
#43 • *A Fury Scorned* • Pamela Sargent & George Zebrowski
#44 • *The Death of Princes* • John Peel
#45 • *Intellivore* • Diane Duane
#46 • *To Storm Heaven* • Esther Friesner
#47-49 • *The Q Continuum* • Greg Cox
  #47 • *Q-Space*
  #48 • *Q-Zone*
  #49 • *Q-Strike*
#50 • *Dyson Sphere* • Charles Pellegrino & George Zebrowski
#51-56 • *Double Helix*
  #51 • *Infection* • John Gregory Betancourt
  #52 • *Vectors* • Dean Wesley Smith & Kristine Kathryn Rusch
  #53 • *Red Sector* • Diane Carey
  #54 • *Quarantine* • John Vornholt
  #55 • *Double or Nothing* • Peter David
  #56 • *The First Virtue* • Michael Jan Friedman & Christie Golden
#57 • *The Forgotten War* • William R. Forstchen
#58 • *Gemworld Book One* • John Vornholt
#59 • *Gemworld Book Two* • John Vornholt
#60 • *Tooth and Claw* • Doranna Durgin
#61 • *Diplomatic Implausibility* • Keith R.A. DeCandido
#62-63 • *Maximum Warp* • Dave Galanter & Greg Brodeur
  #62 • *Dead Zone*
  #63 • *Forever Dark*

Star Trek: Deep Space Nine®

Warped • K.W. Jeter
Legends of the Ferengi • Ira Steven Behr & Robert Hewitt Wolfe

Novelizations
  Emissary • J.M. Dillard
  The Search • Diane Carey
  The Way of the Warrior • Diane Carey
  Star Trek: Klingon • Dean Wesley Smith & Kristine Kathryn Rusch
  Trials and Tribble-ations • Diane Carey
  Far Beyond the Stars • Steve Barnes
  What You Leave Behind • Diane Carey

#1 • *Emissary* • J.M. Dillard
#2 • *The Siege* • Peter David
#3 • *Bloodletter* • K.W. Jeter

#4 • *The Big Game* • Sandy Schofield
#5 • *Fallen Heroes* • Dafydd ab Hugh
#6 • *Betrayal* • Lois Tilton
#7 • *Warchild* • Esther Friesner
#8 • *Antimatter* • John Vornholt
#9 • *Proud Helios* • Melissa Scott
#10 • *Valhalla* • Nathan Archer
#11 • *Devil in the Sky* • Greg Cox & John Gregory Betancourt
#12 • *The Laertian Gamble* • Robert Sheckley
#13 • *Station Rage* • Diane Carey
#14 • *The Long Night* • Dean Wesley Smith & Kristine Kathryn Rusch
#15 • *Objective: Bajor* • John Peel
#16 • *Invasion!* #3: *Time's Enemy* • L.A. Graf
#17 • *The Heart of the Warrior* • John Gregory Betancourt
#18 • *Saratoga* • Michael Jan Friedman
#19 • *The Tempest* • Susan Wright
#20 • *Wrath of the Prophets* • David, Friedman & Greenberger
#21 • *Trial by Error* • Mark Garland
#22 • *Vengeance* • Dafydd ab Hugh
#23 • *The 34th Rule* • Armin Shimerman & David R. George III
#24-26 • *Rebels* • Dafydd ab Hugh
  #24 • *The Conquered*
  #25 • *The Courageous*
  #26 • *The Liberated*

Books set after the series
  The Lives of Dax • Marco Palmieri, ed.
  Millennium Omnibus • Judith and Garfield Reeves-Stevens
    #1 • *The Fall of Terok Nor*
    #2 • *The War of the Prophets*
    #3 • *Inferno*
  A Stitch in Time • Andrew J. Robinson
  Avatar, Book One • S.D. Perry
  Avatar, Book Two • S.D. Perry
  Section 31: Abyss • David Weddle & Jeffrey Lang
  Gateways #4: *Demons of Air and Darkness* • Keith R.A. DeCandido
  Gateways #7: *What Lay Beyond:* "Horn and Ivory" • Keith R.A. DeCandido
  Mission: Gamma
    #1 • *Twilight* • David R. George III
    #2 • *This Gray Spirit* • Heather Jarman
    #3 • *Cathedral* • Michael A. Martin & Andy Mangels
    #4 • *Lesser Evil* • Robert Simpson
  Rising Son • S.D. Perry
  Unity • S.D. Perry

Star Trek: Voyager®

Mosaic • Jeri Taylor
Pathways • Jeri Taylor
Captain Proton: Defender of the Earth • D.W. "Prof" Smith
The Nanotech War • Steve Piziks

Novelizations

Caretaker • L.A. Graf
Flashback • Diane Carey
Day of Honor • Michael Jan Friedman
Equinox • Diane Carey
Endgame • Diane Carey & Christie Golden

#1 • *Caretaker* • L.A. Graf
#2 • *The Escape* • Dean Wesley Smith & Kristine Kathryn Rusch
#3 • *Ragnarok* • Nathan Archer
#4 • *Violations* • Susan Wright
#5 • *Incident at Arbuk* • John Gregory Betancourt
#6 • *The Murdered Sun* • Christie Golden
#7 • *Ghost of a Chance* • Mark A. Garland & Charles G. McGraw
#8 • *Cybersong* • S.N. Lewitt
#9 • *Invasion! #4: The Final Fury* • Dafydd ab Hugh
#10 • *Bless the Beasts* • Karen Haber
#11 • *The Garden* • Melissa Scott
#12 • *Chrysalis* • David Niall Wilson
#13 • *The Black Shore* • Greg Cox
#14 • *Marooned* • Christie Golden
#15 • *Echoes* • Dean Wesley Smith, Kristine Kathryn Rusch & Nina Kiriki Hoffman
#16 • *Seven of Nine* • Christie Golden
#17 • *Death of a Neutron Star* • Eric Kotani
#18 • *Battle Lines* • Dave Galanter & Greg Brodeur
#19-21 • *Dark Matters* • Christie Golden
#19 • *Cloak and Dagger*
#20 • *Ghost Dance*
#21 • *Shadow of Heaven*

Enterprise®

Novelizations

Broken Bow • Diane Carey
Shockwave • Paul Ruditis

By the Book • Dean Wesley Smith & Kristine Kathryn Rusch
What Price Honor? • Dave Stern
Surak's Soul • J.M. Dillard

Star Trek®: New Frontier

New Frontier #1-4 Collector's Edition • Peter David
    #1 • *House of Cards*
    #2 • *Into the Void*
    #3 • *The Two-Front War*
    #4 • *End Game*
#5 • *Martyr* • Peter David
#6 • *Fire on High* • Peter David
The Captain's Table #5 • *Once Burned* • Peter David
Double Helix #5 • *Double or Nothing* • Peter David
#7 • *The Quiet Place* • Peter David
#8 • *Dark Allies* • Peter David
#9-11 • *Excalibur* • Peter David
    #9 • *Requiem*
    #10 • *Renaissance*
    #11 • *Restoration*
Gateways #6: *Cold Wars* • Peter David
Gateways #7: *What Lay Beyond:* "Death After Life" • Peter David
#12 • *Being Human* • Peter David

Star Trek®: Stargazer

The Valiant • Michael Jan Friedman
Double Helix #6: *The First Virtue* • Michael Jan Friedman and Christie Golden
Gauntlet • Michael Jan Friedman
Progenitor • Michael Jan Friedman

Star Trek®: Starfleet Corps of Engineers (eBooks)

Have Tech, Will Travel (paperback) • various
    #1 • *The Belly of the Beast* • Dean Wesley Smith
    #2 • *Fatal Error* • Keith R.A. DeCandido
    #3 • *Hard Crash* • Christie Golden
    #4 • *Interphase, Book One* • Dayton Ward & Kevin Dilmore
Miracle Workers (paperback) • various
    #5 • *Interphase, Book Two* • Dayton Ward & Kevin Dilmore
    #6 • *Cold Fusion* • Keith R.A. DeCandido
    #7 • *Invincible, Book One* • David Mack & Keith R.A. DeCandido
    #8 • *Invincible, Book Two* • David Mack & Keith R.A. DeCandido
Some Assembly Required (paperback) • various
    #9 • *The Riddled Post* • Aaron Rosenberg
    #10 • *Gateways Epilogue: Here There Be Monsters* • Keith R.A. DeCandido
    #11 • *Ambush* • Dave Galanter & Greg Brodeur
    #12 • *Some Assembly Required* • Scott Ciencin & Dan Jolley
No Surrender (paperback) • various
    #13 • *No Surrender* • Jeff Mariotte

#14 • *Caveat Emptor* • Ian Edginton & Mike Collins
#15 • *Past Life* • Robert Greenberger
#16 • *Oaths* • Glenn Hauman
#17 • *Foundations, Book One* • Dayton Ward & Kevin Dilmore
#18 • *Foundations, Book Two* • Dayton Ward & Kevin Dilmore
#19 • *Foundations, Book Three* • Dayton Ward & Kevin Dilmore
#20 • *Enigma Ship* • J. Steven York & Christina F. York
#21 • *War Stories, Book One* • Keith R.A. DeCandido
#22 • *War Stories, Book Two* • Keith R.A. DeCandido
#23 • *Wildfire, Book One* • David Mack
#24 • *Wildfire, Book Two* • David Mack
#25 • *Home Fires* • Dayton Ward & Kevin Dilmore

Star Trek®: Invasion!

#1 • *First Strike* • Diane Carey
#2 • *The Soldiers of Fear* • Dean Wesley Smith & Kristine Kathryn Rusch
#3 • *Time's Enemy* • L.A. Graf
#4 • *The Final Fury* • Dafydd ab Hugh
Invasion! Omnibus • various

Star Trek®: Day of Honor

#1 • *Ancient Blood* • Diane Carey
#2 • *Armageddon Sky* • L.A. Graf
#3 • *Her Klingon Soul* • Michael Jan Friedman
#4 • *Treaty's Law* • Dean Wesley Smith & Kristine Kathryn Rusch
The Television Episode • Michael Jan Friedman
Day of Honor Omnibus • various

Star Trek®: The Captain's Table

#1 • *War Dragons* • L.A. Graf
#2 • *Dujonian's Hoard* • Michael Jan Friedman
#3 • *The Mist* • Dean Wesley Smith & Kristine Kathryn Rusch
#4 • *Fire Ship* • Diane Carey
#5 • *Once Burned* • Peter David
#6 • *Where Sea Meets Sky* • Jerry Oltion
The Captain's Table Omnibus • various

Star Trek®: The Dominion War

#1 • *Behind Enemy Lines* • John Vornholt
#2 • *Call to Arms...* • Diane Carey
#3 • *Tunnel Through the Stars* • John Vornholt
#4 • *...Sacrifice of Angels* • Diane Carey

Star Trek®: Section 31™

Rogue • Andy Mangels & Michael A. Martin
Shadow • Dean Wesley Smith & Kristine Kathryn Rusch
Cloak • S.D. Perry
Abyss • David Weddle & Jeffrey Lang

Star Trek®: Gateways

#1 • *One Small Step* • Susan Wright
#2 • *Chainmail* • Diane Carey
#3 • *Doors Into Chaos* • Robert Greenberger
#4 • *Demons of Air and Darkness* • Keith R.A. DeCandido
#5 • *No Man's Land* • Christie Golden
#6 • *Cold Wars* • Peter David
#7 • *What Lay Beyond* • various
Epilogue: Here There Be Monsters • Keith R.A. DeCandido

Star Trek®: The Badlands

#1 • Susan Wright
#2 • Susan Wright

Star Trek®: Dark Passions

#1 • Susan Wright
#2 • Susan Wright

Star Trek®: The Brave and the Bold

#1 • Keith R.A. DeCandido
#2 • Keith R.A. DeCandido

Star Trek® Omnibus Editions

Invasion! Omnibus • various
Day of Honor Omnibus • various
The Captain's Table Omnibus • various
Double Helix Omnibus • various
Star Trek: Odyssey • William Shatner with Judith and Garfield Reeves-Stevens
Millennium Omnibus • Judith and Garfield Reeves-Stevens
Starfleet: Year One • Michael Jan Friedman

Other Star Trek® Fiction

Legends of the Ferengi • Ira Steven Behr & Robert Hewitt Wolfe
Strange New Worlds, vol. I, II, III, IV, and V • Dean Wesley Smith, ed.

Adventures in Time and Space • Mary P. Taylor, ed.
Captain Proton: Defender of the Earth • D.W. "Prof" Smith
New Worlds, New Civilizations • Michael Jan Friedman
The Lives of Dax • Marco Palmieri, ed.
The Klingon Hamlet • Wil'yam Shex'pir
Enterprise Logs • Carol Greenburg, ed.
Amazing Stories • various

STCM.02